ffesmire @ Comcast.net

Nashville Skyline

Nashville Skyline

Francis Fesmire

Hardback: 978-0-557-94017-2

Paperback: 978-0-557-69779-3

To all my friends,

        past,

               present,

                      and future.

To my amazing sons.

And most of all,

        to my loving wife,

               my moral compass,

                      the light of my life.

ACKNOWLEDGEMENTS

I would like to thank Gary Layda for the photograph of the Nashville skyline that appears on the cover of this book and Charles Gaushell of Paradigm Marketing & Creative for his rendition of the Signature Tower that appears on the back cover. I also would like to thank Dr. Philip Coyle of Richmont Graduate University for his spiritual guidance and for giving me the courage to see this project to completion, Lantz Powell of the Literary Agency for Southern Authors for his wisdom and helpful advice, and my son, Forrest, for assistance with plot development and copy editing.

THE PAST

PART ONE

A stone, a leaf, an unfound door;
Of a stone, a leaf, a door.
And of all the forgotten faces;
Naked and alone we came into exile.

Thomas Wolfe

CHAPTER 1

I, John Gabriel Rutherford IV, scion of a once-noble southern family, adjust my steadfast telescope on the distant double star Sirius. Silence looms all around, except for the occasional clang of barges, the occasional shouts of men, carried by the brisk wind over the nearby river. The crescent moon hangs low above the horizon, forming a thin, rippling streak of light across the icy waters. Shadows of barren trees recline on all sides, protecting me from the earth below. The bitter wind numbs my cheeks and pervades my scorched nose with the burning smell of winter.

As I stand on my secluded roof, I feel as if I am suspended in a womb between the heavens and the earth but present in neither one. Isolated and alone, my senses miss nothing. I can feel the granules of the shingles pressing through the firm soles of my leathery boots; I can smell the pungent odor of hickory smoke in my ragged sweater; I can see the reflections of single stars in the river beyond.

In the dim light I employ to adjust the telescope's dials, my warm breath fills the air with every exhalation. Looking down at the reddish glow of my waxen hand, I wonder if I am just a phantom in another dimension of the universe, a nightmare in someone else's dream? My bones ache from the need to convince myself of my reality. The stars convince me of my reality.

You see, I am a watcher. I have always been a watcher, and I will forever be a watcher, incapable of the kind of action the heavens demand. And yet the possibility remains that I can act, that I can join this world and assume responsibility for myself as well as for others. But now I am just a cosmic voyeur, a peeping tom of the universe. I should be struck down by the gods for gazing upon so much history, upon so much splendor and magnificence. I see every star I look upon as it existed years and years before. Even the light reflected off my hand is from the past.

You see, there is no present. It is just an illusion. The present implies a time full of pleasant possibilities for the future, a time where every step signals the beginning of an infinite number of steps from which to choose, a time that someone can take with such ease that he does not even have to be aware of its existence.

But in this world, I do not have those infinite possible steps to embrace. I exist on an imaginary tightrope and must watch every step, lest I fall into the cold, dark abyss. I live in constant fear of the future, in fear that the inevitable will take place, and I live in constant fear of the past, in fear that what has already happened will happen again. How can the present exist in such a world?

As I look for Sirius, I ponder what the reserved scientists would say about this beautiful star. They would tell me that it is the brightest star in the sky, at magnitude negative one-point-forty-six. That it is nine light-years distant—or fifty trillion miles—and that it is orbited by a white dwarf star that gives out one four-hundredth as much light as our sun but is thirty times denser. A pint of this dwarf companion star would weigh almost twenty-five tons—amazing even to us watchers.

Now, a scientist finds Sirius by going into his neat little lab packed full of pristine scientific instruments. A stained coffee pot brews on the warmer, and a tiny refrigerator hums in the corner. The aloof scientist saunters over to his beloved computer and punches the following into the keyboard: *right ascension*—six hours, forty-five minutes, and nine seconds; *declination*—negative sixteen degrees, forty-two minutes, and fifty-eight seconds. Motors begin to whir, and now, if the scientist should happen to look through the eyepiece of his telescope, he would see Sirius. But chances are that he has absolute faith in his computer and complete trust in his telescope, and at once he begins spectroscopic recordings, photometric readings, and infrared photos. Instruments flash with multicolored lights, tape-drums hum, shutters click, and miles and miles of data pour forth on little strips of paper and magnetic discs. Once the recording of the data is complete, the cold scientist deigns to look through the scope, as if to pat himself on the back and say, "This truly is Sirius." But believe me, he will have seen everything and anything but Sirius.

But when I look at Sirius, I first look at Orion, a man of great stature and beauty. I feel the pain and sadness when he was blinded by the king of Chios for loving the royal daughter, the joy when the sun restored his sight, and the tragedy when Diana was tricked into slaying him on the eve of their wedding. I see the tears flowing down Diana's cheeks, tears more sorrowful than the Earth has ever known, as the waves roll the lifeless body of great Orion upon the sandy shore.

Delicately, she lifts her departed lover, kisses him on his cold lips, and places him in the heavens for all to see. What an unselfish gift for Diana to bestow upon the dead Orion, to bestow upon the ones now living. There stands mighty Orion in the sky, for me and everyone else to see, wearing his lavish girdle and dazzling sword, his poised arm holding an immense club above his head. The Pleiad nymphs of Diana fly before him, and behind follows his faithful dog, Sirius.

Inhaling some cold air, I scan toward the southern horizon in a line formed by the three stars of Orion's belt. There is Sirius, bright and beautiful and majestic. I then admire the semicircle of stars stationed around Orion. First there are Castor and Pollux, the inseparable twins, one immortal, the other just a man. And next there is Procyon, the little dog whose appearance heralds the imminent arrival of Sirius. After Sirius is radiant Rigel, the left foot of Orion. I return to Sirius and wonder about the unseen companion star, two mismatched lovers forever circling each other.

Now I am ready to spy upon Sirius, the faithful dog star of Orion. I hold my breath in eager anticipation and lower my head to the naked eyepiece. My blond hair stands upright on the nape of my neck. I can feel the prickling of starlight all over my sensitive skin. Tears rush into my fervent eyes. I see it, I see it, I see—

A gunshot rings out.

The heavens and the earth disappear. There is only the here and now. My weighty heart skips a beat. The cold air cuts to my impenetrable bones. It has happened. I have been a watcher for too long. I try to run to the edge of the pitch-black roof, but my legs will not move, and I fall to my knees. The shot rings in my head in dizzying proportions.

"Father! Father!" I scream, but only a whisper comes forth from my strangled larynx. I crawl on abraded hands and knees to the roof's edge and blindly grope for the hidden ladder until the cold aluminum cuts through my tender hand. I start my descent. Down below, I cannot see the earth, just darkness, a world of no light, a world of no hope. I miss a step and hang suspended above the dark void by my right hand. Then my grip gives way, and I fall.

As I land, pain shoots up my right leg. The shattering sounds of bone splintering in the frigid air pierce my ears. The pain feels pure and honest. My hands claw at the ground as I wait for my senses to return. I feel the sharp blades of the frozen grass, the smoothness of the round pebbles, the texture of the frozen dirt. Tears fill my eyes. I sit up and grasp the stinging handle of the sliding glass door and pull myself up. I limp into the dead house. The lights are extinguished, and the only sounds I hear are the dull groans and creaking of wood bending in the cold wind, the ticking of my grandfather's clock in the hallway, my harsh breathing. I switch on the dim hallway light and work my way to my father's study, my ghostly shadow leading the way.

"Father, Father, can you hear me? Are you all right?"

There is no response.

"Father, Father … please …"

Again there is no response.

I open the brass handles on the double doors to the study and stagger inward, the pain in my leg searing like hot firebrands on open flesh. The room is unlit, and the hallway light sends a faint ray of hope inward. Dozens upon dozens of rows of silent books lurk overhead. As I approach the 150-year-old oak desk, a desk scarred by the pain of the past, I am in a state of limbo between hope and fear. Again pain shoots up my right leg and hurls me to the floor. My face glances off the sharp edge of the ancient desk, which opens up a thin slice of red along the angle of my right jaw. While I am paralyzed in a fetal position, my left hand rests in a warm puddle of wetness.

I scream.

* * *

I sit up, gasping for air, and clutch my chest with trembling hands. My temples throb with every heartbeat, and adrenaline pours through every cell. I concentrate, intent on slowing my rapid breathing, calming my racing heart, steadying my quivering fingers. I stare upward at the ceiling, at every little crevice, every shadow. My boat rocks in the fading winds. I pull back the matted quilt and notice that sweat covers my body. Even the silky sheets are drenched.

I crawl out of the bed gently, so as not to disturb my girlfriend, Sis. I stand over the crumpled mattress, over the sweat-stained image of a human figure. The moonlight streams in through the window and bisects the ghostly imprint of my body on the mattress. The left half of the impression hides in darkness, and the right half gleams like the summit of Mount Everest on a clear day. Sis sleeps nearby with a smile on her face. I turn and tiptoe onto the deck of my houseboat, into a dim world, isolated and alone.

The warm summer breeze dries my drained body. The lake is so peaceful. Not a ripple breaks the surface, and a soft wind blows from the south. It beckons me with a mysterious aura, a call of peacefulness, security, and strength. I dive in and swim down deep before breaking the surface, and I exhale the spent air in one long sigh. The reflection of the moonlight is fractured into a dazzling array of sparks and shimmering. I feel cleansed and purified, baptized by the mighty lake.

I gaze into the sky and try to find Sirius, but it is not present; but that is something from my past. I'm still a watcher, but not of the sky anymore. Now I'm a watcher of people. People teem upon the earth as the stars teem in the heavens. But people are so much more difficult to see. It is the remoteness of the stars that makes them so much more tangible and alive, whereas people are just here, nearby, readily touched if you just stick out your arm, but oh so difficult to feel, to see.

I pull myself out of the water, dripping, onto the rear deck and look out over the lake one last time. The moon sits low on the horizon and reflects off the glass-smooth lake in a dazzle of brilliance. The warm summer breeze wraps around me, drying me, taking away the pain of the nightmare, the pain of the past.

I crawl back into bed, refreshed and relaxed, and grab the adjacent pillow, pulling it toward me like a lover.

Sis stirs. "Gabe, are you all right?"

"I'm fine. I'm okay. I'm … it's just … just one of those crazy dreams again."

Sis shifts over to my side of the bed and embraces me with warmth and gentleness, with security and love. I fall into a deep, peaceful sleep.

CHAPTER 2

I crack the thin slits of my eyelids. The sun shines with faint, radiant heat; birds chirp with an earnest fervor; the reborn summer wind blows hard from the north. My houseboat gently rocks to and fro, secured by a determined anchor in the midst of the awakening lake. What could be more perfect?

You see, my houseboat is my grandest discovery, my own little universe, my own little microcosm, one step removed from reality. My houseboat guarantees a world of freedom, a world of infinite hope. I am isolated, cut off from the pressures and demands of day-to-day living, and the resulting freedom creates a world of no constraints, a world of no limits. The possibilities are endless, and with the inhibitions of the surrounding world removed, one can enjoy the experience to the fullest, one can move closer to themselves, and one can move closer to one another. These are the reasons I spend a large part of my life as an exile on the water.

Hearing the gentle breathing of Sis, I roll over to my left and lightly kiss her soft cheek. "I love you, angel," I say, but there is no response. Her long, brown hair is frizzled, and the sun dances around the edges, forming a shimmering halo. Pressing my morning hardness against her soft bottom, I place my lips close to her ear.

"Wake up, beautiful."

Sis peers through her squinting eyelids and smiles at me while looking over her shoulder. "Good morning, love," Sis says.

Again I press myself against her. Sis turns, gives me a peck on the cheek, and then pushes me away. "I'm not that easy."

In vain, I try to nuzzle up against her, pushing myself in desperation.

"Gabe, stop that. You have to earn it first."

"But Sis, I—"

"I'm hungry, and it's your turn to fix breakfast. Then maybe we will see about taking care of *your* hunger."

Grinning, I force Sis back into her pillow and pin her arms above her head. I try to kiss her, but she turns her head from side to side. In desperation, I stick my tongue in her ear and blow warm air. Sis shrills in laughter and then gives me that mischievous glare of hers, full of ominous overtones.

"I surrender," I say. "You win. May the gods wreak vengeance upon the founder of women's liber—"

A pillow smacks me hard across my face.

"Whatever happened to that age when beautiful women served their masters with undying allegiance?" I say as I leap, laughing, out of the bed and dash into the safe confines of the adjoining room. A pillow follows the shadows of my footsteps, just barely missing the mark.

In the kitchen, I am surrounded on three sides by the shimmering lake. My boat rocks in the gentle summer breeze. I look about and see that the lake is ours. Inspired by the beauty, I forget the tension between my legs and decide to be ambitious this morning and cook eggs Benedict. I remove the simple ingredients for my wonderful hollandaise sauce: eggs, butter, and lemon juice.

While melting the butter over low heat, deftly I whisk two egg yolks in a smattering of water. My mind wanders back to college chemistry class, back to a time when chemicals were mixed with chemicals, a time filled with fear of imperfection, fear of not getting into medical school. Everything was precise, everything exactly weighed and volumes precisely determined. That is how I first started cooking, measuring out every food substance painstakingly, annoyed when the recipe called for a pinch of this or a pinch of that, calibrating the oven temperature to preciseness, frustrated when the food never tasted like it was supposed to taste. And then I made a discovery. Cooking is not a science. Cooking is an art, a religion, a philosophy. It cannot be quantified by milligrams or cubic centimeters, or degrees Fahrenheit. It is a spiritual medium, to be respected and awed over. One simply has to let go, to feel the weight in one's hand, to smell the odors, to look at the colors. An intermingling of water, egg yolk, and butter here, a smattering of lemon juice there, now a pinch of salt and a dash of cayenne. It is so easy.

I put the sauce aside and call for Sis, who soon arrives at my side. She has already dried her hair and is wearing a pink satin robe. I prepare the poached eggs and ham as Sis slices up a tomato and an assortment of fruit. Once again the Fates have smiled on my poached eggs. The Fates and I have a peculiar relationship. If I pay my respects, they smile favorably on me, but as soon as I step out of line, the Fates are there to greet me with many "unpleasantries."

Leaving the finishing touches to Sis, I retrieve a folding table from the storage compartment and place it on the forward deck. After draping a colorful embroidered cloth on the table, I sneak out a chilled bottle of champagne and a dazzling flower bouquet, which I had hidden in the forward compartment the day before.

I return to the kitchen and take Sis in my arms. "Close your eyes."

Sis complies, and I lead her out to the deck.

Standing behind her, I whisper in her right ear, "Do you hear the sounds of the birds, the lapping of waves? Do you feel the dancing of wind in your hair, the prickling of sunlight on your body?"

Sis's body relaxes; a sigh escapes from her slackened mouth as her mind and body concentrate on the surroundings.

"Now you may open your eyes."

Sis's eyes light up with joy, and her smile beams in the bright sunlight.

"Gabe, they're beautiful. And champagne ... what's the special occasion?"

"Only you. Now let's eat."

Sis pulls my head down toward her heart-shaped lips and gives me a kiss. "You're so sweet."

I soon return with two plates loaded with eggs Benedict and an assortment of sliced fruit. The sun is not yet hot, and we eat at a leisurely pace, consuming vast quantities of food and champagne. Needless to say, the alcohol goes to our heads, which seems a great way to start off a Sunday.

Breakfast could not be more perfect. The eggs Benedict tastes like ambrosia, Sis delights in her flowers, and we both reel with laughter. Soon we divide up yesterday's evening newspaper and take pleasure in reading each other articles of interest.

"Listen to this. Associated Press. Ann Hardwood, a thirty-eight-year-old housewife in Jacksonville, Florida, was hospitalized yesterday for injuries sustained from having her arm caught in the toilet bowl. Mrs. Hardwood—"

"Gabe, are you making that up?"

"No, I'm not. Now let me finish. Mrs. Hardwood was attempting to retrieve her wedding ring when her arm became lodged. Her husband was on a business trip in North Carolina and returned two days later to find his wife passed out in the bathroom. Paramedics and plumbers summoned to the scene were forced to dismantle the entire toilet bowl before Mrs. Hardwood's arm could be freed—"

"Gabe!"

"Honest, it is right here," I say and hold up the paper to show her the headline. "Doctors at University Hospital state that Mrs. Hardwood suffered moderate dehydration and some vascular impairment in the injured arm over the two-day ordeal. They do not feel Mrs. Hardwood will suffer any permanent—"

"I don't know why you take such delight in reading such absurdities. Maybe you should subscribe to the *National Enquirer*. At least you would know when you are dealing with fiction. Now, here is truth, not fancy. Associated Press. Two thousand pro—"

"Now you are going to make me depressed. Don't you get enough of this at work?"

"Hush. Now listen. Two thousand pro-independence students rioted beneath the Jokhang Temple in the Tibetan capital of Lhasa yesterday, the holiest shrine of Buddhism in Tibet. Police used tear gas and stun grenades to control the unruly mob. One student was killed in the confrontation. Chinese officials stated ..."

We continue like this for the rest of the morning and banter about politics, movies, books, people, and each other while munching on fruit and drinking coffee. The boat rocks in the morning breeze, straining ever so gently against the tense anchor. Waves lap against the sides and dappled birds dance high overhead in the light blue sky. Every now and then, the peace is broken by the drone of a passing fishing boat or the roar of a jet engine high above. Straight ahead, the wide-open lake is framed by beautiful hills and billowing clouds. A half-mile behind us, one can just make out my dock on the distant shore. Since this is one of those rare days when we both are off for the entire day, we decide to make the most of it, just the two of us, alone.

"Gabe, I have discovered the most wonderful place. Relax, and I will take us there."

"Sounds great to me."

Sis revs the engine while I draw the anchor's crooked flute from the deep sea bottom. The boat lurches forward before I am settled. I totter on the deck and nearly fall into the glassy water below.

"Hey, turkey, you did that on purpose."

Sis winks at me and increases the throttle. My glorious boat leaps from wave to wave. The sun shimmers on the freshly broken water. The wind dances in my hair. The roar is deafening. I sure do love my boat. I named her *Helen* after Helen of Troy, and I have placed her name on the stern. *Helen* is painted white on the outside with a sky-blue deck all around. A single blue stripe dances around the entire perimeter, and a sunburst is painted on her port side.

The inside of *Helen* is just as resplendent. A large master bedroom lies in the aft compartment and accommodates a low canopy bed surrounded by blue and gold tapestry up high. In the bow sits the kitchen and the main steering wheel, the den in between. Thick blue carpeting covers the floors. Underneath the forward deck is an extra bedroom, and the den contains a cream-colored sofa bed, so there is plenty of room when the need arises. On the roof is a sky-blue deck with an outdoor steering wheel. Wired all through the boat are elaborate speakers for my hi-tech stereo, which I employ to calm the angry seas. And of course, I would go nowhere unless I had my Yamaha keyboard.

As I come through the side glass door, Sis tips her white captain's hat and pulls back the throttle as if she were stopping, and then, all at once, she guns it forward, throwing me backward into the den. Laughing, I throw a flip-flop at her back, but it bounces harmlessly to the floor. Sis becomes such a child whenever she pilots *Helen*. And myself, I am a … a ….

Onward we fly on the great blue sea, past the lazy fisherman, past the agile waterskiers, past the carefree joyriders.

"Where in the world are we going?"

Sis smiles and turns up the volume on the stereo. Neil Young is singing "After the Gold Rush," an apt song for the mood I am in now. So I just relax and let the words filter through my consciousness, as onward we rush through the foamy waters in our own little vortex of happiness. Sis is intent on finding her secret spot, and I am just content being here. I sneak up behind Sis and wrap my arms around her fervent body.

"Tell me, where are you taking me? Am I being ferried by Charon to the Elysian Fields?"

Sis grins at me over her shoulder, and I plant a big kiss on the nape of her neck, lingering there, sucking gently, biting softly. I raise my head and gaze at the turbulent water jumping out of the way. I can see little white caps of tiny wavelets dancing on the surface; I can smell the distinct but not unpleasant odor of freshwater fish. The onward motion of the boat sends tiny vibrations through every nook and cranny of my receptive body. Mesmerized by the rushing vortex of sea below me, I feel as if the boat is standing still, the world passing by. My head reels with dizziness, and my whole body aches with the desire to become one with the sea, one with nature.

We travel like this for thirty more minutes, past numerous islands, around jutting peninsulas, until I am thoroughly lost. Sis eases back on the throttle and turns down the stereo. She steers for the naked shore. Here, to my wonder and amazement, is a magnificent cove whose narrow mouth is blocked from view by a tree-covered island. The boat idles through the narrow channel, and the sea opens into a huge arena of paradise. White cliffs stand high on all three sides. The rocks begin beneath the water's surface and extend a good fifty feet before leveling off. On top, just back from the topmost ledges, beautiful pine and hickory trees hang suspended from the sky. The island at the mouth affords protection from all waves, from all winds. No anchor is required to moor our boat, but I cast it out anyway.

Sis kills the engine, strides onto the forward deck, and places her arm around my waist.

"Beautiful! Amazing! This has to be the Elysian Fields. How did you ever find this place?"

"It is Eden, you silly pagan, and how I found this place is my little secret."

Chuckling, I grab Sis in my arms and hold her suspended above the quiet liquid glass below. "I bet you came here with one of your old boyfriends. You probably even lost your virginity here."

"Wouldn't you like to know? Now, put me down before I bite off one of your ears."

Thinking of Garp and Bonkers, I sit Sis back on the deck and jump back before she can push me into the still waters. I suspect Sis had her television station's helicopter fly her over the lake, looking for a place to surprise me, and this secret knowledge fills me with inner joy and happiness.

Staring below, I see the shark-like fins of a silent garfish cutting the surface of the still waters. Slowly the fins sink into the oblivion below. Only a small ripple remains, spreading in all directions, like a pebble thrown into a pond.

The ripples beckon me, and after changing into a bathing suit, I dive into the greenish-blue waters below, gliding on the smooth surface like a skater on ice. As the shock of the cold wears off, I realize that the water is quite warm and comforting. Lazily I swim forward, turning every now and then onto my back, looking skyward. A soft splash sounds behind me, the sounds of beaten water draw close, and then the gentle strains of Sis's breathing enter my ears. Isolated, alone in our beautiful cove, we swim side by side in unison, our feet leaving a trail of foaming wake as our arms glide effortlessly through the silky waters. And as if our minds are one, we turn to face each other and, entwining our arms and legs, kiss long and hard.

And just as Leda and the swan performed a maddening dance in the sky, our dance continues in the sea. Oh, this is paradise. This is life. Not that doctoring stuff where people die every day, where a never-ending stream of people demands my time and attention. No, this is life ... love and beauty and magnificence and splendor, and all that these words entail.

Loosening our grips upon each other, we continue toward the edge of the cove, towards the one area of cliffs that seems climbable. Swimming down to the bottom, we find that the water is clear, unobstructed, and deep along the edges where the cliffs join the sea. We pull ourselves out of the dripping water and find that nature has built an almost perfect stairway to the top. Sis leads, I follow.

Upward we travel, intent upon the task. Sis's feet mark the spots for my feet; craggy rocks jut along the edges. Here and there, baby trees grow in the nooks and crannies, and moss hangs over the damp rock, chipping the solid foundation away with time. From time to time, tiny rocks break loose and run headlong down the steep slope, the splash resounding upward into our ears.

Looking down, I notice an arrowhead in a crack between two rocks. I stoop to pick it up, but I find it is embedded in the stone, too tight for me to remove. *Maybe on the next trip,* I think to myself, and I rush to catch up to Sis.

"We are almost there. Watch this last bit of loose rock."

Winded, I reach the lofty summit. Down below is my miniature houseboat, its presence dwarfed in comparison to the splendor around. Half naked, we sprawl out on the rocks. Our thoughts give rise to words, and our words give rise to new thoughts.

"Being on this cliff reminds me of a time when I was a little girl. There was a group of boys in my neighborhood who used to tease me about the way I dressed and the way I looked. They liked to call me 'chipmunk' because of the buck teeth I used to have, and they said I dressed 'like poor white trash' since I hated to wear dress—"

"But you became a beautiful swan, didn't you?"

"Yes, I guess I did. Well, one day I became super angry and challenged them to a tree-climbing contest. I remember being real high up, almost touching the clouds, much higher than any of the boys would go—."

"Penis envy."

"Hush."

"Okay, okay."

"Suddenly there was a loud crack as the branch I was sitting on splintered. As if in a slow-motion movie, I remember falling down the tree, bouncing off branch after branch, desperately trying to stop the fall. With a loud thud, I landed on the ground, flat on my buttocks."

"I won't say a thing."

Sis laughs and then continues. "I jumped up and ran around in circles, cussing and shouting until the pain went away. And then I laughed uncontrollably, and the boys laughed with me, not at me. And from that moment on, they treated me with respect, and they treated me as a friend."

Sis grows silent as she stares out over the distant, amorphous landscape.

This is why I always love coming to beautiful, unexpected places. The experience always seems to bring up past memories; the present and the past become one. If only this present could beget the future, life would be so much easier.

Sis continues to stare out into the distance.

"I remember when I was in high school," I begin, "when some friends took me hiking in the Smokies. We came to a dazzling waterfall, the drop over one hundred feet. While everybody was swimming at the base of the falls, I decided that I had to climb to the top of the falls. There was a warning sign at the base, reporting that four people had been killed on these falls and saying to please use the marked trail to the top. But I climbed anyway, straight up the edge of the falls, the challenge having arisen. When I was almost at the crest, the laughter from below creeping up, the cool mist of water spray in the air, my grip slipped."

"Oh, god! What happened?"

"Downward I slid. My life was over, and I was filled with not fear, but peace and calm. Time ceased to exist. In my tranquil state of mind, I noticed a small pine tree growing from between the rocks. I reached outward and grasped this tree, checking my descent. Catching my breath, I continued my ascent."

"Were you out of your mind?" Sis says while shaking her head.

I smile and continue, "On the summit, I gazed down at my swimming friends. I was filled with ecstasy and exhilaration and energy and vigor, because I had faced death and I had conquered it. I felt more alive at that moment than at any previous moment in my life."

"I hope you took the marked trail to the bottom."

"Of course! Do you think I'm crazy or something?"

Sis gives a sigh and gazes into my eyes as if searching for something, a look of sadness in her eyes. She says, "I'm glad you made it."

Sis lays her head in my lap, staring at the sea. She says, "You know, Gabe, when my parents died in the car accident just before my high school graduation, I thought the world was over. No grandparents, no sibling, no aunts, no uncles … no one … nobody. I was alone and totally lost. The following fall, I went off to Sewanee, feeling sorry for myself, wondering what I had done to deserve this. That first semester, I tried everything I could to flunk out—skipping classes, partying too much, avoiding homework. But I discovered two things—friendship and God. My friends kept me from flunking out, and they helped me stop feeling sorry for myself. God took away my loneliness and helped me trust in his divine plan. Without God and my friends in my life, I never would have discovered my hidden talents. Whoever would have believed that a Southern belle from Memphis would be elected Phi Beta Kappa and graduate magna cum laude from the University of the South? Whoever would have thought that me, Elizabeth Halcyonn Morgan, would become chief editor of the school newspaper and later anchorwoman for Nashville's CBS station? Despite everything, life has been good to me."

Caressing her soft hair, I say, "You are a remarkable woman, and I'm glad I have you in my life. I'm envious of your faith, and I'm envious of your blind devotion. Though I am not able to share your belief in God, I want you to know something. I will always be your friend—forever."

Sis and I exchange a few more stories, a few more thoughts, and then we lie back and bask in the sun like two mountain lions on a jagged peak. The heat of the sun rains down on my face, a gentle wind dances around my ears, and the sounds of unfettered birds pour forth from all around. It is times like these that make us realize that every little experience has contributed to who we are. Every little event, every little motion, every little sensation that our eyes, ears, skins, and noses pick up has gone into making us. And yet we are more than just the sum of our experiences. Each of us interprets the significance of our own experiences in his own manner.

The interpretation of the experience itself has the most import. What we think happened is much more important than what actually happened. And each year, as we grow older and accumulate more experiences, more wisdom, we have the option to go back and reinterpret the past. The past therefore is constantly changing. It is no more a static entity than the sea flowing beneath us.

Opening my eyes, I turn my thoughts aside. I see Sis standing on the cliff's edge. The sun spreads over her bikini-clad body, outlining her perfect form. I cannot help but believe I am looking at a beautiful bronze statue, sculpted by the gods themselves. Sis gazes at me as if trying to read my thoughts, her brown eyes piercing my green eyes. Then, looking at the waters below, she raises her palms upward, as if supplicating the ancient gods, and springs forward with a loud scream that trails her to the waters below, cut off by the resounding splash of agitated water. Laughing, I run to the cliff's edge, preparing to jump, when a shadow passes through the edge of my eye. Sis's lithe form waves from below for me to follow. I look up and see a magnificent, multicolored bird circling high above. It looks like a kingfisher with its broad wings and beautiful blue neck. Shouting, I point to the sky above. "Hey, Sis, look! A kingfisher."

The bird continues to fly around the cove in an ever-widening circle, full of a mysterious aura. Suddenly it shoots straight upward, hangs for a moment suspended, and then sharply turns downward, streaking straight as an arrow toward the water below. I gasp as the bird crashes into the glasslike surface. Water sprays forth in all directions, foam covering the entry site. Where is the bird? It is nowhere to be seen. Puzzled, I am about to shout to Sis when, as if by magic, the spectacular creature reappears from beneath the surface and flies westward, grasping a struggling fish in its fierce talons.

"Wow, did you see that? I cannot believe it."

"God, that was incredible," Sis responds from afar.

I gaze toward the distant waters below and once again prepare to jump. A strange foreboding comes over me. I am so high, so very high. I try to calm my fears, but it is not enough. "I can't."

"Come on, Gabe. I will catch you."

"I can't, I can't," I say, shaking my head repeatedly. "I can't."

Feeling a little dejected at my cowardice, I take one last look at the magnificence around. My boat rests in the middle of the cove, the blinding afternoon sun reflecting off its roof. Shadows of the cliffs creep across the waters' edge, and idle fish swim just under the glassy surface.

I climb down the way I came up.

* * *

At the bottom of the bluffs, Sis has pulled herself onto a hollowed-out ledge and plays with the water with her toes, sending ripples outward in multiple arrays. I pull myself beside her.

After catching my breath, I stand and back up a few feet. When Sis seems totally relaxed, I take a running dive into the water while grunting, "I'll race you to the boat." Furiously I plow the foaming waters, desperately trying to outrace Sis. I hear the crash of Sis's body in the water behind, and the sounds of flattened water draw close and then pass me by. As I touch the boat, Sis has already pulled herself onto the deck, her feet dangling just beside my face. Panting, I am too exhausted to pull myself out of the water.

"I'm an old man, weak and tired. Please help me."

"Okay, old man, but you better find your strength soon."

She gives me a hand and drags me out of the water. We hug, and then I stretch out on the deck, feeling the warmth of the boat underneath, the rays of sunlight on my chest. Soon my strength returns, and I gaze at Sis's tan figure standing on the deck, her face upturned toward the sun, feeding on the radiant heat. My eyes follow a bead of water on the nape of her neck, which hangs there for an instant and then winds down the curve of her muscular back and over the roundness of her buttocks before disappearing into the shadows of her inner thighs. Her beautiful brown hair shimmers in the almost nonexistent breeze. As if sensing my eyes upon her, Sis turns and stares into the depths of my soul, her eyes feeding on my eyes, burning with a passion as intense as the center of the sun.

I reach out with my hands, and Sis kneels beside me. I kiss her on the soft folds of her neck, blow warm air on her earlobes, and whisper words of love to her as I lower her onto the deck of my affectionate boat.

"Come to me, Gabe. Come to me now."

* * *

Sis sleeps on the couch as I guide my boat through the murky waters. At every point, I feel as if I am at the limits of the universe; the Stygian blackness lurks all around; the thick fog presses inward. But with each few yards traveled, a few more yards of glowing sea shimmer under my searchlight; a few more yards of discovered territory, a few more yards to travel.

I am filled with sadness and dread at leaving this dream world, leaving this world full of happiness, togetherness, and best of all, full of possibility, to return to a world where the only real change that occurs is the ticking of a clock.

These feelings remind me of the pain of growing up, the pain of giving up all that childhood represents. Childhood, like the world of my houseboat, is a time of your life when every bit of the world is full of possibility, that time when ignorance and naiveté serve to make everything more real than real, more glorious than glorious, and more alive than alive. But with the coming of knowledge and experience, ignorance and naiveté are disposed of until one is left with an empty shell of lost dreams, hopes, and beliefs. The world has been disposed of, and you yourself have been disposed of, until you forge ahead and create a new world of dreams, hopes, and beliefs. If this process could just stop. If only the world could be on your side, be what you want it to be. Oh, to be a child again, to be able to reject reality and live in your own dream world, safe and protected from harm.

I still remember as if it were yesterday: I was a child of four, watching cartoons, making discoveries, forming ideas and thoughts. I remember seeing the cartoon character, Mr. Magoo, dig his way to China. What a discovery. Excited at the prospect, I journeyed the next day with a compass, shovel, and tape measure. I remember the ritualistic labors I performed to determine the exact spot where to dig for China, measuring angles, measuring distances, looking at the sun for assistance. And there was the spot, right in the middle of our next-door neighbor's front yard. With fervent energy, I dug for what seemed like hours, my young body burning with heat, too young for sweat, with smiles of growing excitement. My limbs ached, But I persevered until I could no longer continue that day. I returned home filled with excitement. Tomorrow I would reach China.

The next day, with a smile on my face, I returned to the same spot, shovel in hand, ready for discovery. But to my consternation, I found that my hole had been filled up with dirt. Confused and dismayed, I soon realized that I must have been close, for it must have been the Chinamen themselves who filled my hole. With greater energy, with greater excitement, I dug onward, but again I had to call it quits for the day.

Soon after arriving home, there was an agitated knock on the door. It was a man with an excited, flushed face, our neighbor.

"Mrs. Rutherford, your bratty kid has been digging in my front yard. I will have none of that. If he comes into my yard one more time, I will spank him myself."

"I'm sorry. I will have a talk with Gabriel," my mother managed to squeak out as her cheeks turned red. And just as he had come in a whirlwind, so he departed, and all was silent.

It was then that I realized that it was the adults who were against living in a world full of possibility. They had no curiosity. They had no desire to visit with Chinamen. They just wanted to eat, work, and sleep. But I still had my curiosity, and I still had my dreams, and I swore that I would never give them up, and it would be many years before my father would take that from me.

CHAPTER 3

Squinting, my sluggish eyes adjust to the brilliance of the hospital corridors. Light pours forth from all around, reflecting off the white floors, glistening on the surrounding walls. The hallways are filled with the commotion and flurry of people intent upon their tasks. Orderlies push supply carts and patients in wheelchairs, nurses in immaculate white uniforms hurry to their stations, doctors scurry this way and that with charts in their hands, and idle patients with haggard expressions pace the hallways in pajamas and slippers while puffing on cigarettes. The air is filled with the incessant drone of voices. Overhead, a speaker cracks through the chatter intermittently, paging doctors, paging orderlies. All is in a bustle, all in organized turmoil, like bees in a hive, some intent on storing honey, others returning from a busy day's work, and still others whose job is to drive away lazy drones from idle hives. Such is our hospital. Such is our task.

Looking down, the floor is covered with multiple colored lines, crisscrossing the hallways in an endless array. The red line leads to the emergency department, and I follow. My footsteps give rise to new footsteps; the echoes of my feet sound the way.

The sickening smell of antiseptic solution pervades the air: the smell of cleanness, the smell of sterility. I cannot help but contrast this smell to the pleasant odor of fresh lake water, the not unpleasant smell of fish, the smell of open air. How can something so sterile and clean smell so rotten and dead? A sickness wells in my stomach, and I wish to vomit. But onward I go, following the red line, past the hum of the radiology department, past the ghastly odor of the pathology lab, past the drone of the chemistry lab.

I turn one last corner and am greeted by two stark doors with bold lettering that reads, EMERGENCY ROOM: AUTHORIZED PERSONNEL ONLY. The red line ends, and this is where I begin. The sickness rises again in my stomach. I enter.

* * *

The emergency department stands out in contrast to the rest of the hospital. The walls are painted light blue, the linoleum floors glow softly, and the overhead lights give off a peaceful incandescence. Nurses and aides, intent upon their tasks, stop to greet me, stop to make me feel welcome.

"Well, here comes my precious baby doctor," calls out Mrs. Jones, our oldest nurse on staff.

"Hi, Mom. Are you going to be looking after me today?"

"You bet. I will be watching you all day to make sure you don't get in any trouble," she says and gives me a gentle squeeze on the shoulder.

Mrs. Jones is one of my favorite nurses. She is widowed and wealthy, and she should have retired ten years ago, but onward she works. She thinks I am just a little child, and compared to her, maybe I am.

I enter the staff lounge, intent upon a cup of coffee. A round table sits in the middle, where doughnuts and a newspaper greet me. Sitting on the couch against the wall, all bloodshot and stubble-faced, is Dr. Jim Cleburne, exhausted after an evening's work.

"How was the night?"

"Just awful. The patients just never stopped coming in, there were two codes on the floor, and one of our nurses called in sick," Jim responds while nodding his head in frustration.

I pour myself a cup of coffee and imagine that Jim must have been a lieutenant general for the Confederate army in his prior life. He walks with a limp, but with pride and conviction. His face is weather-worn; there is a scar on his forehead, and he has gray, thinning hair on top. I can picture him at Gettysburg, leading Pickett's Charge, the falling of men all around, the cannon and rifles booming in front. But onward he charges, in desperation, with pride and courage; onward he charges.

"Are there any turnovers?"

"Just a little old lady in Room 4 with pancreatitis. Dr. Newman is on his way to admit her."

"Go home, and get some sleep."

"Okay, buddy, I'll see you on the flip-flop," Jim says and then goes limping down the hallway, his cowboy boots resounding with every step.

I snatch a doughnut and glance at the morning paper. Ireland is still in turmoil, planes continue to fall apart in the sky, a company is being sued for illegal dumping, and Dolly is singing on national television tonight.

With a loud noise, a nurse unknown to me comes barging into the lounge, reaches for a doughnut, and says, "It is going to be a busy day, Dr. Rutherford. I hope you brought your running shoes." I look up and notice a faint scar extending from just in front of her left ear and running downward, along the curve of her jaw, stopping just beneath the chin. From the angle I am sitting, the scar seems to be grinning at me, mocking me. Then, just as quick as she had come, she disappears into the bright light of the hospital corridor.

I carry the coffee in one hand, the doughnut in the other, and walk out to see what the day has in store for me. Already patients are filing into the waiting room, one by one. An old man holds a bloody rag on his forehead; a small child cries incessantly, vomit dripping down his chin. It is going to be one of those days.

"Good morning, Dr. Rutherford," a cheery voice says to me. It is Lynn, one of our more experienced nurses, bringing me another doughnut.

"You are going to make me fat."

"Fat? Ha! You will need these extra calories today. The crazies are going to be out, I can feel it," Lynn says and then turns her swift body in the opposite direction, intent upon her chores.

Today I am working a seven AM to seven PM shift. I will be working twelve hours a day for seven straight days, and then I will have seven days off. What could be more ideal? Two vacations a month, twenty-six weeks of escape from the world every year.

In the daytime, patients just seem to come in an endless array, never seeming to stop, never seeming to slow down; all demand my attention; all demand my time. People come into the emergency department with all kinds of complaints, all kinds of ailments, both serious and minor, and sometimes they come just to have someone with whom to talk.

Some days I grow so tired of treating sore throats and flu and rashes that I cannot wait for a real emergency to come. But when I watch the life pour forth from some hapless soul dying before my very eyes, with nothing I can do to stop it, I wish that sore throats and only sore throats would come in.

Most physicians think I am crazy for working in the emergency department. There's no regular patients and no regular schedule, just constant change. But what a world, to be able to meet challenge after challenge, to be able to bring back people from the brink of death, to live in a world where there is only death and life and nothing in between. Sometimes I feel not so much like a doctor, but more like a paramedic in the field of battle; the only difference is that there are no bombs bursting overhead, no whine of helicopter props spinning in the wind.

Oh, if only my life were so simple. If I knew what is right and wrong in my life—if only I knew. But here in the emergency department, my life is simple: I save everybody. It is not my job to question why; it is not my job to decide whether to resuscitate a one-hundred-year-old bedridden, demented widow; it is not my job to wonder why this drug dealer was shot. No, it is just my job to save them, to keep them breathing, to keep their hearts pumping. I'm just a repairman, not a philosopher or poet, just a repairman whose skills are tempered by the fallibility of mankind.

A gentle tap on my shoulder breaks my thoughts.

"Dr. Rutherford," a voice calls from behind.

I turn and see the pleasant smile of Mrs. Carol Davis, the head nurse in our department. She is a short, heavy-set woman in her forties, with a rotund face and deep blue eyes. A round, flattened nose completes her face. Though she is not very attractive, her vivacious personality and glowing smile make up for her physical shortcomings.

"Good morning, Carol. What's up?"

"All our rooms are ready. All are fully stocked. And best of all, we have an extra nurse today," she says, casting furtive glances this way and that, making sure that all is going as ordered.

"Terrific. Let's just hope it is not as busy a day as we expect," I say as Carol excuses herself to return to her duties.

The nurses here are great. They make my job so much easier. I do not know how I could do my job without them. Many are extremely bright and intelligent, and if they had grown up in a different part of the country, with a different set of parents, I have no doubt that they would be doctors, and damn good ones. I guess, though, I should be glad that they are not doctors, because my job would be so much tougher without them.

I am just about to light up a cigarette in the ambulance bay when Carol runs up to me.

"Dr. Rutherford, EMS is running emergency traffic with a forty-six-year-old male with crushing chest pain. They are two minutes out. They have given him sublingual nitroglycerin and morphine, but they state his pain is still a ten."

"Great, I like how they give us a little warning. Let's put him in Room 1 when he gets here, and go ahead and get some more morphine from the drug box. Have the tech ready with the EKG machine."

A little excitement, I think to myself, as the shrill oscillations of the ambulance siren resonate with growing energy. I walk into the resuscitation room and inspect the equipment, making sure all is ready. Mrs. Jones glances at me with fear that something is out of place, but I give her a nod of approval. That is enough; she relaxes.

At once the screeching of tires echoes through my ears, the doors swing open wildly, and the paramedics rush in with a stretcher that contains an obese, ashen-colored man. Sweat pours forth from every pore of his body. He huffs and puffs with every breath.

"Sir, I am Dr. Rutherford. We are here to help you."

His eyes plead for me to help him. The nurses meanwhile place nasal oxygen, hook him up to monitors, and determine his blood pressure.

"What time did you start hurting in your chest?"

"It started this morning, just after I got to work ... about thirty minutes ago. Doc, help ... the pain—"

"Are you on any medicines at the present time?"

"No, no, I hurt, the pain, the—"

"Do you smoke?"

"Yes, yes ... about two packs a day."

"Have you ever been told you had high blood pressure or high cholesterol?"

"Yes, yes, yes ... I hurt, I hurt."

In the meantime, Carol has given him ten milligrams of morphine, and the patient relaxes.

"Have you ever had any chest pains before in your life?"

The patient shakes his head and looks up at me, fear on his face.

I examine him and hear the ominous hoof-beats of extra heart sounds, and the fine crackles of moisture building up in his lungs. His veins pop out on his forehead and rise and fall with his respirations.

I look at his vitals and see that the patient's pressure is remaining stable.

"Mrs. Jones, give him forty milligrams of Lasix and start a nitroglycerin drip. Let me know if his pressure falls too low," I say. Just as I am about to leave the room, I turn and say, "And don't forget to give him two baby aspirin."

I stride out into the main hallway to talk with the paramedics while the tech obtains the EKG. "What can you tell me about what happened?"

The paramedic's blue eyes light up with fire, and his face glows with inward confidence. "His secretary told us that he arrived at work this morning and looked as healthy as ever. A few minutes later, he asked for some Maalox for indigestion. When the secretary returned, she found him on the floor, clutching his chest and covered with sweat. We got him here as soon as possible."

"I'm glad you arrived there so soon. He is one sick man. It will make a big difference."

I smack him lightly on the shoulder and turn my attention back to my patient. A nurse hands me the EKG. I look at the peaks and valleys on the tracing, which indicates a massive heart attack, the widow-maker. Looking at my sick patient, I see that he is quite ordinary in appearance, at least if you are an American. He is in his mid to late forties, with a thick crop of jet-black hair, obviously dyed, combed to cover a balding scalp. Around his midriff runs a thick band of fat in even distribution. There is no question that he is an American. Our obesity is the greatest monument to our great technology.

The patient turns his head toward me and fixes his pale gray eyes upon mine. They are filled with fear and uncertainty. Sweat pours down from around his eyebrows, and his muffled voice echoes through the oxygen mask. "Help me, Doctor. Don't let me die. Please don't let me die. The pain is coming back."

"Mrs. Jones, give him five more milligrams of morphine and mix the streptokinase ASAP," I say as I give the patient a reassuring squeeze on the shoulder. I turn toward Carol. "Ask the unit clerk to phone the cardiologist on call and to notify the ICU that we will need a bed."

I am just about to leave the room when the patient screams in terror. "I'm dying! I'm dying!" I look up and see that the monitor tracing is a blur: ventricular tachycardia—fast, regular waves of ominous portent.

"We need some assistance here!" I shout. "Do we have a pulse?"

"We have a strong pulse," says Carol.

"Doctor, I hurt! I hurt! Help me."

"Mrs. Jones, give him four more of morphine and seventy-five milligrams of lidocaine. Carol, charge up the paddles."

The regular waves fade to oblivion; now, only fine oscillations are seen on the tracing, and the monitor alarm gives off a steady drone. The patient loses consciousness.

"We have ventricular fibrillation. Start CPR. Carol, hand me the paddles," I command as two other nurses rush into the room. One pumps on the chest; the other gives breaths of oxygen with a bag-valve mask. I look up and now recognize the nurse pumping on the chest by the faint scar on her face, but I am unable to see her name tag.

"Seventy-five of lidocaine is in," I hear over the commotion.

"Okay, everybody clear," I say and then press the life-giving paddles onto his chest and push the button. The electricity flows in one massive jolt, and the patient's lifeless body contracts, throwing him slightly into the air. There is no response, merely the fine, quivering line on the monitor. I recharge the paddles and give him one more jolt. Again the electricity flows, and this time there is a partial response, but then the heart fades once again into oblivion.

I charge the paddles once again and whisper to myself, "Come on, you bastard, don't quit on me now."

Sweat pours from my armpits, my pulse bounds through every part of my body, and the energy reels in my head. I place the paddles on his chest and prepare for another try. The nurse with the scar has left the room. Oh, number three, do not fail me this time; you are the only chance this man has, the only chance his family has, his friends have. For the third time, I yell *clear* and deliver a charge to his chest. The smell of burned flesh and hair filters up into my nose. For the third time, the body leaps off of the table.

"Look, he is in sinus rhythm," I say. "Do we have a pulse?"

"We have a strong pulse, one hundred and ten systolic," responds Carol.

"Mrs. Jones, let's give him another fifty milligrams of lidocaine and start him on a drip at two milligrams per minute. And Carol, get the streptokinase going as soon as possible." I turn my attention to the awakening patient. He is confused and scared, but he is alive.

"Sir, you are going to be all right. We will be sending you to the intensive care unit in a few minutes. Your wife will be here shortly," I say in a reassuring voice, trying not to let the patient know the severity of his condition, his near brush with death. "Just try to relax and get some sleep. You are going to be just fine," I say, wondering if I am right, knowing he can die at any minute. Would it be better if he knew he had just been dead a few minutes ago? Would that instill in him a desire to survive, or is it better for him not to know? Would the knowledge of impending death start him praying to God, whoever that may be, for his survival, or would he be filled with a feeling of despair and bitterness? Would he feel guilt over all of his past wrongs and feel regret at all the things in life that he never had time to do, or would he be filled with a sense of accomplishment and rejoice at all of his wonderful experiences in life? I guess what I am really asking is, would knowledge of your impending death create a sense of victory or a sense of defeat?

Knowledge is a weird entity. It can make a person, and it can break a person, and whichever effect it has on a particular person depends on every little experience he or she has ever encountered in life. It depends on the very root of your self-identity and your position in the surrounding world. It depends on the very essence of what we call living and how that living is conducted. Remember, man was cast out of Eden for gaining knowledge, and Pandora's box released all sorts of knowledge, including evil, upon this world. We all have knowledge, and the most significant piece of knowledge that we have is the fact that we all know that we are going to die someday. It may be ten minutes from now, or it may be one hundred years from now, but we all are destined to die. It is how we relate this piece of knowledge to our existence on this planet that determines our very way of life. Do we accept this knowledge and take responsibility for this world, or do we decide that life is short and that every little moment must be lived for self-satisfaction? This is the most important question we face today, and this will still be the most important question we face ten thousand years from now.

The patient's heart is stable now; the patient is without pain. Lynn enters, carrying his old medical records to me. His name is Daniel Lee Bernard. Now I have a name for this patient. It is funny how I never thought to ask him his name; he was just one member of the species *Homo sapiens*. But now he is a real person: a person with a past, a person with a family, and, I hope, a person with a future. Dan is married and has three children, all in their teens. Nothing here indicates that he has a heart condition; nothing here indicates his impending fight with death. Of course he smokes, and of course he eats too much, but Jesus, he is just forty-six. I guess now he will have many days in the hospital to reflect on whether or not he changes his lifestyle.

I turn my attention to what is in store for me for the rest of the day. I have seen almost everything in the emergency room, much of it stranger than fiction. I have seen atrocious murder victims; I have seen the bizarre, one-in-a-million oddity accidents; and I have seen some things that are downright funny. Just last week, I took care of a beautiful blonde, blue-eyed woman who had injured her leg in a car accident. As I approached the gurney with a smile, she said in a thick southern accent, "Please be gentle with me, Doctor. I have real tender skin."

Looking at her, the face was a bit odd, a bit out of proportion, and there was a trace of an Adam's apple underneath the dress collar. It was then that I realized that a set of male genitals was staring at me from underneath her dress. My god, *she* was a *he*. What a mind blower. But like a good doctor, I chuckled to myself, maintained my medical composure, and treated him/her to the best of my abilities.

"My horoscope said tonight was going to be my lucky day," he/she said.

"I don't think your horoscope was right today," I replied.

"Sure it was. I was lucky enough to meet you. I bet I could show you a real good time," he/she said and then, ever so gently, licked his/her upper lip.

"Sorry, I already have a girlfriend."

"I won't tell if you won't tell," he/she said, and then he/she let out a shrill scream as I pressed on the mid-portion of his/her thigh, feeling the crepitus from the edges of broken bone grating against one another.

The clatter of rolling wheels brings my attention back to the present. The nurses are wheeling Dan off to the intensive care unit. His breathing is unlabored, and he is resting comfortably. "Good luck, my friend," I whisper.

* * *

The rest of the morning is as routine and monotonous as the emergency department can be: sore throats, and colds, and people who partied too hard, hoping they can talk me into giving them an excuse for missing work over the weekend. I try to contain my anger and frustration. Where is the glory in treating this crap? Why can't these people see a family doctor in his office? But this is part of being an emergency physician: the excitement and the boredom. I tell that to myself over and over again, over and over … over and over …

Around noon, I am just about to sneak off for a bite to eat when a hulk of a man is wheeled in on a stretcher. There are multiple stab wounds about his shoulders and thighs. He is about the biggest and meanest-looking man I have ever seen. He skin is covered with tattoos, and his eyes are like two huge airport beacons. His hands dwarf my hands. A thick beard covers his face, and a broad nose, crooked from previous fights, sticks out. Incredible muscles with bulging veins protrude from under his T-shirt. My, who would ever take on this man in a fight?

The nurses start two IVs and cut away his clothes. A small stab wound is just above his belly button. Strapped to his upper thigh is a large cucumber, above a minuscule penis.

I walk into the hallway and approach Mrs. Jones.

"Mrs. Jones, can you please go into Room 4 and remove that cucumber?"

Mrs. Jones looks at me with confusion and then strides into the room. Within a few seconds, she runs out, all red-faced and embarrassed.

"Doctor, I can't do that. It's near his privates."

Chuckling, I reenter the room and remove the cucumber. The patient tries to hide his embarrassment. I turn to Lynn and say in a low whisper, "You know what they say about the size of a man's hand," holding my small hand next to his enormous palm.

"Hush, Doctor, you are going to get us all killed."

I repair his superficial wounds while waiting for the surgeon-on-call to arrive. Soon the patient is whisked off to the operating room for exploratory abdominal surgery. I hope I do not ever meet that man in a dark alley. I retrieve the cucumber and place it in a jar of formaldehyde: my trophy dedicated to the male ego.

Hungry, I sneak off to the lounge for a bite to eat. Ellen Moore, one of our bolder and younger nurses greets me. "Hey, Doctor, I heard you saved that cucumber. Does that mean you have the same problem?"

I grab her around the neck and give her a few shakes. "Hey, Ellen, I thought you knew better than that. I thought I was famous over the entire Southeast for my abilities."

"I sure would like to find out for myself," Ellen says with a seductive grin, and then she blows me a kiss. After a nervous laugh, my face blushing, I turn my back to her and place a cold hamburger in the microwave, not so much to heat it up as to kill any germs that it may contain. I hear Ellen chuckle, followed by the sounds of her rummaging through the refrigerator, looking for her lunch.

As I take my first bite of the fibrous, stale beef, I cannot help but think of the time I read in the newspaper about a man who discovered a human thumb in his packaged hamburger. It appeared that some unfortunate individual had a little accident at the processing plant and sliced off the end of his thumb while cutting up the beef. I can picture him running off screaming for help, everyone in a state of panic, but no one calm enough to think to look for his thumb. I can see the conveyor belt continuing on its way, a patty with a thumb on top, until at the end of the line, it is all packaged inside a bun and a neat cellophane wrapper. Well, as I recall, the unlucky finder of the thumb sued the company for mental anguish, as he was now no longer able to eat any beef. The unfortunate company was forced to pay him five hundred thousand dollars, and off the hapless gentleman went, happy as a lark, hoping that he would find a big toe in his next can of Campbell's soup.

Isn't it amazing how we Americans deal with misfortune? Americans do not so much deal with bad luck—or adverse Fates, as I like to think of it—as they just ignore the possibility of its existence. If any accident occurs, if any quirk of bad luck happens, no matter what, Americans think that is somebody else's fault.

Now, in Mexico, things are totally different. Take, for instance, last year, when a bus careened off the road into a gully, killing all aboard. The family members of the deceased collected their lost love ones and prayed that their souls would go to heaven. They grieved over their deaths and asked the Lord God to help them understand the purpose of this misfortune. But did they sue? Hell no, because they knew it was part of God's mysterious plan, and anyway, would the money bring back their lost loved ones?

Now, in this country, these great United States, if such an accident were to occur, the surviving relatives would sue for millions of dollars. The wives would sue for the loss of the breadwinner—it wouldn't matter whether their husband had ample life insurance. The husbands would sue for loss of companionship and sexual services— even if they were in the process of divorcing. Survivors would sue for traumatic anguish. The courts award the money, the insurance company pays the claim, the bus company informs the public of its higher rates, and the plaintiffs and their lawyers run off to their banks with smiles on their faces and money in their hands. It is just the great American way of redistributing the wealth.

"Earth to Dr. Rutherford, do you read me?"

I look up and see Ellen gazing at me with a wry grin on her face. She must be in a great mood, for the better she feels, the more obnoxious she is.

"Oh, Ellen, are you ever going to leave me alone?"

"Not likely, as least as long as you as you keep rejecting me."

"But you're forgetting my vow of celibacy."

"What vow?"

"The vow I took when I became a Tibetan monk."

"What are you talking about? I always see you flirting shamelessly with the lab and x-ray techs. What about us nurses?"

"I'm too much of a sinner to consort with women in white," I say and head for the doorway.

"Oh, Doctor, don't go. I can't make it through lunch without you," she says and then throws her hand on her forehead and swoons like Scarlett O'Hara.

Laughing, I throw up my arms in pretended disgust and exit the room with as much speed as possible. Ellen sure is a crazy little girl. If I weren't hopelessly in love with Sis, I suspect I would ask her out. But Ellen knows I'm taken, and that just makes our flirtation more fun.

I call Sis at the television station to find out how late she will be tonight. They put me on hold, and I have to listen to that horrific music they play, worse than that obnoxious alarm tone, worse than fingernails on a chalkboard, before a voice cuts in.

"Hi, Gabe, guess what? It looks as if that Turner deal is going to go through. It is going to take a lot more work, though."

"That's great. I guess you won't be home until late tonight."

"I am sorry. I hope you don't mind."

"Of course not. I'm ecstatic for you, and I hope everything works out. I will try to stay up, but it has been a long day."

"Okay, sweets, I have to run now. I love you."

"I love you too."

The phone clicks, and the connection goes dead.

I'm so happy for Sis. She has been trying for months to arrange a deal between her station and Ted Turner's station to produce a series on the problems in the rural South, and now it looks like it's a done deal. This will give Sis national exposure and be a great boost to her career. And to be associated with Ted Turner cannot hurt either. Ted Turner is the classic American go-getter, what everybody dreams of becoming. In a few years, America will be owned by the Saudis, the

Japanese, and Ted Turner, and Ted Turner will most likely find a way to buy out the others.

Hurriedly I down one last cup of coffee and then sneak back into the emergency department. The patients are backing up now in the waiting room. The hamburger smolders in my stomach, and I ponder whether or not I should sign myself into the ER as a patient and have my stomach pumped. No, I guess not. I can endure a little hardship now and then, I hope.

After hours of endless lines of patients and endless lines of complaints, my day is drawing to a close. The sun is setting on the unseen horizon as I ponder tonight's activities. Abruptly, my concentration is broken by the frenzied screams of a man being pushed through our entryway in a wheelchair. He is a slender man, about my age, wearing a nice gray three-piece suit. We grab him and restrain him on a stretcher, his Adam's apple undulating with every scream. But he continues to scream, each scream piercing my inmost soul.

I examine him from head to toe; nothing is wrong with him, but still he screams. After I administer five milligrams of Haldol, he soon calms down.

"Sir, why are you screaming? Are you in pain? Are there voices in your head?"

He cocks his head to one side, looks at me with his left eye, ponders my question for a moment, and then says, "Why do you ask me that? I think you should be asking yourself, 'Why am I not screaming?'"

Puzzled, I consult the psychiatrist on call and bid all farewell.

CHAPTER 4

Driving homeward, I fight the glare of the setting sun in my rearview mirror with my right hand, my left hand on the wheel. The Nashville skyline taunts me with memories of the past, a constant reminder that the world is always changing, that my world is always changing. Before me looms the Sheraton Hotel with the obnoxious spaceship restaurant on top, finished when I was still in college. I still remember taking a date to that restaurant during Christmas break. The date was a disaster, and the girl spent the whole drive home telling me about her sinus drainage and sore throat. If only I could go back in time, I would say, "That's okay, I don't want to kiss you either."

Nearby is One Nashville Place, which looks like R2-D2 from *Star Wars,* and the Third National Financial Center, which looks like a palace for the gods. These two buildings greeted me when I returned to Nashville following my medical training, a reminder that I had been gone for so long. On the opposite end of the skyline, blotting out the horizon, stands the Renaissance Hotel, a monstrosity that I had to endure on an ongoing basis as I watched its construction going to and from work.

But standing in the middle, like a lighthouse for a troubled world, what I see now, and what I always shall see when I look at the Nashville skyline, is the thirty-floor Life and Casualty Tower with the large L&C on the top, a building that was finished when I was just a small boy, a building that will always be the beacon of my youth. Which letter symbolizes me, the *L* or the *C*?

The honking of a truck brings me back to the present. Cars zoom this way and that way, and the rush of the air through the open window deafens my ears. The vibrations of the road tingle through my bones. Onward I fly, in my red Mustang convertible, the sweet smell of leather all about. Today I have healed the bums and the hardworking, the wicked and the kind of heart, the demented old and the crying infants, the broken-down whores and the beautiful mothers. I have healed all without regard of whether I am doing anybody any good. But do I really think that I can make a difference? Or do I really care? Horseshit!

Maybe that is why that man was screaming. Maybe he had discovered the futility of the human condition. I do not know, and I really do not care. At least I have a good-paying job, and I have my houseboat on the lake, and I have Sis.

A whiff of putrid air rises to my nostrils. I look to the side of the road and see a dead opossum, its guts having spilled out, and a shadowy bird picking on its innards. Fascinated, I follow the bird in the mirror; the bird pecks a few more times, pauses, and then looks about searchingly. It spreads its long, black wings and alights into the air, flying along the highway, over my car, a black speck disappearing into the glare of the sun.

O bird, are you that vulture that torments Prometheus? That bird that day after day, plucks out his passionate liver with your ravenous beak and claws? And O Prometheus, what secret do you hold that enables you to survive such endless torture? What secret could be so great as to enable you to endure such pain and hardship? What secret is so indisputable as to allow you to suffer such undeserved punishment until you might submit to the will of the gods? You can free yourself anytime, but no, you would rather suffer eternal agony than sell your soul. If I could just discover what you have learned, O Prometheus.

Byron's verse on Prometheus filters through my mind:

> *Thy godlike crime was to be kind*
> *The sum of human wretchedness,*
> *And strengthen man with his own mind.*
> *And baffled as thou went from high,*
> *Still in thy patient energy*
> *In the endurance and repulse*
> *Of thy impenetrable spirit,*
> *Which earth and heaven could not convulse,*
> *A mighty lesson we inherit.*

A mighty lesson we inherit … that is the key. If I can dissect these lines, dissect the story of Prometheus, I can arrive at the truth; I can learn the secret of life. But what if this verse is just pretty lines of poetry? What if the story of Prometheus is just propaganda to give meaning to the life of sufferers? Oh, my mind aches from abstraction. I must stop thinking of such absurd ideas.

Luckily, the Country Kitchen lies just ahead. I think I will have a good old Southern dinner to calm my frayed nerves. My car leads the way, dust rising from the spray of gravel as its relentless wheels plow through the foamy entrance.

I park my Mustang off to the side, between a splintered telephone pole and a white Cadillac. A spindly brown dog wags its frayed tail, begging for food. I kneel briefly and pet it, hoping it will find a home soon. The large black letters of the restaurant's logo loom overhead.

Entering, I am greeted by a cheerful waitress, wearing a knee-length plaid dress.

"How are you doing there, sir? Table for one?" she says in a quaint country accent.

"I'm doing just fine," I say, leaving out the T on "just" as I fall naturally into her accent. "Yes, I will be dining alone."

"Well, you just follow me right over here," she says and then leads me to a small table in the far corner. The table wobbles, and a fern leaf tickles my left ear. "Would you like to see a menu?"

"No, thank you. I just want the catfish special and a large Coke."

"It will be just a few minutes, sir," she says, and before I have a chance to respond, she is off to another table, quick as a fox.

Looking about, I examine the surrounding folks methodically, intent on what I may discover. At the table in front of me sits a rotund family of three, chomping down on the fried chicken special. The father wears a white shirt, no tie, and black cotton pants. The shirt sticks to his sweaty sides and reveals mounds and mounds of fat. His breathing is loud and raspy, and a vein on his temple swells with every breath. Beads of sweat hang from his temple. With his nicotine-stained fingers, he pours copious salt onto his chicken and mashed potatoes. I have already diagnosed hypertension, hyperlipidemia, diabetes, morbid obesity, sleep apnea, anxiety-stress disorder, and cigarette abuse from just looking at him. Taking all factors into consideration, I suspect he will die from cardiac disease within the next five years, ten at the most.

"Pass some more of that gravy over here, boy," he says to his chubby son, who sits across from his father.

"Sure, Dad," he replies with a mouth full of chicken. "This place sure makes the best chicken in the world."

The adolescent son is almost as overweight as his father, but his voice is high-pitched and cheery. He face glows with the radiance of youth and innocence. He wears a plaid hunting shirt and reminds me of the hero in *Confederacy of Dunces*.

The wife sits on the husband's right, a little overweight, but more from lack of exercise than eating. Her face is covered with layers and layers of makeup, and the rouge on her cheeks reminds me of fresh bruises. She chatters endlessly in her husband's ear, and he responds from time to time with a nod or a few words, intent upon eating.

"Did you know that Jack and Mary bought a new station wagon yesterday?" she intones in his ear. "They are going to take it to Florida next month."

"That's nice, dear."

"Jack's sister-in-law owns a timesharing condominium in St. Augustine."

"Pass the potatoes."

"Mary says she is going to drink from the Fountain of Youth and get rid of her wrinkles."

The father winks at his son and continues eating. The chattering continues. The son giggles silently, and I see mounds and mounds of ballooning fat oscillate in subdued spasms, like Jell-O in an earthquake.

"Jack doesn't believe in the Fountain of Youth, but Mary said ..."

So this is the typical American family. I wonder why we rarely see families like this on TV. Is it because TV is to allow us to forget what real people look like, what real people do, and how real people behave?

I close my eyes and imagine this family at home tonight. I see Dad in front of the TV, his labored respiration as he smokes, drinks beer, and eats potato chips while watching the Dodgers clobber the Atlanta Braves once again. Mom sits in a wooden rocking chair knitting a sweater for winter, talking in an endless drone to her preoccupied husband. The son lies in his bed, drooling over his collection of *Penthouse* magazines.

Abruptly, the image becomes a TV commercial. The camera pans over each family member, including the dog, until it stops on the mother. She smiles, leans forward, and whispers, "I have diarrhea." Then she pulls out a bottle of medicine. "But fortunately I have Kaopectate." Unable to control myself, I start laughing out loud at the thought. My unsteady table wobbles with my convulsions; the fern dances in my ear.

A tap on my right shoulder interrupts my laughter.

"You sure look like you're sitting in a mighty uncomfortable spot," a smiling gentleman in overalls drawls in a rich country accent. "Why don't you come join us over here? We have plenty of room."

I look past his pointing finger and see a large table dwarfing two pleasant-looking folks, laughing and carrying on.

"I will be glad to. That's right nice of you, sir," I say as I stand and walk over to the nearby table while shaking his hand. "My name is Gabe."

"Nice to meet you, Gabe. My name is Connor, and this here is Lori and Wayne," he says, and I greet and shake hands with each one in turn.

Sitting between Connor and Lori, at the head of the table, I am struck by the charisma that these people generate. They are dressed in simple country clothes, but more importantly, they seem to exude life. Connor wears faded overalls and a checkered shirt. Lori has on jeans and a tight, colorful cotton shirt that accentuates her full figure. Wayne wears black leather pants and a Davy Crockett brown leather jacket. The gaps in their teeth seem to shine, and the wrinkles and scars of farm life glow. Suddenly I realize that all of these people are country music stars. I cover up any hint of recognition and put on my good ol' Southern boy behavior, thankful that I did not wear a tie today.

"So, Gabe, what kind of work are you in?" Connor inquires.

"Well, I'm a doctor of sorts."

"A doctor? Lordy, good for you," Lori says.

"What kind of doctor are you, a brain surgeon?"

"No I'm just a lowly ER doc."

"God, you must see all sorts of gruesome things," Wayne says with a grimace on his face.

I shrug and change the subject. "So what kind of work are you folks in?"

"Oh, we all like to sing and pick guitar," Connor replies.

"You wish, Connor," Lori says. "You don't even know the front of a guitar from the back, and when you sing, my bird dog covers her ears with her paws. Now, I will tell you who can play the guitar here. That's Wayne, and I have the sweetest voice in these here parts."

"Hell, Lori," says Connor, "I taught all of y'all everything you know, and don't forget it."

"In your dreams."

"So, Doc," says Wayne, "how did you get to be a doctor?"

Remembering a joke from my father, I begin, "Well, back when I was about fourteen, I went out hunting with my best friend. His name was Roy. Yes, that's right—Roy Smith it was. We were having us a great time in the woods, shooting at everything that moved, drinking stolen beer, and smoking my father's cigars—"

"I bet you were hunting snipe," says Connor.

"Yeah, yeah," I say. "Well, my friend—that's Roy—had to take a leak. Pardon my language. So he was standing there wetting this tree when a rattlesnake jumped up and bit him. I blasted the snake right away with both barrels of my twelve-gauge shotgun, and then I looked at my friend there rolling in the grass, holding his crotch, screaming and yelling up a storm. He yells at me, 'Go get me a doctor, quick—'"

"That must've hurt," says Wayne.

"So I drop my shotgun and take off running through the briars and thorns, running and running until I come barging into Doc MacCabe's office. 'Doc! Doc, come quick! My friend has been bitten by a rattlesnake,' I said to the old country doctor. But he said, 'Sorry, son, I have a baby to deliver, but I will tell you what you do. You go take—'"

"Whew ... this is going to be a good one," says Connor.

"Will you be quiet?" says Lori.

"The doctor then said, 'Take this here scalpel back to your friend, cut two holes over where the snake bit him, and suck all the venom out.' 'But Doc,' I said, 'He got bit on his—!' The doc cut me off right then and said, 'Get out of here, boy, and go save your friend.'"

Connor starts laughing good and hard. "Shut up, Connor, let the doc here finish," Lori says and gives Connor a friendly pinch on the ear.

"Okay, Doc, I'm sorry. Go on with your story," Connor says, winking at me with his right eye.

"So I take off running through the woods again," I say, pumping my arms as if I were running. "Back through the thorns and briars, through the leech-infested swamps. And finally I reach my friend, still moaning, rolling around in the grass, holding his groin in desperation. 'Where's the doctor?' Roy asked. 'What did he say?' Well, I look Roy straight in the eye with a real serious look, and I firmly said in a grim voice, 'Well, I'm sorry, Roy, but the doc says you are going to die.'"

Everyone bursts out in laughter, and Connor gives me a friendly slap on the knee.

Wayne, his laughter having subsided to a lean grin, presses me again. "So why did you become a doctor?"

"Well, to be honest with you, I felt so guilty about letting my best friend die that I vowed I would become a doctor and make up for it, and I'm still trying."

"That's a good one, Doc," says Lori. "I wouldn't even be surprised if it were true."

It's a terrible joke, but these people have accepted me. We all go on telling jokes, teasing each other, talking about old Martins and Gibsons. I gaze at their animated faces, amazed at how great they look, amazed at how they look more real than life. Is this what TV and stardom does to somebody? Does it fade the wrinkles and brighten the missing teeth, strengthen the voice? Is this what makes Sis so marvelous?

I feel a bump on my shoulder and see that the waitress has brought out our food: mounds of fried chicken for Lori and Wayne, country ham for Connor, and catfish for me. All of this food ... *it is like being in heaven,* I think as the first taste of catfish dissolves on my tongue. Immediately my mind is flooded with images. I remember the first catfish I ever caught as a boy, fishing with a warped cane pole off the steep riverbank, with gooey worms as the bait. I still have a jagged scar on my right thumb, a reminder of the thorny barb. Biting into my first hushpuppy, a spicy heap of batter, I think of the hunters in days gone past, hunched over the blazing campfires, frying up the day's kill, their frantic dogs yelping in the background. I can smell the pleasant smell of burning hickory wood, and see the light reflecting off oily gunmetal. I see the smudged faces of joyful hunters and the shimmering moonlight through the trees. I can picture the hunters spooning out the extra fried lumps of cornmeal, throwing them to their frenzied dogs, exclaiming, "Hush, puppy!" It is all there with every bite, with every swallow.

"Hey, Doc, are you off in the twilight zone?" asks Wayne.

"I just love catfish. It always reminds me of my youth, of my heritage."

"I sure do miss catfish," Connor says. "For the last five years, whenever I eat it, my gallbladder doubles me over in pain."

"Well, Connor, if you weren't such a chicken, your doctor would have taken that sucker out years ago," says Lori.

"I know, Lori, but I'm afraid I won't wake up, and then where would all of y'all be without me?"

A chorus of hoots and hollers follows his last remark, and Connor just grins and grins, the gaps from his two missing teeth looking like eyes peering from within. Connor starts talking politics, between bites of chicken.

"I'll tell you what we ought to do to the Russkies," Connor declares, waving his arms. "We ought to fill up a few spy planes with kudzu, fly over Moscow, and dump it out. Kudzu will accomplish more in one summer than either that Napoleon fellow or Hitler were able to do. Not even the cold Russian winter could kill off kudzu."

"That's right," says Wayne. "I used kudzu to get rid of my first wife. One night when she was asleep, I gently carried her out on the back porch and set her in her favorite rocking chair. The next morning, I awoke to find a heap of kudzu all over the porch. Never did hear from my wife afterwards."

"That kudzu is tough," I say, "but I'll tell you what's tougher. Elect Billy Graham president, give him control of the atomic arsenal— then those Russians will be crawling on their knees to us." Luckily they laugh. I had forgotten the one rule of country living: never mock religion. It is not worth the risk.

We continue eating at a leisurely pace, savoring every bite, passing food around, eating off each other's plates. I am going to miss tonight, these people, this food. But there will be other nights. I look at my watch and see that it is getting late. Remembering my friend outside, I discreetly wrap some leftovers in a napkin and slide them into my right pocket. I stand and shake Connor's and Loretta's hands, and then I lean over and give Wayne a pat on the shoulder.

"I sure enjoyed meeting all of you tonight. Maybe I will see you here again sometime. Take care."

I have won, I think to myself as I exit the restaurant. I went a full meal without acknowledging that I knew they were famous, without asking for their autographs. I met them on an equal level, and I was accepted. I have earned my own right of existence.

The scrawny dog wags her frantic tail by my Mustang, eager for friendship, eager for food. I kneel down on one knee, the pitiful dog now whining as tears form in the corners of my eyes. I gently stroke her while placing each bite of food into her searching mouth with my right hand.

"Hush, puppy. Hush, puppy," I whisper, stroking her thin, matted fur. If only I had a place for her.

CHAPTER 5

As I turn the key to Sis's apartment door, a feeling of warmth comes over me: a feeling of being at home. I enter, and the flick of a switch reveals the spacious living room. The warm light invites me with its comfort and security. A large blue couch sits along the right wall, and plush, pale gray carpet lines the floor. On the left wall are antique hardwood cabinets topped by rows and rows of glassed-in bookshelves. The wall across has two grand windows with large French doors lying between, opening onto a balcony. A baby grand piano sits atop a Persian rug in the far left corner, and an antique brass telescope stands in the right corner. All is quiet because Sis has yet to come home from work.

As I look through the French doors, the Nashville skyline is alight with activity. The L&C Tower shines as a beacon for all to see; the lights of planes crisscross the distant sky. The sight mesmerizes me, beckons me, summons me to reach into my soul. I open the balcony doors and walk out into the warm summer breeze, thinking of Sis. I remember, as it if were yesterday, the first time I met Sis. It was five years ago, almost to the day. A tornado had ripped through a small Tennessee community lying in a steep gully north of Nashville, near the Kentucky border. I was bored and had nothing better to do, so I drove to the scene to see if I could be of any assistance. I arrived there as soon as possible, ready to give aid in whatever form I deemed necessary, when I was struck by the sight of a godlike woman who, through sheer charisma and brute force of will, led the search through the rubble for survivors. I recognized her as a reporter for a local news station. She was twenty-five at the time and had been sent to cover the crisis. But after arriving at the desperate community, she had been overwhelmed by the devastation wrought by the ravenous tornado. She had junked her role as a reporter and used her talents in an attempt to save any lives that might be hanging on a thread.

"I know you're scared. I know you're exhausted," she announced to a tearful and panic-stricken crowd gathered nearby; a fallen schoolhouse lay before them in a heap. "But there are family and friends trapped beneath this rubble, and we can help them. We can save them. You, you, and you are the biggest; help pull the rubble from the heap and pass it down." She turned toward another group of men. "Now, you four men line up here and pass the rubble from one to another to the schoolyard, out of the way." She pointed toward some grieving women and said, "Go find sheets and bedding, and anything that will serve as bandages."

And just as when a commotion has arisen in terrified mob, and rocks fly, and gasoline bombs burst, and all the world seems a frenzy, when perchance a man known for his wisdom and piety may stand and address the mob, and calm their angry spirits—thus Sis calmed the panic-stricken community, and they listened and set about the tasks given them. Sis scurried this way and that, divided out the deeds, appointed order, and helped these people help themselves. She led, and we followed. I have never admired any person in my life so much as that moment when I first watched Sis in action.

When the last living victim had been sent away by ambulance, I noticed for the first time the extent of the destruction. Not a building was standing. The ground was littered with twisted metal and paper. Tattered insulation from the destroyed buildings flapped in the moaning wind. A station wagon tottered high above on a nearby cliff. The remains of a church cross were impaled in the only standing tree.

I still can close my eyes and see the image of the survivors weeping over the covered bodies of their lost loved ones, crying about the destruction of their homes and the pain of loss. A fire burned on the east end of the town at the apex of the gorge. A country preacher roamed among the survivors, seemingly always trying to maintain himself between his audience and the fire.

"O my brethren, a calamity has befallen on you, and you, my brethren, deserved it. Ponder this well, and fall on your knees, my friends. The scourge of God has humbled the proud of heart and slain those who have hardened themselves against him. Oh pray ye now—pray to the lord almighty, that he may take pity on you and forgive you for thy sins."

I stopped listening. Sickness arose in my stomach, and I wanted to vomit. Some of the survivors now joined the preacher in prayer. Others stood around with hollow eyes and blank expressions. And then I saw Sis in the distance, isolated and alone, weeping. I walked over to comfort her, her TV camera lying at her feet, a broken tricycle lying face down in the mud nearby. Sis looked up with tears in her eyes and then gave me a smile that I will never forget: a smile full of hope and possibility, a smile that still is etched into my soul. I smiled back, fighting back tears. I placed my hand on her shoulder and wept. I wept for the dead, I wept for the broken-hearted survivors, and I wept for Sis.

And the next day, when I saw Sis's story on the evening news, I wept again, for it was not a story glorifying the destructiveness of the tornado, the number of buildings destroyed, the number of people killed. It was just a simple tale of human tragedy, a tale of people with lost loved ones, a tale of people with no place to go, a tale of the pain and tragedy of loss.

I realized right then that we live in an age not of heroes like Odysseus or Aeneas, but of simple heroes like Sis who are capable of doing what is right, simply out of a matter of common decency. This is the Sis that I first met; this is the Sis that I have grown to love.

Well, to make a long story short, I was the shy type who never would have had the guts to ask someone as grand as Sis out. But Sis, being a good investigative reporter, tracked down my name and called me one night out of the blue. I have never been so delighted and so terrified as I was when I answered the phone that night.

On our first date, we met at a local restaurant for a drink. When I walked in nervously, I saw a woman sitting at the bar that I thought might be Sis. As I approached, the bartender brought out a drink and pointed to a patron sitting at the end of the bar. I saw the woman give a nod of thanks. The patron smiled and gave a silent toast in return. I paused, unsure how to best approach this woman, wondering whether it was Sis. I saw the patron at the end of the bar stand, preparing to launch his attack. Then the women turned her head toward the advancing man, paused, and as if she sensed my steadfast gaze, looked over her shoulder at me and gave me that smile again. Sis reached out, grasped my arm, pulled me close, paused, letting me feel her warm breath in my right ear, and said, "Saved by a knight in shining armor." The patron at the end of the bar shrugged and sat down to nurse his drink while waiting for other prey.

Our drink soon turned into a *few* drinks. When closing time came, we moved to a nearby hangout for college students, where we drank coffee for hours, talking like we had been friends all of our lives. I knew I had met my best friend, and I hoped that Sis thought she had met her best friend. Just before dawn, sitting in front of her apartment in my bashful Mustang, I so wanted to kiss Sis, but I was afraid of rejection, afraid that she just wanted to be friends, as had so many other girls in my life. Sis, finally tiring of my shyness, took my face in her hands and kissed me with more passion than I had ever known in my life, our tongues intermingling, her teeth lightly biting my tongue, our soft noses rubbing. It was like the birds singing, the sun rising, a rose unfolding, a newborn crying, a rainbow smiling—all at the same time. And when I remained too much of a gentleman, Sis grabbed my left hand and placed it on her right breast. The universe and I were at peace.

And the next day on the way to work, I stopped by Sis's apartment unannounced, with a solitary red rose. Sis answered the door in gray sweatpants and a white sweatshirt, her unwashed hair pulled back and no makeup on her face. To me she looked like a goddess. On Sis's face I saw shock and embarrassment over being caught unprepared, but I also saw delight and joy in knowing that the previous night had been real. And if Sis had any doubts regarding my intentions, they were gone now.

Over the next few months, we saw each other rarely. Sis was always on assignment—a flood here, a devastating fire there. Whatever calamity God had brought on Tennessee, you could be assured that Sis was there to cover the story. And when Sis was in town, it seemed I was always working. But when we did spend time together, it was like the heavens and earth came together into one. And when we weren't together, we wrote passionate letters. The letters went back and forth, regardless of whether she was in town or out of town.

One cold weekend after we had been dating for several months, Sis came over and pinned me (a "hapless youth," as I would later tease her) to my bed, holding my arms above my head, and with a veil of her hair draped around my shadowed face, professed her undying love. And that spring, at Lake Lanier, we exchanged commitment vows and silver pinky rings by candlelight to symbolize our newfound love.

I believe that Sis and I will marry someday, but she still is tentative about taking that next step. She is terrified at the thought of having children, and she is always talking about respect and trust, and how respect and trust are the only things that matter in a relationship. But I think it is her fear of losing her complete independence, her fear of even partially relying on someone else for her needs. I think it must relate to her parents dying, but sometimes I think something dark and terrifying happened to her in her past, a secret that she is too scared to share, even with me.

The summer breeze is cool now, and goose bumps appear on my naked arms. I look one last time at the Nashville skyline and then stride into the peaceful living room and set myself in my burnt-orange recliner chair, my own misfit addition to this glorious apartment. I lean back and rest my weary body. I close my eyes and try to feel every part of my body. I flex my toes and fingers, I wiggle my scalp, lick my lips, like a newborn infant discovering its own body limits. I visualize where each appendage of my body lies, where every hair and mole lies.

I focus on my taste buds. What tastes are in my mouth? Can I distinguish between self and non-self tastes? What noises do I hear? Can I hear the sound of blood rushing through my ears? Common sense seems to tell me that the noise must be deafening, but why can I not hear it? I concentrate hard, trying to break through the barrier of my mind. But what if I break through? Will I ever be able to shut off the roaring sound, or will I be merely a lunatic frozen in a paralyzed state, unable to focus on the real world? It sounds like an interesting science fiction story to me. I file that one away for future reference.

Thoroughly relaxed now from my mind's wanderings, I decide it is time for a bath. I fill the tub with hot water and pour myself a glass of Jack Daniel's on the rocks, adding a twist of lime to numb the taste. I grab *Our Mutual Friend* from the bedroom and reenter the steamy bathroom. Whenever the world gets too complicated, I like to read Dickens because he is so clear-cut. Only good and evil exist—only good deeds and bad deeds, and nothing in between. There is no confusion as to what is right or wrong. If only life could be so simple. And what could be better than reading about the marvelous characters he invents, all too outrageous to be believable and too outrageous to ever be forgotten?

I sit on the edge of the tub, reading, testing the water with my toes, then my ankles, the Jack Daniel's filtering through my head. Dizzy and relaxed, I set the book aside and slide into the long tub, the warm water rising to greet me.

I flip on the whirlpool switch, and at once the tub is alight with activity, churning and boiling, melting my skin away. The screams of the jets remind me of my screaming patient. Maybe he does know something after all. I have been searching all my life for the answers to life, but maybe I have not been searching hard enough; maybe I have been searching in the wrong places.

I remember in high school when I believed that all the answers to all questions could be found in books, for had not the world's greatest thinkers been writing and thinking about these matters for thousands of years? I pored over all the great intellectual novelists and philosophers: Dostoyevsky, Camus, Sartre, Kierkegaard, Kafka, Mann, and many others. Like a scientist, I would dissect these great writers' works, convinced that I could find the answers in their wisdom, line by line, word by word, letter by letter. Surely there was an answer to the great questions in life. Surely these writers did not obscure the truth merely because there was no truth.

At the completion of high school, I was still convinced that all answers could be found in intellectual enlightenment. So like all good Southern gentleman who do not quite fit into the fraternity life of places such as Vanderbilt and the University of Tennessee, I packed myself off to Harvard University, like Faulkner's Quentin Compson, intent upon discovery.

I remember being in complete awe of the campus the first few weeks. I would walk around the old buildings, past the statues and monuments, through the museums, gazing in admiration at all the famous people who had been there before me. I trod ever so lightly, afraid that perchance I might offend one of the many great ghosts that still haunted these hallowed grounds. I could not sit in the library without wondering what renowned person had sat in the same spot. I would press my head against the table and hope that some of the knowledge it contained might flow into my soul. I would lie in my bed at nights, wondering who had been there before me. But though I was in awe of my predecessors, most of all I was in awe of my classmates, the future Nobel laureates, Supreme Court justices, poets, philosophers, scientists, and the list goes on forever.

And here I was, neither brilliant nor charismatic, with no hope of future greatness, merely hoping to share in the glory of others, hoping to find some answers to the meaning of life. But gradually I began to become alienated. Why was everybody so happy? Where were the students like myself? Where were the great debates on knowledge and existence and purpose? Why was everybody having fun but me?

And so I fell into despair. I became an exile, hanging out with the blacks and the Arabs and the Asians and the Jews. I felt comfortable and safe in this group. And at night, as I lay awake in bed, I would ponder my nonexistence. I would plan for the following day, and take delight that I could go completely unnoticed. I could go from classes to lunch to the gym to dinner, and no one paid me any attention whatsoever. I soon became convinced that I was only an illusion. I constantly had to ascertain my own existence. Could I scratch this desk and leave a mark? Could I feel the heat of a match? Could I shout out my window and have someone answer, other than a heartless echo?

And then I moved into an eighth-floor room at Leverett House. I spent my free time sitting on my windowsill, staring down at the depths below, at the tiny trees, the hard pavement, the sharp barbs of the wrought-iron fence. Here was a choice that was mine. I could jump or I could not jump, and with this realization that I had a choice came a new substance to my reality. I now felt that I had some control over my life. I could live or die, and that choice was mine and only mine.

And in this fragmented state of mind, one day I met this crazy girl with a boy's name: Chris. She was smart, beautiful, kind, and silly, and I believe she thought the same thing about me. And one cold summer night, while standing on the walk bridge over the Charles River, I kissed her for the first time. And then I knew that my new symbol in life was love. Forget being intellectual, forget trying to find the answers to life in books; there was just one meaningful goal in life, and that was to love and be loved.

But I refused to see the shadowy existence I was creating for myself. I refused to see that I wanted to fuse my identity with someone else's. Of course I was soon rejected by her and forced to face the folly of my mistakes. It was the nearest to the abyss that I have ever come. It was the closest to jumping out the window that I have ever been.

And now what is my symbol in life? I have no idea. It certainly is not intellectualization, and I do not think it is love. Maybe my symbol in life now is pleasure. Should not that be everybody's goal in life, to seek pleasure and enjoy life? To forget the sordidness of the real world, to live life to its fullest? But why was that man screaming? I feel as if there is some new aspect of myself, heretofore completely unknown, being subjected to some sort of cosmic tension. Could it just be the transition from early adulthood to mid-adulthood, just a mini mid-life crisis? After all, it is my thirty-third birthday next week.

My mind and body ache from these clouded thoughts. I try to shut them out, but I am unable. I close my eyes and lie back in the water, the bubbles from the jets intent upon my knotted muscles. Yes, *just a mid-life crisis*, I think to myself as I try to relax, try to clear my mind.

CHAPTER 6

My peaceful slumber is disturbed by the bright morning sunlight pouring through my crimson eyelids. I feel the gentle oscillations of waves through the keel of my serene boat. Splitting my eyelids, I see thirty-three red roses lying on the pillow to my side. It is Sunday, my birthday.

Sis is the one woman in the world who knows that guys like to be given flowers, though most would never admit it. The only other time I have been given a flower was when I was thirteen, just before I kissed my first girl. Or, should I be truthful, after my first girl kissed me. I remember standing in a crowded room, surrounded by dancing teenagers, when unexpectedly this amorous girl walked up to me with a red rose, placed it in my hand, and then planted her ruby lips on mine. Confused and scared, I took a step back and tripped over a sitting couple. Feeling like an idiot, I soon composed myself, and before long I was French kissing as if I had been doing it all of my life, braces clashing, tongues intermingling. Those were the days.

I rise up in the bed, still a little disoriented, and inhale the fresh morning air. The air is full of the smell of fresh pancakes and bacon. The clanging sounds of Sis cooking in the kitchen filters through my ears.

Sis enters the room with a present wrapped in golden foil and tosses it on the bed beside the flowers. "Happy birthday, love," she says while hanging on my neck. "I love you."

"Sis, you're wonderful. I just love the flowers."

"I knew you would. Now hurry up, breakfast is almost ready."

"Not until I coerce you into giving me a real kiss." I roll her over my lap and pin her shoulders to the bed.

"You win, but only because it's your birthday," she says, and then she kisses me with her probing mouth, her soft lips sucking mine, her moist tongue searching for my tongue, a gentle bite, the sweet smell of roses all about. As I start to unwrap my present, Sis chides me, "Not until tonight."

"Have you no mercy? This better be better than the present you gave me last Christmas."

"What do you mean?" Sis says, her eyebrows furrowed in dismay.

"Sis, get real. Last Christmas, you tortured me with the biggest present that I had ever received in my entire life ... sitting by the tree all December long. You even went so far as to dress it up like a house with roof and—"

"I thought it was quite clever. I bet—"

"Shush. Every day I would heft the weighty box and try to guess what it could be. I knew it had to be—"

"Now you are making me feel bad."

"Let me finish. I knew it had to be the most magnificent present I had ever received. The pressure was on, and I had to make sure that I had a magnificent present for you. So what did I do? I made up clues—very witty I might say—and sent you on a scavenger hunt throughout your apartment. And what did you find but a beautiful and expensive—really, really expensive, I might add—emerald bracelet. Now that was a present."

"I have to give you that one."

"But me, no ... I opened the present, thinking something wonderful was inside the box, and what was in the box but a suitcase. Initially I was shocked and disappointed, but then I realized it must be a trick, you clever one. And then I opened that suitcase, thinking something wonderful was inside, and lo and behold, there was another—"

"I just want you to know that it was a very expensive luggage set."

I stare Sis into silence and continue, "My excitement continued to grow as I opened three suitcases, one after another, until I got to the toiletry bag. I knew then that something wonderful was in that bag, but no, it was empty except for tissue paper. I was in shock. I'm still in shock—empty, nothing, not a thing. How could you have not taken advantage of such a wonderful opportunity?"

"But Gabe, I thought you liked that present."

"Sure I did," I say, feeling guilty on seeing the hurt in Sis's eyes, "but not for Christmas."

"Maybe I'll do better today," she says, and gives me a wink. A sweet kiss is fixed on my forehead, and then she departs.

Soon I am in the warm shower, the spray of water washing the evening's grime down the drain, refreshing me, awakening me. It is going to be a big day. Sis has invited my best friends over for a party on the lake.

* * *

Breakfast is wonderful, and Sis and I spend the morning lounging about, sipping on mimosas, until my friends start to arrive in the early afternoon.

Ken Grande drives up first in a black Porsche, which I assume he rented at the airport. And of course, out steps the most stunning blonde I have ever seen, dressed in a long, sleek, blue cotton dress. Ken was my college roommate at Harvard, born and raised in California. He has short, curly black hair, brown eyes, and Mediterranean skin. Girls have always drooled all over him.

In college, he was one of those confused guys who would not sell himself out for anybody. All that he wanted to do was to take pictures, and that is about all he ever did. He was always frustrated that school kept getting in his way. And when the photography department insisted that he take a course on the theory of art, Ken insisted otherwise. "How can you teach the theory of art?" he would exclaim to me, time after time. "No one can teach you a theory that doesn't exist." And so, being the principled man that he was, he never went to the class, and he never wrote any of the papers, and like all men of such principles, he took a resounding F and earned himself a one-year probation from the dean.

The next year, he took the course defiantly, attending the lectures but never taking notes, writing glorious papers but turning them in late. He used to take great delight in receiving his graded papers with comments like, "This was the most outstanding paper in the class, but unfortunately you were a week late, so I must give you a B." This would delight Ken to no end. This was his method for beating the system.

Well, I graduated ahead of Ken, thinking all the time that he might graduate by his tenth year, but Ken surprised me by finishing after five years. In college, his greatest fear was that someday he would end up shooting wedding pictures for a living. His father wanted him to be an engineer, but Ken liked living on the edge, and I guess he proved to his father that he has what it takes. Now he is a famous photographer who travels back and forth between New York, Los Angeles, Paris, London, and the like, in his personal jet, always surrounded by beautiful models. Every time I see him, he has a different girl on his shoulder: an actress, a violinist, a Zen Buddhist, and the list goes on.

"Hey, Ken," I shout across the dock. "I'm glad to see you've made it."

"I wouldn't miss it for the world."

His beautiful blonde leads the way up the gangplank, the nipples of her proud breasts protruding through her thin cotton dress, her deep blue eyes outshining the sea around, her long blonde hair trailing down her back. Ken follows, a small camera case across his left shoulder and a leather suitcase in his right hand.

"Gabriel, I want you to meet Dawn, Dawn Reese. She's a model from New York," Ken says with a sly grin on his face.

I give Dawn's hand a gentle squeeze as my roving eyes admire her full cleavage. "Hey, Dawn, I bet you are one of the new Black Velvet ladies, for why else would somebody as beautiful as you hang out with such a lowlife."

"Hey, watch who you slander," Ken says with a pretended look of hurt on his face.

"Just speaking the truth. I—"

"Well, Gabriel," Dawn interrupts as she presses me away with the palm of her right hand, "you better be careful. Ken has been telling me all the dirt on you for the last three hours. You are not so innocent yourself."

"Oh, I'm so hurt that anybody could think such a thing about me." I turn and yell for Sis.

Sis soon comes up, and after the introductions, she takes Dawn and her suitcase down below. Ken and I lounge on the front deck, the sun shaded by the overhanging roof.

"That is quite a girl you have there."

"She sure is, and you're close to being on the mark—she's one of the new Victoria's Secret models." His smile disappears, and his face turns serious. "So how have things been going?"

"I don't know. This birthday is having a strange effect on me. I guess I just don't like getting old."

Ken nods his head in an understanding fashion, and then we both look out over the lake, at the swift boats splashing by, at the joyful skiers, at the crying birds.

I wonder if Ken has found the secret to life. All through college I used to think Ken knew something I didn't know; he exuded a mysterious aura, an aura he still exudes now. Or is it possible that Ken has become so detached in life that nothing is important any more, that nothing can faze him?

The girls come up from below wearing beautiful bathing suits. Both are godlike; both dwarf the sea with their beauty.

"Hey, here come Mark and Mary," Sis calls out.

Mark Goldsmith pulls up in his 1975 Jaguar XJ6, its sides rusting, the steering wheel on the wrong side. His long black hair ripples in the wind, and his taut muscles bulge through his tank top. Mary jumps out first with her long, wavy black hair pulled back into a ponytail. She wears a light aqua sundress, flapping in the breeze, and bright pink flip-flops. Mary has pale white skin with cute freckles on her nose. Her eyes are dark brown, almost black in color, enticing, inviting. Mary is a rising young painter in Nashville, with talent galore. She is so bashful about her work that it is almost funny. She never can understand why anyone would buy one of her paintings, and she often hides them in her attic until her frantic agent talks her into bringing them down.

Mark is an interesting sort of fellow, one of the most relaxed and sedate guys you will ever meet. He was my classmate through medical school and another one of my partners in despair. Mark almost never opens his mouth except to say something sarcastic, and he rarely expresses any serious emotion, except for affection to his wife. Back in medical school, Mark had this strange philosophy about tests. He believed that every point above passing was time wasted on studying, and thus he would study for a test until he was sure he could pass it, and then he would later chastise himself for the twenty points above passing he received.

Mark and I were big on pranks, and one of them almost ensured our dismissal from medical school. During the first month of our second year of school, we heard that a friend of ours in the first-year class was going to be dissecting in the anatomy lab that night. Well, we borrowed a key and arrived about an hour earlier than our friend. Mark stripped down to his underwear, and I covered him with baby powder, and then he crawled underneath a sheet on an empty table, near our friend's table. I found the circuit box and disconnected about half of the lights in the room. Next, I tied a thin string to the skeleton in the corner and hid across the room, string in hand. We waited in silent vigil for the arrival of our friend.

Soon we heard the creaking of the lock being opened, and in walked a shadowy figure clad in a white coat. From my hiding place, I saw the figure look about the room; a slight shiver seemed to travel up his spine. Soon he was patiently dissecting, oblivious to all. First I gave the string a tug. The skeleton began to shake. Confused, the figure looked up, looked around, and started to leave the room, but soon he turned his attention back to his cadaver. Again I gave the string a tug. This time the figure jumped, startled and scared. I gave a low moan from my spot, a signal to

Mark. Mark then sat bolt upright, the sheet falling from his white torso. The figure shrieked and crumbled to the floor. Laughing, I ran to him and found, to my dismay, that it was not our friend. Oh, shit, we were in deep trouble; it was his lab partner.

The next day, we found ourselves in the dean's office, on probation, an apology forced upon our lips, ordered to give hours of private tutoring in the dreaded anatomy lab to struggling first-year medical students. I know our prank had gone a little too far, but how could we resist?

Mark now is a country club radiologist who likes to sit around reading up on computer science and drinking his Johnny Walker Black on the rocks. He claims he will retire at age forty-five, but if you know the life of a radiologist, he wouldn't notice the difference.

Mary's laughter, as she walks up the gangplank, brings me back to the present.

"Mark, Mary, great to see you've made it," I say as I shake Mark's hand and place my left arm around Mary affectionately, low on her waist, almost too low.

Sis eyes me suspiciously and then she introduces Mark and Mary to Ken and Dawn. We all walk to the rear of the boat, the girls chattering all the way.

"Dawn is a model in New York, although she just told me that she is also a poet. She has a publisher considering her first book of poems now," Sis says with a look of admiration on her face.

"How neat. I'm an artist of sorts, although I hate to admit it," says Mary. "Sis and Gabe are my greatest fans. Sis keeps trying to do a story on me, but I'm just not that great of an ..." Her voice fades into the wind.

"So Ken," Mark begins, "I heard a lot about you over the years. Gabe says you're the one who kept him from jumping off his 'abyss seat'."

"Yeah, Gabriel sure was one fucked-up dude back then. He used to think that he was the one looking out for me."

"Y'all folks better hush up, or I'm going to kick you off my boat and take the girls out by myself."

"You would love that," says Ken.

"So who else is left to come?" Mark asks.

"Only Christine Sanders, a lawyer in town, a friend of mine since high school, a real sweetheart. She used to claim she was a lesbian, then she said she was bisexual, and now I think she is omnisexual."

"Sounds interesting," Ken says.

"She is. But beware. She's a die-hard idealist, something neither of you know anything about."

While I am in the cabin fixing drinks, Christine pulls up in a black Bronco jeep, the top down. After she gets out of her car, I see that her dishwater blonde hair is tied behind in braids, her small tan figure framed by tight cutoff blue jeans and a pink T-shirt with GREENPEACE emblazoned on its front. Her tiny breasts bounce ever so gently as she strides up the gangplank.

All have gathered now on the front deck. Sis pulls up the anchor, and I rev the engine. The boat idles forward, past the safe confines of my boathouse, past the safe confines of the calm bay. A sailboat crosses in front, and then I hit the throttle. *Helen* flies forward, jumping wave after wave, the long V trailing behind.

I direct the boat to the middle of the lake, casting out the anchor, absorbing the full weight of the sun, the full impact of the watery breeze.

We all move to the upper deck, bathing suits in place, the fresh smell of coconut oil filling the air. I sit in a lawn chair, the sun beating down on my neck. Mary stands and removes her sundress; there is a conservative matching aqua bikini underneath.

"Mary, please put some of this 15 sunscreen on. I'm not going to be a part of your demise due to skin cancer," I say, not able to escape the physician within me.

"Okay, but only if you will rub it on my back."

"Gladly," I say as I give Mark a wink. Mark winks back. Sis again eyes me suspiciously.

Sis and Dawn spread out on the rubber mats. Dawn wears a rainbow-colored one-piece bathing suit that is cut very low in the back, with a large V-shaped front that barely covers her breasts, tantalizing me whenever she leans forward. Sis is wearing a skimpy floral bikini that leaves little to the imagination. Mark sits in the opposite corner, facing the sun, his metallic *Terminator* sunglasses hiding his eyes, revealing the reflection of my distorted self, the misshapen houseboat intermingled with the glare of the sun; he has a wry grin on his face. I bet he is having fun, ogling all of these beautiful girls, with nobody really knowing where he is looking.

Christine sits to my right, wearing cutoff blue jeans and a bikini top. Her braids are now undone, and her beautiful dishwater hair flaps in the wind.

"Get me a beer, Gabe," Mark demands.

"Forget it, it's my birthday."

"I'll get the beer," says Ken. "Gabriel's bones are fragile from old age, and I wouldn't want him to hurt himself."

Ken yells to Mark from the rear of the boat and passes up a cooler of beer. Soon the air is filled with the pop and fizz of beer cans opening in the summer breeze. All are content; all are happy.

Dawn sits next to Sis. "Is Sis your real name?"

"No, my true name is Elizabeth, Elizabeth Halcyonn Morgan, but all my friends call me Sis."

"Why Sis? Did you have an older—"

"Oh, no." I interrupt. "Like I've never heard this story before."

Sis stares me down and then begins, "It's a long story. When—"

"A very long story, which I have—"

"Gabe, hush. When I was little, my dad called me his 'little Beth.' But my mom had a maid name Willie Dell, who had—"

"Maid? More of a slave, if you ask me."

"Yes, I do admit that I grew up in a pampered lifestyle. Willie Dell cooked all our meals, took care of the household, and was more of a mother to me than my real mother. Anyway, Willie Dell had a son named Sammy who was three when I was born. Sammy thought I was his little sister and started calling me 'Sis.' Soon Willie Dell began to call me 'Sis,' and thereafter my mom. My dad insisted on calling me 'Beth' but finally gave up by the time I started grade school, as he realized I would never respond to any other name but the one given to me by my beloved playmate."

"Were you and Sammy always friends?"

"When we were little, we were best of friends. He's the reason I'm such a tomboy. He taught me how to throw a football, dribble a basketball, fish, go frog gigging, and even how to catch a snake with my bare hands. But as we got older, things just weren't the same. I think he thought it was not cool to hang out with a rich white girl, and I know my parents weren't too thrilled with our friendship, so it just died out over time. Sometimes I ..."

Sis stands and nods her head, a look of sadness in her eyes. She says, "I'm hot." Then she walks to the edge of the boat, raises her sleek, muscular arms toward the heavens, and as graceful as a swan, dives off the stern and slices into the still water. No splash or sound follows.

Mark, never to be out-machoed by a woman, jumps up and follows Sis. Immediately a loud splash rises high like a geyser, spraying all of us. I throw a few life preservers into the water, and soon all of us splash around merrily. Dawn swims up to me and grasps a nearby floating jacket.

"I'm sure glad Ken and I could come. Your boat is wonderful, and this lake sure beats the hell out of life in New York."

"Thanks." I pause and look about and then look back to Dawn. "So what do you think of Ken?"

"Strange, sexy, intelligent, thoughtful, inquisitive, very mysterious, and a wonderful photographer. Does that answer your question?" she says, ending with a lighthearted laugh.

"I always knew that was Ken's secret to attract women. Keep them puzzled."

Dawn's laughter fills the air. "You're probably right."

"So, what made you want to become a model?"

"I'm not sure. It gives me a sense of power, of responsibility. I try to mirror other people's souls in my work. I try to be a reflection of the world, so to speak. Do you know what I'm saying?"

"Sure," I reply, not having the slightest clue as to what she is talking about.

"I'm trying to put that same sense of power into my poetry," she says and then stares at the still horizon.

Ken, Mary, and Sis are now having a water fight. Dawn and Christine hold onto a life jacket and talk in hushed tones. Mark floats on a flimsy raft, his left hand grasping onto the anchor's rope, oblivious to all. I pull myself up onto the back deck, dripping water, and remember that I better turn on my gas grill. Sis bought me a stainless steel gas grill three years ago. The first grill I owned was a charcoal one, but that turned out to be a disaster. Every time the wind changed direction or the boat rotated, the cabin became flooded with smoke. It was months before the charcoal smell left my cabin. Now I have a gas grill: not as tasty, but very practical.

I retrieve the T-bone steaks that I have been marinating all day long in my secret sauce: three parts Worcestershire sauce, one part soy sauce, lemon pepper, and a dash of garlic. Staring at the steaks, I am mesmerized by the intricate marbling of the meat, and my mind wanders over the events of my life, over my successes and failures, over the meaning of life. Have I been placed on this planet for a reason? Is there a God out there who directs the course of our destiny? Has my future been mapped out already by this cosmic entity, or am I free to choose how I lead my life? Do I owe the world any kind of repayment for being here? Or in fact, does the world owe me repayment for placing me on this ghastly planet?

And what if there is no God? What then? I certainly do not owe the world anything. Then is existence just for the sake of existence? Is life only here to be enjoyed? Should anything else matter?

"Hey, everybody, it's almost dinner time," I shout to the misfit swimmers and set the steaks on the grill. I sear each side patiently before placing them away from the flame. I pour some hickory chips on top and close the grill, allowing the smoke to permeate every crack and crevice, every molecule of meat. The smell is alive and passionate.

The lazy swimmers have, by this time, each one in turn, pulled themselves onto the back of the boat, greeted me, and headed off inside to clean up.

I look through the window and see that Sis is making one of her famous mint juleps: a half-inch of sugar on the bottom, two sprigs of fresh mint on the inside, crushed ice to the glass's rim, straight bourbon until frost forms on its sides, and a bit of grated nutmeg on top. Now, that is a mint julep, or so Sis says, straight out of a recipe from William Alexander Percy's novel *Lanterns on a Levy*. She passes the glass to Christine, who brings the glass out to me.

"Try this."

I take one long, deep swallow. The alcohol rushes through every joint in my body and floods my mind with warmth and peacefulness.

I look at Christine and say, "So what new projects are you working on now?" Christine is always up to something, whether it is "save the whales" or "homes for the poor."

"I'm working on a law program for the needy—free legal advice, that sort of thing. Poor people don't have any idea what their rights are, how not to be taken advantage of, how to start their own business, all sorts of things," she says, searching into my eyes for a response. "We haven't come up with a name yet. Maybe you can help me."

"That's a tough one. How about the People's Legal Clinic?"

"Sounds too communistic," she says in a serious tone, missing my sarcasm, and dips her head as if intent upon a solution.

"So why do you want to help the needy? Is it guilt or something?"

"Maybe it is a little from guilt. I grew up in a rich, spoiled family and was given everything I ever wanted. And school was always so easy for me. Now I feel like it is not fair that everybody has not been given the same chances that I have. It is just my way of saying thanks to the world for being so nice, my way for repaying the world for its kindness."

"But shouldn't we want to do good for the sake of doing good, and not because we are filled with guilt over our upbringing or our success? Otherwise, disadvantaged people have no reason for being good," I say, hiding my anger that guilt seems to be the major force in most human actions.

"The source of our actions is not important, just the net result. Why are you always such a cynic, Gabriel? Try letting go. Stop fighting the world so hard. It's not as bad as you think. And besides, guilt is not such a terrible thing. I think it springs from a source greater than our inner psyche. I think that it springs forth from the collective soul of mankind. I think guilt may be the only force that may save this world from blowing itself up."

Oh no, I have stirred her soul, and there is no telling where this conversation is going. Why should I feel guilty that I have this nice houseboat, and a good job, and a beautiful girl? My life is not so wonderful. Each of us adapts to the lifestyle to which we are accustomed. It is not my fault that people are starving all over this planet. It is not my fault that millions are dying from disease and malnutrition. It is not my fault.

"Blame it on God," I blurt out.

"What did you say?"

"The steaks are ready." Whew, saved by the bell.

* * *

Dinner was wonderful: tossed salad, blissful steaks, and lots of beer and whiskey. Our burps resound across the waters.

"Do you have Sis's electric guitar on board?" Mark inquires.

"Of course. Sis brought both her electric and acoustic guitars."

"Then let's jam."

Mark sets up Sis's Fender guitar on the back deck, and I retrieve my Yamaha piano. Mark leaves his shirt off and puts on his *Terminator* glasses. I wear a bandanna on my head. Sis takes her acoustic guitar, a 1945 Gibson, and Mary and Christine provide the chorus, wearing scarves on their right wrists.

We play some Neil Young, Rolling Stones, and the Band. Boy, do we sound terrible as the noise reverberates across the open lake. I suspect the fish are suffering a slow and painful death. Dawn sits in

Ken's lap, enjoying our performance, a Mona Lisa grin on her face. While I am trying to concentrate on playing the piano, I become aware that Ken's mischievous hand is creeping up Dawn's thigh. Her breathing intensifies; her muscles weaken; smiles of joy appear on her face. That little rascal. Suddenly Dawn is transformed. She leaps up and takes the mike.

"Play 'Lola,' now," she demands. Dawn first hums the opening verses until we get some semblance of the music and rhythm. Dawn pauses, looks at us to make sure we are ready, and then shouts, "One, two, three, hit it," and we begin playing. Dawn leads the way with a voice full of passion and purpose, and the rest of us just try to keep up.

L-O-L-A Lola, lo-lo-lo-lo Lola ...

Dawn's energy electrifies us. At once we are transformed into a real band.

Lola, lo-lo-lo-lo Lola, lo-lo-lo-lo Lola ...

The music pours forth, and the other girls sing in the background. Dawn is in control; her voice resounds with earnest fervor, and then it is over. Ken's shouts and hoots reach my ears.

"Dawn, that's great. Give us one more," I say.

"No more. I just know that one song," says Dawn as she returns the mike. She sits back on Ken's lap and plants an amorous kiss on his receptive ear.

The band disbands, and we all lounge about, drinking and talking. The sun is now low on the west horizon, a full moon just beginning to show on the east horizon. The lake is abandoned except for ourselves anchored in its midst. Mark approaches me and sits down.

"This lake reminds me of our trip to Greece—the beauty and peacefulness, the booze and the women," he says.

"There were no women."

"Well, there could have been, if we had been a little more diligent."

At the completion of medical school, Mark and I had spent a month in Greece, just prior to our residency. We slept in dollar hotels, hung out in the old cafes, and ate in out-of-the-way restaurants.

"Remember how we first saw the Parthenon?" I say.

"Wasn't that great?" Mark replies, his face shining bright.

When we first arrived in Athens, it was late in the afternoon. The gates to the Parthenon were sealed. So we scaled the rear wall, the cliffs above, full of danger and excitement. It took us over an hour, and there we were, on top, by ourselves, standing before the Parthenon. We had found the secret to being a tourist. There were no cameras clicking, no tourist guides going on with their endless drone, just us and the great ruins before us.

"Yeah, it sure was, and remember the celebration we had after our climb?" I say.

"Yeah, we got shit-faced drunk."

"And what else do you remember?"

"Gabe, are you ever going to give up on that story? There is no way in hell that I peed on your backpack."

Mary's ears perk up, and she wanders over.

"What's that about Mark?"

"Mark got so shit-faced drunk on German beer and ouzo one night in Greece that he peed all over my backpack, thinking it was the john."

"Well, I will never believe that is anything but a figment of your imagination."

We all laugh, and Mary wanders off. In our silence, I think about the old Greeks we met in the cafes, the old Greeks who taught us how to drink Turkish coffee, down shots of ouzo, the proper attitude for playing chess. I remember being fascinated by the similarity to sitting around small country restaurants in rural Tennessee, listening to the farmers talk, watching them chew tobacco and play checkers, hearing the stories of their youth. I never once forgot the tradition of this once-great people. These people were all descendants of the greatest culture of mankind. They were not common fisherman and farmers and shopkeepers; they were the progeny of heroes like Achilles and Agamemnon and Ajax and Ulysses. They were gods in their own right.

And I knew right then that I would never be able to travel to another country and stay in a Hilton, and visit fancy restaurants, and take guided tours. The people were the essence of the experience. The people were more important than the museums, and the buildings, and the nightclubs, and the like.

And when I returned to America, I returned with an exalted sense of perception. I had a telescope into other people's souls. I could hang out in cheap bars and dirty restaurants and see local people for their greatness, for their heritage, for what they represented. I could—

"Gabe, you sure have changed from medical school."

"What?"

"Remember how idealistic you were? You were going to 'save the world.' You were going to make the world a 'better place to live,' but I always told you that you would change."

"I wish you had convinced me earlier, and then I would be a radiologist now, and be rich like you."

"Poor baby," Mark says, nodding his head with a smug look on his face, rubbing his right index finger on his thumb in a circular motion.

"What are you doing?"

"This is the world's smallest record player playing 'My Heart Bleeds for You.'"

"Very funny ... I thought you were playing with your booger."

Kristin and Mary are over in the corner, rolling a joint. It's been a long time since I have smoked, not since college. Mary soon comes over to my side and gives me a hug and a kiss.

"Happy birthday, old man. You get the first hit." Mark wanders off to the others, and Mary sits down. I cup my hands, and Mary lights me up. I take a long drag, and Mary does the same.

"Why do you paint, and why are you always so damn embarrassed over your work?"

"I guess I paint for myself. It is hard to share yourself with others. I can't really explain it, but when I pick up a brush, something comes over me, a sense of longing, a sense of longing not of the past or present or future, but a sense of longing for something more."

"This is getting deep."

"And out of this longing comes an image, and I strive to make my image and my painting one, and if I do, I feel whole, and if I don't, I'm disappointed and must try again and again."

"Too deep for me. As Bob Dylan would say, I feel like I am knockin' on heaven's door."

After taking a long drag on the rolled paper, she continues, "Don't you have a force in your life that pushes you, that beckons you, that makes you create something out of nothingness?"

"You've been smoking too much."

The drug enters my mind, slowing down time, filling the room with a dense fog. All about are voices chattering, forgotten faces beckoning me. I look at each one in turn, trying to see who they are. I feel naked and alone. Everybody here is a stranger. Sis approaches.

"Relax, Gabe, it's only the drug. We are all friends here."

Feeling her hot breath in my ear, feeling her warm body against mine, feeling her arm about my neck, I relax. My mind starts to wander. I wonder if there is any way to prove whether or not God exists. I could design an experiment, carry it out, become famous. What if I took a sample of dying patients, randomize them into two groups? One group would have a set of priests and nuns hovering over them, praying non-stop for God to heal. The other group would have a band of atheistic poets and philosophers wishing them well. Of course we would have to dress them in the same clothes, to control for the placebo effect, and all prayers and entreaties would have to be silent. Would not God, if he existed, listen to nuns and priests before he would listen to a bunch of atheists? I wonder how many patients I would need for this study. Just think, I could prove or disprove God's existence with a simple statistical test, a chi square test or a Fisher's exact test. All the mystery of the world could be solved by elementary mathematics, all the ... all the mysteries ... all the ... all ... now, what was I just thinking? Something about God ...

Oh, hell, I always come upon the greatest ideas when I am stoned, and then I forget them. I look at the sexy body of Christine in the distance. God, is she beautiful. I wonder if she is still bisexual. Just think how great it would be to get Sis and Christine in bed together. Just think of all the possibilities ...

... An artist sees an image, and out of the image comes a form ...

... How can you teach a course on the theory of art ...?

... My, you've changed ...

... One, two, three ... *Lo ... la ... Lo ... la* ...

... Just think, I kissed my first girl. Wasn't it wonderful? Braces clashing, tongues intermingling ...

... Let's see, if I move my knight here, I can beat this old Greek, I know I can ...

... Remember how idealistic you were? You were going to make the world a better place to live ...

… Oh, God, look at that cleavage …

… Gabriel sure was one fucked-up dude back then …

… Let's see, I wonder if God exists. I wonder if I can invent an experiment that would settle, once and for all, the question of whether or not God exists …

… Please put some of this 15 sunscreen on …

… But why shouldn't you do good for the sake of doing good …?

… Why are you such a cynic? If you would just stop fighting the world …

… It's not my fault that people are dying all over this planet …

… *Lola, lo-lo-lo-lo Lola, lo-lo-lo-lo Lola* …

… You were going to change the world. Don't you remember …?

… It's not my fault …

… Just think of the elegance, to be able to prove or disprove God's existence with a simple statistical test. Just think …

… Don't you have a force in your life that pushes you, beckons you, makes you create something out of …?

… Relax, Gabe, we're all friends …

… Blame it on God …

… I wonder if God listens to atheists …

… But I always told you that you would change …

I realize that my eyes have been closed, and I open them. I try really hard to focus on the present. The images of my friends seem to swell and recede like waves on the ocean shore. Gradually, time seems to speed up; the drug seems to be wearing off.

Sis wanders off toward the others, dragging her hand along my scalp as she leaves. Ken and Dawn walk over, hand in hand.

"Having a good time?" I say to Ken.

"Sure am," Ken says and gives Dawn a squeeze around the shoulders while gulping down a sip of beer. Ken turns to Dawn and says, "Gabriel here was my introduction to the South. We drove down to his parents' house one spring break and partook of such activities as drinking JD and shooting STOP signs. I was almost arrested for taking photographs of the nuclear power plant. They thought I was one of them Yankee liberals, one of them protestors about to show up with thousands of die-hard liberals. It was real tough, though, trying to convince them otherwise when I had Massachusetts plates on my car. And the thing that amazed me the most was that everybody had guns— shotguns, pistols, assault rifles, muskets, all kinds of guns. The Russians sure would be in for a surprise if they ever tried to invade the South."

Dawn and I laugh, and I start to wander back to the safety of Sis. Ken interrupts me halfway.

"Hey, Gabriel, what's the problem? I know you're on the edge. Remember how you were always so depressed in college? I used to joke about your 'abyss seat,' but I was really worried. Now I see that strange look in your eye. Are you okay?"

"I don't know. Something's just out of whack."

"But why? Everything in your life is perfect. You're a doctor, have great toys and a beautiful girlfriend."

"Just perfect," I say with a frown on my face. "If I only knew your secret."

"Gabe, there is no secret." Ken points out over the majestic lake, at the rising moon, at the revolving stars. "Just look about. What more justification do you need in life?" He pauses and then continues, "But just remember, Gabriel, you have one great talent. You are a survivor, and nobody will ever take that from you."

He pats me on the back, pokes me in my ribs, and then pushes me over to Sis, who catches me in her outspread arms.

"Got you, love, and I'm not planning on ever letting you go."

"Oh, Sis, you're the best," I say as I give her a gentle squeeze.

Sis looks into my eyes with her deep brown orbs, kisses me with her fleshy lips, and then gently nibbles on my ears. Her nipples become erect under her thin cotton dress. All of a sudden she screams and holds her eye.

"Oh, shit, something flew into my eye. Will you help me?" she says and takes my hand, leading me to our bedroom, holding her eye in pain. The door closes behind. Sis turns and laughs, her hand fondling my crotch.

"I saw you checking out all the girls," Sis says while unbuckling my pants. "Well, you are just going to have to be satisfied with me." Sis throws me onto the bed and, like a woman possessed, pounces on me and continues in her heated state. Time starts to slow down, and the bedroom walls starts to expand. We moan, but there are no sounds. We gaze at each other, and I see veil after veil of stars, and then there is nothingness.

I feel the sweet sighs of Sis's breath in my ear, the gentle heaving of her breasts against my chest, the pounding of her heart against mine. And then we hear the applause outside, the hoots and hollers.

"More, more! We want more!" Mark yells.

Hiding our embarrassment, Sis and I exit the bedroom.

"Is your eye all right?" Christine says.

"Just fine," replies Sis, and then she gives me an affectionate hug.

Mary places a hand over her right eye. "Gabe, I think something's wrong with my eye."

Everyone laughs but Sis, and then Mary leaves the room and returns with a cake full of candles. All break out into that obnoxious "happy birthday to you" song.

"Make a wish! Make a wish!" Sis exclaims.

I hope I am someday rich … no … I hope I give Sis an engagement ring next Christmas … no … I wish I could forget about life and just enjoy it. Yes, I want to enjoy life to its fullest. Inhaling deeply, I blow out all thirty-three candles with one breath. I guess I'm not so old after all.

"Now, Gabe, here is your present, just for you," Sis says and hands me my golden gift.

What could it be? What could it be? My excitement grows. I shake it next to my ear and think of the disappointment of last Christmas. After ripping off the paper, I find inside a little wooden box made of cherrywood, a small brass latch on the front. I open the box, and inside lies an antique gold compass. There is an engraving on the back of the compass:

Now you can never become lost.
Always yours,
Love, Sis

After I read the engraving out loud, Sis hangs a kiss on my neck. "Gabe, I am always yours, and I will never, ever let you forget that."

"It's beautiful, thank you," I reply with a tear forming in the corner of my right eye.

* * *

Soon the cake is all gone, and it is getting late. Sis navigates the boat toward my boathouse, and I enjoy the company of my friends. The lights are out, and we sit on the forward deck. The mighty moon hangs high overhead, and Scorpio gleams to the right, its huge claws clutching the heavens. The water is motionless, and the only noise is the muffled whine of the engine and the splash of water against the bow. Sis gives a long tug on the horn, like the mighty wail of a great beast, the wail of the god of the sea.

"Look over there, to the south," I say to Mary, who seems to hang on my every word. "That is Scorpio, one of the easiest constellations in the sky to find. See the great claws? And that red star there is Antares, the rival of Mars in Greek myth."

"And what did Scorpio ever do?"

"There are all sorts of myths. But the myth I find the most interesting is that he was the slayer of Orion—stung him to death. Orion and Scorpio are antagonistically opposed in the sky. Orion sets in the west just as Scorpio rises. However, we all know that mighty Orion could never be overcome by a scorpion."

"And what is that bright star?" Mary says, pointing high in the sky, near the bright glow of the moon.

"That is not a star. That is Jupiter, and if I had my telescope, you could see its moons and the famous red spot."

Mark walks up. "That is enough star talk, Gabe. I had to listen to this nonsense all through medical school."

I turn toward Mary and say, "We all know Mark is uncultivated and ignorant of worldly things. One night soon, I will drag out my telescope and dazzle you with the beauty of the universe."

"I'm not sure if Mark will trust me with you."

"I'm sure he wouldn't do anything that I wouldn't do," Mark says, a mischievous grin on his face.

* * *

Sis deftly maneuvers the boat into its home. Mark, Mary, and Christine bid their farewells, and I find myself resting in the comfort of Sis's arms.

"So Gabe, dear, what's been troubling you? You just don't seem to be yourself."

"I'm sorry, I just don't know what the problem is. I have the best friends in the world, a good job, and most of all, you, but something seems to be missing. Don't you think it is time we get married and have children? You know, start a family ..." My voice drifts off into silence.

"Is that a proposal?" Sis says with a look of apprehension on her face.

"Don't you think it is time to take the next step?" Caressing her hand, I press my cheek into the softness of her breast and hear the pounding of her heart, beat by beat.

I feel her whole body shudder and notice that goose bumps have appeared on her arms. She pushes me away and searches my eyes. "Yes, Gabe, I think it is time we start talking about marriage and children. But I have to admit, though, the thought of marriage terrifies me. I'm scared of losing my independence and individuality. I'm scared that if we marry, then you will want to leave me, like other people in my life have left me."

"I won't ever leave you. I promise."

"But I'm also scared that I will be a terrible mother, and—"

"You'll be a great mother."

"It's more than that. Don't take me wrong, but I'm scared because sometimes I'm not sure who you are."

Whew, what a bombshell. "What brought that on?"

"I'm sorry, Gabe, I always feel nervous when the subject of marriage comes up. I'm sorry—it's your birthday. I think your problem is that you just have your priorities in life a little confused."

"What?"

"And as for my insecurities, they will take care of themselves. All I ask of you is just love me for who I am, and always show me respect."

"That's easy," I say and give Sis an anxious hug, wondering how this conversation ever began. I just have my priorities confused. That's all.

That's right, I just have my priorities a little confused. God help me. I'm thirty-three and I still have no idea who I am. What gives?

What am I failing to understand? If only I can discover the truth. Hey, world out there, hear me. I exist; I am real.

World, hear me …

Hear me …

* * *

Sis and I fall asleep in each other's arms, the sounds of love from Ken and Dawn filtering through the thin walls.

* * *

My compass lies silently on the nightstand.

Its needle points directly at me…

PART TWO

Turning and turning in the widening gyre
The falcon cannot hear the falconer;
Things fall apart; the centre cannot hold

W. B. Yeats

CHAPTER 7

The noise is deafening, as jackhammers blast, cars honk, lightning thunders. In vain, my hands cover my ears, but still the incessant noise pours through the webs of my fingers. Then there is nothing, just darkness and silence as a thick fog creeps through my exhausted limbs. In the distance I see a dull glow and force my immobile body to move. I can feel the crunch of sodden grass with every step, as I wade through the thick air like a pelican mired in an oil slick. I look about, hoping to find an exit, but my legs are weak, my muscles are tired. Then my thigh collides with a fixed, cool object.

Oh, God, help me, help me. Get me out of here.

The fog clears, the sun is set low on the horizon, morning dew covers the grass, and there in front of me is my father's tombstone.

Oh, God, please, please help me.

A wooden door lies on the surface of the grave, and then it opens, and a mysterious figure beckons to my terrified self. His ashen-colored face jars my fragile bones; his deep gray eyes pierce my soul; the thin scar on his left jaw laughs at my every move.

Wake up, wake up, I plead. But no, I follow the figure to the edge of the grave. I look down and see a winding staircase, down and down, around and around, as far as the eye can see.

"Who are you? What do you want?" I call to the mysterious figure, his Adam's apple undulating with every swallow.

He is silent.

"Leave me alone. Go away … please."

He points toward the weathered tombstone, and then he is gone, rushing down the winding staircase.

"Don't go! Come back! You haven't told me who you are," I beseech him and take off down the spiraling staircase after him. The door slams above with a resounding echo. Around and around and around I go, as the dark, damp air whistles through my terrified ears, but the shadowy figure always remains a few steps ahead. Down and down and down I go; darker and darker and darker it grows; faster and faster and faster I run.

"Stop, stop, stop! Where are you taking me, taking me, taking me?" I shout.

My voice echoes back to my senseless skull, and then there is nothing, only my harsh breath in the damp air, only the dull thud of shoes on the winding stairs.

A light grows in the distance; just a little farther, I tell myself. The ghostly figure is gone. But onward I push, down and down and down, around and around and around, until I find myself standing in a huge, candlelit room. The figure now stands across the dim room against the wall, expressionless, staring at me with his steely gray eyes. The room is cut out of black volcanic rock. Weeping moss grows in every crevice; the floor is smooth glass; and there, there in the middle of the room is a decayed table, and at the head of this table sits my father. There is my father, my father, my father.

"Father, Father, Father, how are you, are you, are you? I have missed you so much, so much, so much," I say, rejoicing, but my father stares straight ahead, a silly Gomer Pyle grin on his unmoving face. "Father, Father, Father, don't you see me? It's your son, your son, your son!" But again there is no response.

I stand there looking at him as he sits before me with that obnoxious grin. A faint, round scar on his forehead stares at me like a third eye, and then there is anger. I boil inside; I am filled with hate.

"Just who in the hell do you think you are?" I say, not waiting for a reply. "Just what right did you have to ruin my life, to steal my childhood, to make me grow up before I was ready?" I yell, as my passion grows, but still he stares straight ahead with that shit-eating grin, the third eye mocking me, laughing at me.

"You are scum, scum, scum, and I hate you, hate you, hate you." I spit in his face, but still he does not move. "I wish you were never born, never born, never born. You are the most pitiful excuse for a human being that ever was, ever was, ever was. I hope you rot in hell, rot in hell, rot in hell." And then, out of control, I start hitting him and hitting him and hitting him; my fists pummel his head in a blur, right and left, right and left; my punches pound against him, trying to make him look up at me, trying to make him notice me, trying to wipe that grin off of his face. The flesh tears away from my frantic hands with every blow, the pearly white bones of my bleeding knuckles gleam in the air—

I scream.

* * *

My heart pounds in my chest as I struggle to breathe in the thick syrupy air. My T-shirt is soaked with sweat and clings to my body with a viselike grip; my limbs tremble like a chandelier caught in an earthquake. Thank God, it is only a dream, only a dream, only a dream. Thank God … only a dream … only a dream … *Father, Father, why hast thou …*

I relax and fall back asleep, forgetting the pain of the past.

CHAPTER 8

S is and I awake to the feel of the cool autumn morning air creeping through the open window, to the sound of the occasional honking horn from the nearby Nashville skyline.

"Good morning, Gabe. Did you sleep well?"

"Just perfectly," I say, trying to remember a dream I had last night, something about my father, my father, my father …. I give Sis a great big hug and say, "What do you say to a picnic, in Murfreesboro? I know just the spot."

"Wonderful. We can go by KFC and pick up some chicken, coleslaw, and potato salad."

"And let's not forget the pecan pie."

"You are going to be the downfall of my figure, and then I will be out of a job," Sis says as she grasps the imperceptible layer of fat on her smooth stomach.

"Well, we better exercise now to burn off some calories," I say as I roll on top of Sis and press my warm breath into her ear.

"That feels so good," Sis whispers into my impatient ear.

* * *

We roar down the old Nashville highway in my unbridled Mustang, the top down. The warm autumn air rushes through our chaotic hair, our loose sweaters flap in the steadfast wind, music pours forth from my stereo. Onward and onward we go, in the blast of the oncoming wind. All around us are cars going this way and that. Empty farmhouses line the roadway. The sun gleams off the green glass insulators, sitting high on abandoned telephone poles like tiny pagan statuettes to an unknown god. We approach a train on our right, drawing close, and then pass it by.

"Look, it has a red caboose," I shout through the deafening hurricane and point.

"Wow," Sis shouts back and waves to the conductor on board.

Near Murfreesboro, the traffic slackens. Soon we are the last travelers on the road. Gone are the tourists and cargo trucks; gone are the businessmen and housewives. We are in our world, our world alone, like Robinson Crusoe and Friday on their tiny island, their universe within a universe. On our left grazes a herd of beautiful brown horses, heads down, chewing on the browning grass. On our right a couple of yelping dogs roam at the feet of a slovenly hitchhiker, a determined man who holds a sign saying CHATTANOOGA.

I look at Sis and notice that her blazing eyes are knit at the edges and her symmetric jaw is held rigid. Then she fearlessly slaps her knee and nods her head fervently, off in her own dream world.

"What are you thinking about?" I shout through the blast of the wind.

"I'm overwhelmed with confidence right now. I've just realized that I have never failed at anything I have ever tried to do. There are no limits to what I can accomplish. I'm going to take this world by its horns, wrestle it to the ground, and make it a better place to live."

Her mood spreads to me, and I open up a can of Budweiser, let out a cheer, and toast the sky. "Here's to you, world! May you always be as great as you are now."

A brown bird with a white belly circles high overhead, and I applaud its beauty. "Hey, great bird, may you watch over my every move."

A grazing horse looks up at the honk of my horn, and I salute him. "O wise horse, may your wisdom and beauty always surround me."

Two children are perched in the rear window of a passing Ford, and I wave to them. "O great children, may you be the leaders of tomorrow."

Sis is now laughing at my silliness, and she raises her head full into the wind. Her hair whips back and forth in disarray; her cheeks are flattened. My car slows down, as my turnoff lies just ahead. Sis's long brown hair settles, and her cheeks resume their former shape.

"I've never been here before. Where are we going?"

"To the playgrounds of ghosts and forgotten children," I say and give a gentle laugh.

Sis looks at me with a puzzled expression on her face.

I steer my Mustang down a narrow road. Farmlands and farmhouses line both sides, the changing leaves of fall flutter in the breeze, and ahead stands a large monument with cannons all around it.

"This is it—the cannon monument, the playground of our once-proud ancestors. And just over the crest is Stones River. Wait until you see how beautiful it is."

"Whose cannons were these?"

"Yankees." I pause. "I will tell you about the whole battle later on," I say as I pull up my car just beneath the huge obelisk, which looms high overhead like a miniature Washington monument.

The peaceful cannons are perched all about, three-inch ordnance rifles, six-pound 1841 field guns, ten-pound parrot cannons, twelve-pound Napoleons. The distant turbulence of water colliding with pebbles resonates with the gentle breeze.

Sis and I spread out a blanket on the grassy plain in front of the river, the air now warm as the sun shines down with a steady radiance. After we remove our sweaters, we take joy in our solitude, in the splash of fish in the water, in the call of birds preparing to depart for the coming winter. Sis has brought her old guitar, and I spread out the feast.

"Sis, we haven't been on a picnic in several years."

"You're right—since you have a houseboat, we haven't felt the need, have we?"

"No, I guess we haven't. I remember the last picnic we went on was to one of your favorite spots in Sewanee."

Sis eyes brighten. "Yes, wasn't that beautiful? Sitting on my favorite lake, soaking up the sun and the nature around, pouring down the champagne, and singing 'Joy to—'"

"And sneaking off in the woods to make love."

"Yes, those sure were good days. I should have known then that you were such a bad boy."

"I just get naughtier by the minute."

We both laugh and then pause, serene in our present, and look out over the rippling river, rejoicing over the past.

"Tell me about the battle? I never learned much about the Civil War."

I kneel next to Sis and clear out a small area in the earth below. I grab a nearby stick and inscribe a map in the knotted earth.

"Here we are, and here is the river. Both the Confederate lines and the Union lines stretched out north and south, facing each other on the eve of the battle. General Braxton Bragg—an idiot, by the way—was the Confederate general, and General William Rosecrans was the Union general. On the opening morning of the battle, December 31,

1862, both generals had the notion of a surprise attack on the enemy's right flank, but the Confederates were quicker. At dawn, they charged here, catching the Yankees completely by surprise, like at Shiloh."

"I don't know anything about Shiloh."

"That's okay. Someday I'll take you there. Well, anyway, the Confederates charged first, and it was a complete rout. The Union forces were jackknifed against the Nashville and Chattanooga Railroad, here," I say and make a V in the dirt to show the position of the Yankee army.

Sis follows my every word, attentive and absorbed, the perfect student, sharing in my growing excitement. "What happened next?"

"It should have stayed a rout, but no, Bragg ordered attack after attack on an area called the Round Forest. The troops here were well fortified and had plenty of cannon protection, but no, Bragg kept trying the impossible. If he had only had the foresight to send Breckinridge to this spot right where we are sitting, he would have been attacking the jackknifed Yankees from both sides, and they would have all been captured, or forced to retreat."

"But wouldn't these cannons have slaughtered the Confederates?"

"Of course, if they were here, but they were not here on that opening day of battle." I pause in deep thought, pondering what could have been if I had been the Confederate commander, how history could have been changed. There would have been no Lookout Mountain, or Missionary Ridge, or Atlanta, or March to the Sea. But then what would we have? Surely slavery would not exist? Surely the South knew slavery was a dying institution? But what if it did not know any better? Would the new South be like South Africa, with apartheid and students and nations all over the world protesting against our inhumanity? Hmm. I am glad I wasn't the general back then.

"So they fought all day long over that stupid forest," I say as my stick jabs into the ground, grinding into the soil with a touch of animosity, "and nothing happened but lots of wounded and dead soldiers. On January the first, there was no fighting. Both sides buried their dead, took care of their wounded. Bragg rejoiced in his victory, unaware of the day to come. On the morning of January the second, Rosecrans crossed the river and occupied the crest beyond those houses. The shallow here is called McFadden's Ford." Again I inscribe the dirt with my upturned stick and jab the ground with growing frustration. "Whether out of foresight or military genius, Captain John

Mendenhall occupied this knoll where this cannon monument lies, with every Yankee cannon he could muster. Fifty-seven cannons in all."

"Are these cannons from the battle?"

"I'm not sure. We'll have to check with a park ranger. I'm sure some of them were here that day. But anyway, that afternoon, Bragg, dismayed to find that the Yankees had advanced upon his right flank, ordered Breckinridge to charge. Onward he rushed, up these hills, and the terrified Yankees turned and fled. It was another rout. It was victory for sure this time, or so Bragg thought. Just as Breckinridge's men descended upon these fields in front of us, these now house-covered suburbs, the Yankee cannons opened fire. It was a slaughter. Worse than anything anybody had known up to that point in the war. It reminds me of a passage in the Aeneid, a passage in which Virgil compares the treachery of the Greeks at Troy to the devastation that happens when a flame has fallen among standing corn, the winds raging—"

"Didn't you take a lot of Latin?"

"Yes, seven years … I also took three years of ancient Greek. I was such a nerd. Had I believed in God, I could have been a priest."

"Gabe, I wish you would give God another chance. He's out there if you would just let him in."

"Why? Just look at the world, at all the injustices."

"I do look at the world, every day, and I see God all around me. Do you remember the first lines of John? 'In the beginning was the Word, and the Word was with God, and God was—"

"Ha! What a lame translation. I bet you were also taught that the Word is Jesus."

"What do you mean?" she says, taken aback at my harsh tone.

"In the original Greek, the correct translation is 'In the beginning was *logos,* and *logos* was with God, and God was *logos.*' Heraclitus used *logos* to represent order and knowledge. Aristotle considered *logos* to represent one of the modes of persuasion, along with *pathos* and *ethos,* and the Stoics considered *logos* to be the logic pervading the universe. Oh, I almost forgot about Philo. Philo believed that God was an indeterminate and impersonal being and that Logos was a second god that helped bridge the gap between man and God. There have been dozens of books written on the meaning of *logos* in the ancient world, and none of them have anything to do with your God or with your Jesus."

Sis gives me a faraway look, a touch of sadness in her eyes, and then smiles and says, "That is enough religion and philosophy for one day. I want to hear more about the battle."

Relieved, I continue with my story. "Anyway, the charging Confederates were decimated. A few managed to make it to the river to be slaughtered by bursting shells. A few more unlucky ones are said to have crossed the river, to be met by grapeshot. The dead covered the ground. The moans of the wounded filled the air. The roar of cannons was deafening."

"How many were killed?"

"In only one hour's time, over eighteen hundred Confederates were killed or wounded in these fields before us. Just think, eighteen hundred young men, their lives ruined in an eye blink. And to what avail? Nothing. The next day, both Rosecrans and Bragg declared victory, although Bragg retreated almost immediately to Tullahoma, calling it a withdrawal to strengthen his position."

I pause, thinking of all the soldiers killed in this futile charge. What did it accomplish? The battle was a draw, although Bragg gave the Union troops victory by default. Just think of all the kids that poured their lives out because they thought war was glorious.

"Pulchrumque mori succurrit in armis."

"What?" says Sis.

"Dulce et decorum est pro patria mori."

"I know that one."

Without realizing it, I trace λόγος in the dirt and then immediately scratch it out. I break the useless stick and throw it aside.

"Did you know that they said the river ran red after the battle? So many dead soldiers floating in its midst, so many wounded soldiers crawling down to its banks to feast on its quiet water with their dying breaths."

I point over the monument to our rear and say, "One half mile that way is the war cemetery. We will drive by it on the way home. Almost seven thousand Civil War dead are buried in that cemetery, all with pearly white tombstones, all forgotten. That is when the reality of war hits you, all those tombstones—" A shudder runs up my spine, and I try to remember something about last night, but I cannot quite grasp it. "All of the graves are Yankee, though."

"How come Confederates are not buried there?"

"Because the U.S. government considered Confederate soldiers traitors," I say with a touch of anger. "Many of them were sent home, to be buried by their families, to be buried next to their loved ones. Others were buried in neighboring cemeteries or where they fell. In 1890, the Evergreen Cemetery in Murfreesboro established a common burial plot called the Confederate Circle, and two thousand unknown Confederate soldiers from the battle were relocated there."

I point forward over the river and say, "And over there are the remains of the Mitchell cemetery. See that clump of high-grown grass and weeds? That family cemetery was there during the battle. First Yankees hid behind the tombstones during the Confederate charge, and then during the cannon slaughter, Confederates took refuge. Vandals have toppled all of the tombstones, but you can still see the jagged indentations in the granite from cannon and rifle fire. After the battle, the Mitchell house was used as a hospital."

Both of us are silent and stare toward the gentle river flowing over the rocks that line its bottom. The rhythmic turbulence relaxes us and fills us with peace, taking away the sorrow of the forgotten dead.

I point up the river and say, "My grandparents used to live about a mile upriver, on the opposite bank. I'll take you there after we eat. I spent many a summer as a young boy playing on this river, playing on these cannons."

"Gabe, did you know I used to kayak on rivers like this? Well, actually they were a lot more turbulent. I spent one whole summer giving raft tours on the Ocoee River in east Tennessee. I was one of the few girls of many guys. I kissed my first boy during one of those summers."

I lean over to Sis, pretending to be about to kiss her. Her eyes closed in anticipation, and then I stick a leg of chicken in her mouth. "Gotcha."

"You're such a goof." She says, "I haven't kayaked in years …" and her voice trails off into oblivion.

"We used to play war games near here, starting when I was about eight years old, over there," I say, pointing, "where those houses now stand. Both sides always wanted to be the Confederates, so there never were any Yankees. We would dig foxholes and trenches and tunnels. Our weapons were dirt clods and BB guns and slingshots. It's amazing none of us were ever killed. See this little scar here?" I point to a tiny mark on my chin. "That's where I was hit by a lead pellet. After I was hit, I chased that poor sucker that shot me all over this neighborhood, pumping my BB gun as fast as it would go, firing shot after shot into his fleeing behind. We outlawed pellet guns after that day."

"Why have you never told me how you got that scar on your cheek?"

Feeling the scar with my right hand, I ponder for a moment with a faraway look in my eyes. "I don't really remember," I lie, feeling a smoldering heaviness in my chest. "Did you ever play any war games?"

"Of course I used to play war games, in the winter, when it would snow. I can remember us building huge banks of snow as fortresses, and making hundreds of tight little icy snowballs. All the kids in the neighborhood would join in, and we would fight for what seemed like hours. I sure made a mean snowball. I was the terror of the neighborhood."

Sis throws a small stone into the river beyond; the *kerplunk* resounds in the air.

"Gabe, tell me about the *second* Battle of Stones River. I vaguely remember you telling me about it long ago."

"That's right, I forgot I told you about that. Well, one summer when I was staying here with my grandparents, a group of us neighborhood kids were marching down the river on a snake hunting expedition, BB guns blazing right and left."

"Did you kill any snakes that day?" Sis asks. "When I was little, I remember playing in my sandbox, when I dug a little hole revealing a long, black snake. It scared me to death. The snake took off in one direction, and I ran in the other. That night I had a nightmare, I dreamed that I opened our front door, and there was that snake, hissing at me, its tongue flickering in the air. God, I haven't thought of that memory in years."

I laugh and begin again, "Here we were, about eight of us kids, BBs blazing back and forth, snakes dying right and left, when about a half mile up the river from where we are now sitting, a loud explosion sounded, and nearby a large splash of water sprayed the air with foam. My god, we thought, what was that? Creeping up to the edge of the riverbank, hiding behind the protection of trees, we saw, to our consternation, a bearded Yankee in full military uniform, a blue wool jacket, with brass eagle buttons gleaming in the sun, and a Springfield musket in his arms. At once we opened fire upon him across the river, our BBs bouncing off trees and rocks. Our Yankee friend let out a yelp and took off running down the bank. We trailed him, seeing a tent in the distance, seeing a whole mess of Yankees, all dressed up, milling about the camp. Deep down, we knew that they were Civil War reenactors, fanatics of the past, living out their fantasy ... but to us, they were Yankees. We immediately sent some of our playmates to fetch some more troops, and by noon we were camped on the opposite riverbank, our band of ill-trained, ill-equipped eight-, nine- and ten-year-olds against this well-seasoned Yankee company. The battle was on. We would fire our BB guns, and they would respond with powder fired from their muskets. We knew they were not firing bullets, but that didn't disturb the fantasy of our battle.

"I still remember that first night of the battle as if it were yesterday, the campfires gleaming across the river, our hushed conversations with the troops. 'So what year were you born?' we asked one soldier. '1840' came the reply. 'What is your name, and what company are you part of?' we asked the bearded leader. 'I'm Colonel William B. Hazen, Second Brigade, Second Division. We've never been beaten by you rebs, and we never will,' he said. 'What did you do before the war?' we asked of another soldier. 'I was a newspaper editor, for the *Sparta Daily*.' Then the colonel said to me, 'Hey, reb, would you trade us some of that Tennessee sour mash whiskey you're drinking for some of this coffee?' This fell upon confused ears, for I was drinking hot chocolate. 'Meet me at the ford, just below us,' he continued. Three of us then took off through the dark woods, the moonlight filtering through the branches, the owl's hoots in the distance. I was glad I brought my flashlight. In the darkness, at the shallow, we met him halfway, he giving us some fresh coffee, we returning some hot chocolate. 'That whiskey sure is good,' he told us. 'Here, why don't you take this newspaper with you? It's news of our impending victory."

"This is so cool. No wonder you remember this event so well," says Sis.

"When I shined my light on his face, a gold front tooth gleamed in the darkness. A thick black beard hid his face. Only the whites of his deep brown eyes were visible, peering from behind tiny gold wire-rim glasses. This was no game. This was real. And when we returned to our camp, by the firelight, we all looked at the newspaper he had given us. It was the *New York Tribune*, dated October 12, 1862. It told of the Union exploits in defeating Bragg at Perryville, and it predicted an early end to the war.

"And the next day, awakening in our sleeping bags to the blast of muskets, the battle was on again. Both sides tried to ford the river in sneak attacks—both sides were beaten back. The action was heating up, and we were outmanned. It was then that the idea occurred to us to build a cannon, a pipe taken from my grandparents' garage, boxes of shotgun shells swiped from the gun cabinets in my friends' homes, concrete-filled beer and Coke cans for missiles, and before long, we had a working cannon."

"Boys will be boys," says Sis.

"That's what my mother likes to say. Well, eager with anticipation, we mounted the cannon in the ground, having drilled a hole in the end of the pipe for a fuse. The Yankees now were milling about the opposite bank, puzzled at our daylong hiatus. Soon we were ready, gunpowder from opened shotgun shells poured down the barrel, next the heavy concrete-filled can on top, and last a fuse from a dismantled firecracker. *Wham* went the cannon, and high overhead arched the missile. Up and up it went, and then it fell like a stone, making a resounding splash in the water near the opposite bank."

"It's a wonder you are still alive," she says.

"Well, we adjusted the angle of our cannon, and *wham,* again went the mortar, again the screaming missile raced high into the sky, crashing down into the middle of the Yankee camp with a resounding thud. Before we fired off our third round, the colonel came to the river's edge, his saber waved high in the air, a white flag on top flapping in the breeze. 'We've won, we've won,' resounded the cheers of our troops.

"Meeting the colonel at the ford, we were eager to hear his surrender terms. 'You boys have gotten a little out of hand. Now, it's all right if you want to shoot tennis balls out of your cannon, but no more heavy objects. Got that? Otherwise my boys are going to start loading their rifles up with real bullets.' The colonel abruptly turned and strode away, all the confidence of a victor carried in his demeanor. Well, Sis, we received his message loud and clear—no more five-pound missiles, but we shot lots of tennis balls."

Sis laughs, nodding her head in amusement.

"Well, the battle continued as before, both sides firing and planning feint after feint. The nights continued to be fun, listening to their stories about their wives, their homes, their generals, and their great president, Lincoln. We listened in rapt attention and, like *The Twilight Zone,* we were transported back in time. This was no illusion. This was the present, flesh and blood.

"And on the fourth morning after the commencement of the battle, we awoke to find they were gone. We searched up and down the river, but they were nowhere to be found. We went into their camp and examined the remains of their fire, where the tent stood, the trees that they hid behind, and we relived the battles again in our minds. It delighted us to no end to examine the deserted places and the abandoned shore. Here the infantry camped, here stood their fire for making bullets, and here was the tent of Colonel Hazen. Nearby were the places where our armies often fought, charging this way and that, hiding behind this tree and that rock. Sis, this will always be one of the greatest memories of my childhood, a chance to fight in the Civil War, a chance to actually time travel."

"That's a wonderful story. You ought to write it down sometime."

Sis and I silently finish our chicken and potato salad. I stretch out in the sun, like a snake in the morning sunlight, and Sis takes her favorite guitar out of its case. It is a 1933 Martin with mother-of-pearl inlay all over the neck. It is an absolute joy to behold. The wood has been mellowing for over half a century, and Sis makes this guitar sing ever so sweetly, like Apollo on his golden lyre, singing out his sweet love for Daphne. Sis sings over the battlefield, over the dead, over the forgotten past, as she plays an old folk tune, her voice echoing off the opposite bank. And then its tune changes, and Sis sings out her undying love, her love for me and the world and everything around us. Her voice harmonizes with the rippling of the water over the rocks, the rustling of the leaves in the autumn breeze, the song of the birds in the distance. And then Sis and the guitar are silent, and I am at peace with myself and the universe ….

* * *

I am awakened by the gentle caresses of Sis as she lets her hands flow through my hair.

"Gabe, you seem to be so much more relaxed lately. It's good to see you not so troubled."

"Yes, I am doing better now. I'm trying to enjoy life. I'm wondering if maybe the whole purpose of life is to seek pleasure, to experience—"

"But Gabe, don't you think there is more to life than pleasure?" Sis says with her eyebrows knit in a waxy frown.

"I'm tired of feeling guilty over the past. I'm tired of worrying about the future. There is only the here and now, as far as I'm concerned."

Sis gives me a look of disappointment and then laughs and says, "You'll see—there's more to life."

Sis replaces the godlike instrument in its case, like a mother laying a newborn babe in its crib, and stretches out beside me. I roll over and face Sis in the glare of the sun. I shield my eyes with my fingers and squint into the blinding glare. The sunlight is broken into a dazzling array of rainbow colors. I discover that by squinting in various degrees, and by varying the angle of my hand, I can control the colors. Look, now Sis is yellow, now blue, now red. Sis looks at me with a puzzled expression.

"What are you doing, Gabe?" Sis inquires.

"Just playing with the laws of nature," I reply, as if I have secret control over the universe.

"Sure." She gooses me in the ribs. "I'm playing with the laws of nature also. See, now you laugh." She pinches me and says, "Now you scream." Then she kisses me. "Now you weep for joy."

"Oh, Sis, life would be so boring without you."

"I hope it would be worse than boring."

"You're right, you're right," I respond and grope my salty mouth against Sis's sweet lips.

While lying on my back, the glare of the sun hidden by Sis's kneeling body, a red oak leaf floats downward and softly lands on my chest. I pick it up and marvel at the multitude of colors and shapes contained in this one leaf, at the multiple lobes and sinuses, the primary and secondary veins, the midribs and stalk, more intricate than my hand. And then I look at Sis, her lean brown face with swirling hair, the frowns and grins, the delicate eyes, the curve of her neck, her well-formed breasts. All about is beauty. Oh, life is so simple; I feel like I'm a kid again.

"Let's go for a walk, Gabe," Sis says and, getting up, walks toward the nearby shore.

"Sure," I say as I follow behind.

Sis picks up a long, thin stick and swirls it in the shallow water. A rock overturns, and out comes a swift crayfish.

"Look, a crayfish!" Sis yells in delight.

"No, that's a Tennessee lobster. Makes great eating."

Sis grabs the squirmy rascal in her hands and holds it in front of my face. "Okay, let's see you eat it."

"It's against the law to eat Tennessee lobster except for the Wednesday after Easter."

"You saved yourself that time with some quick thinking, big guy. Let's see you save yourself this time. I bet I can skip a rock farther than you."

"Five dollars, you're on," I reply, puffing out my chest like a primitive ape.

Downstream, a bass leaps high in the air and catches a hapless insect. A car behind us drives by the monument, pauses, and then speeds off. The sun glitters off the shimmering shallows, creating a mystifying experience. While probing the water for a smooth rock, Sis shouts. I turn and see that she holds a gleaming beer can. Nowhere can we escape the junk of civilization. I have been hiking in places where I was sure no man has ever been before, but my illusion was always shattered by that one beer can. But here, is different. I expect to find beer cans here. It is part of this world.

Sis throws the can onto the nearby shore.

Again probing the bottom of the shallow with my steadfast hand, I feel rock after rock. Here is one, perfect for skipping. It is about the size of a half dollar and perfectly smooth on both sides.

"Sis, do you have your stone yet?"

"Just give me a little more time, I have to have the perfect stone. We each only have one shot."

Soon Sis walks over to my side. "Who goes first?"

"I'll go first," I say, feeling my male ego surfacing.

Looking out over the glass-smooth water downstream, I steady my aim and hurl the stone on a perfect horizontal path. "One, two, three, four, five, six, seven," I count as I watch the ripples spread out on the water's surface from every point of the stone's contact, intersecting each other and forming a dizzying array of patterns.

"That's pretty good, Gabe, but I'm afraid it's not good enough. The technique is all in the wrist. Maybe one of these days, I will teach you how."

"Okay, big shot, let's see if your actions are as great as your talk."

With great deliberation, Sis weighs the stone in her hand, rotating it about her fingers, feeling the texture and grain. With skillful dexterity she hurls the stone a little slanted to the right. The stone hits the water and skips from ripple to ripple in a long line curving towards the right.

"One, two, three, four, five, six, seven, eight, nine."

"Wow, that was great!" I exclaim. "As winner, you are allowed to eat a Tennessee lobster out of hunting season."

"No thanks, I'll take the five dollars."

"What about a passionate kiss?"

"I'll think about it."

We play a few more minutes in the shallow waters, searching for tiny creatures, watching the birds overhead, throwing rocks at the nearby fish. Then Sis calls out, "Let's go for a walk upstream. I want to see your grandparents' house. I want to see where you played as a child."

"Sure, but first let's have some pie."

Sis's face brightens.

* * *

I load our stuff in the trunk of my car while Sis changes into her leather hiking boots. Next I put on my old, worn leather hunting shoes, "my dead Confederate soldier's shoes," as I have always called them because they look like the shoes you see in Matthew Brady's famous war photos of dead Southern soldiers. Then we each cut ourselves a nice piece of pie and crawl astride a twelve-pound cannon.

"Nothing beats a good pecan pie," I say.

"Only a kiss from your sweet lips."

"Is it worth five dollars?" I ask.

"It better be a good one."

After finishing my piece, I jump down from the cannon and walk around the front. Sis sits astride the base, the cannon reaching out like a giant phallus. I look down the barrel and see beer cans, fast-food cups, the junk of civilization. I gaze down at the ground below and see a discarded condom. Well, at least they were practicing safe sex.

"Sis, you finally have a penis almost as large as mine."

"Only in your wildest dreams, little Gabe."

I grab Sis off the cannon, and we dance in merriment around the monument. Then we cross the river at the shallow nearby, McFadden's Ford, and take off upstream. I am thrilled at Sis's interest in my life. Nothing is more wonderful than having someone who is interested in your past, someone who exalts in reliving your life's every movement.

Proceeding along the well-worn trails, I am overjoyed at the sensations pouring forth upon me. Every rapid, every cliff, every rock has significance to me, has memories of days gone by. Looking down, I notice a Confederate Enfield bullet wedged in the crevice of two large rocks. I stoop and try to pull it out, but it's too tight. I grasp a stick and try to pry up the edge, but still it won't come. *On the next trip,* I think to myself, and I rush to catch up with Sis.

"Sis, somewhere up ahead is an interesting rock feature. I never knew if it was manmade or natural, but it looks like an Indian's head. We used to call it 'Indian Chief,' and we were sure it was carved out of stone by the ancient Indians who used to wander these grounds.

I sense that we are nearby, as feelings of déjà vu flood my senses. A bird calls out. It is a bobwhite.

"Bob, bobwhite," I whistle with my lips.

"Bobwhite," the bird returns.

"Bobwhite," I again whistle.

"Bob, bobwhite," the bird returns.

We repeat the ritual a third time. Then all is quiet.

I hear the flapping of wings as the beautiful bird takes off into the distance. Below the rustling branch I see my monument, the huge stone rising into the sky. A strange foreboding comes over me. Maybe these are ancient Indian burial grounds, sacred grounds. The sad face of the weather-beaten chief looks down upon us.

Sis looks up and says, "Wow, this is great. It does look like an Indian chief. I can see the accumulation of all the miseries of mankind etched in its face. Oh, I wish I had a camera."

Maybe this is the Jesus of the wilderness," I reply, not sure why I even said this.

I stare in admiration and wonder as Sis climbs to the top.

"Come up here, Gabe. It has a perfect seat on top."

"I used to do that as a kid, but I'm too old for that now."

"Chicken."

"Yeah, yeah," I say, ashamed at my cowardice.

Sis climbs down, and we proceed upstream. The uneasy feeling leaves me, and again I am rejoicing in my unforgotten youth.

"See that house there, with huge white columns and balcony all around? That was my grandparents' house before they died. I wonder who lives there now."

"Let's go up and ask. I'm sure they wouldn't mind."

"No. I want to remember the house exactly as it was when I was a kid."

Sis and I face the house, holding hands, admiring its beauty. The nearby baby pine trees, which were planted when I was a kid, now stand over thirty feet high. The great oak where my swing hung no longer exists, having been chopped away by lightning. I still remember the exact spot where I buried my pet turtle, Myrtle the turtle.

"We better head back now. It is getting late," I say.

Sis and I hop from stone to stone as we cross a small set of rapids, walk up a slope, and then amble down the road, the easy way back to our car ... back to the present, back to reality.

CHAPTER 9

While sitting on Sis's balcony in the blast of the mid-afternoon wind, in the clamor of cars honking below, I place Faulkner's *Absalom, Absalom!* on the side table and cover my ears, trying to shut out the noise, the final words echoing through my throbbing head:

> "Tell me one more thing. Why do you hate the South?"
> I don't hate it," Quentin said, quickly, at once, immediately; "I don't hate it," he said. *I don't hate it,* he thought, panting in the cold air, the iron New England dark: *I don't. I don't! I don't hate it! I don't hate it!*

I am immediately taken back to my days in college, when I strived to hold onto my Southern identity, the days of my life when I read every Southern novel I could get my hands on, every Southern history book. What was the link between William Faulkner, Robert Penn Warren, Flannery O'Connor, Thomas Wolfe, Walker Percy, Carson McCullough, Pat Conroy, James Agee, Lisa Alther, John Kennedy Toole, Peter Taylor and the like? Why were these writers so much better than anything the North or the West could produce? Why were these Southern writers so prone to drink themselves to oblivion or to place bullets in their heads?

The answer seems so obvious to me. It is guilt ... guilt over the present, guilt over the forgotten past, guilt over the not-yet future. Southerners love guilt. It is part of their heritage. We feel guilty over the injustice of slavery and Jim Crow. We feel guilty over our wish that the South had won the Civil War; we feel guilty over the current racial inequalities; we feel guilty over all the injustices in our own lifetime, in our childhood and our adulthood. You name it, we feel guilty over it. No, Quentin did not hate the South; he loved the South, but he hated himself for loving the South. Is it any wonder that so many Southern writers cannot live in this world?

I ponder over the events in my life that I feel guilty about now. I remember my joy as a little kid in reading about the great exploits of the South and her great generals. I knew every battle and every great charge. And playing in my grandparents' yard, on the battlefield of a great encounter, my mind whirred with imagination. Every cow bone I found was the bone of a dead Confederate soldier. Every large tree marked the burial site of a fallen Southern officer, and every red-colored rock I found by the river was stained by the blood of a fallen comrade. I thought the Civil War was the *Silver* War, something glorious. I did not know that black people had anything to do with the Civil War. I just knew a bunch of Yankees were trying to take away our homeland, so I worshipped the Confederacy and her lost cause.

But in the third grade, I started to learn of the reasons for the war, the injustice of slavery, the South's fear of losing her agrarian way of life, her stubborn Celtic pride. And I was racked with confusion, for I had plenty of black friends in grade school. They were my playmates; they were my friends. I was fortunate in that my parents believed that people were people, and I was not raised to use the term "nigger." I did not know that there were separate water fountains at J. C. Penney. I did not know that there were separate bathrooms for black and white people at the county courthouse. But the South thought these people should be slaves. My young mind was racked with confusion. Maybe it was best the South lost the war; maybe the South was not as great as I thought it was. And I wept tears of sorrow, futile tears of an eight-year-old. But I still worshipped the glorious Southern generals, and her stubborn pride, and the courage that enabled her men to charge upon cannon and breastworks.

And what of Jim Crow? Sure, the South had her injustice in the open. But what of the North? They sent down smooth-talking white businessmen, who promised blacks great opportunities in the North, who enticed them with a lifestyle unknown to them, only to trap them in the cities, trap them in low-paying factory jobs, subjugate them and use them just as the South had done, just as the whole country is doing now.

And as I grew older, I became even more acutely aware of the South and her injustices, and I strived to make up for them. But by the ninth grade, the blacks and the whites had separated themselves. I tried to make a special effort to be friends with my black classmates, to help them with their work, to understand their problems at home. But they did not understand, and I received several black eyes for my vain attempts. But I forgave them for their injustices against me, because I deserved it … the South deserved it.

And what else in my childhood do I feel guilty over? I remember my first real lie, that first significant lie that you carry around with you for the rest of your life. It all began one day when I was playing, watching a bulldozer in a nearby field, thrilled at the power and noise it exuded as it flattened tree after tree. And toward nightfall, I returned to the spot. I climbed on board and, to my delight, found that the keys were still in the ignition. Well, I had watched how it was done, had I not? So why not, I thought as I turned on the ignition. The engine roared like thunder, and after fumbling with some controls, off I zoomed straight forward, making a shallow path in the now-barren field. But then the field was running out, and I panicked. I fumbled with the controls, trying to make the beast shut off. But onward it went. I tried to turn off the ignition. But onward she strode, toward the neighboring woods. I was scared, and so I jumped off, watching the unyielding machine go forward, plowing through a row of trees until it came to rest against some large boulders. I ran home as swiftly as my frail limbs could carry me and hid in my room.

And a few days later, when my mother approached and asked me if I was responsible for the damage done to the Blackburns' field and woods, the damage done to the bulldozer, I said, "I have no idea what you are talking about." I lied. I felt terrible; I prayed to God to forgive me; I wept at nights, afraid the police were going to arrest me. I swore right then that I would never tell another lie.

So what do all of these thoughts have to do with me now, as I look out over the Nashville skyline, at the buildings on the horizon, at the cars and people scurrying back and forth like ants eight stories below? The L&C Tower gleams in the distance; a silent barge travels on the distant river. I remember the past; I see the present; I imagine the future. I see all the injustices of the world, but still I am a selfish person. My only action is not to condone injustices, but what have I ever done to correct them? I look down, and the abyss yawns at my feet.

Tonight I work the night shift: my chance to put right the world. But I want no part of it. It will be Friday night, the night of the derelicts, the night of the murders and alcoholics and rapists, all the filth and scum of humanity, all the misfits. If only I could escape. If only I could refuse to treat them. What good will it do anyway? These people will return to their squalid lives, just as before. The abyss still yawns at my feet. Oh, Father, oh, Father, why was life too much for you?

* * *

Driving in the blast of the autumn air, I pass by a stranded blue Plymouth Barracuda. The hood is up, and the helpless driver stands alongside. As I pass, he turns toward me and glares into my eyes, a scar on the left side of his face grinning at me, but onward I drive, feeling an uncertain queasiness in my stomach for not stopping. The highway gives way to a weathered country road. A large tree lies burnt on a distant hill. A few dead cattle surround the base. Birds circle high overhead, marking the spot.

Why can life not be easier? If I just had something tangible to search for, like the Holy Grail, something solid and real that I could grasp in my two hands.

Up ahead, I see what looks like a factory or a mill on the right side of the road. Two ambulances are on the scene, and three police cars. My concerned Mustang pulls into the parking lot; the dust roars up behind me; a piece of bird dung lands flat on my window. I hit the wipers, and to my dismay, the dung spreads, coating my windshield with a thin layer of mud.

I get out of my car and walk up to one of the policemen.

"Hi, I'm Dr. Gabriel Rutherford, an emergency physician. I wanted to see if I could be of any help."

"Thank God. We have a real problem inside. Come this way."

He leads; I follow. We enter a large warehouse-like room, full of stopped machinery. Over in the corner, a throng of paramedics is arranged in a semicircle. The screams of a man pierce my soul. Coworkers are gathered about in nervous anticipation.

"God, help me. Don't let me die—don't let me die. It hurts, it hurts so goddamn much," comes a call from within the crowd.

We approach the scene, and one of the paramedics turns. He recognizes me at once.

"Doc, are we glad to see you. We got us a real problem here."

The crowd parts, and I enter.

In the distance, an ashen-colored boy kneels on the ground with two paramedics supporting him. He is no older than eighteen, sweating profusely, and trying to catch his breath. His right arm disappears into some sort of machinery. Blood creeps from under the machine like a giant crimson amoeba and spreads outward around his knees. A useless tourniquet has been placed just below his shoulder, and two wide-open IVs pour fluids into his left arm.

"Hey, I'm Dr. Rutherford. You're going to be all right, I promise."

He turns his sparsely bearded face toward me, his green eyes pleading for me to do something. He wears faded blue jeans and a grease-covered T-shirt. On the floor nearby lies a John Deere tractor hat, the puddle of blood just touching the visor. I borrow a flashlight and peer into the innards of the machine. I see the remains of an arm, like hamburger meat, within.

"What are his vitals?" I ask.

"Pulse is 130, blood pressure is 110 systolic," comes the response.

I tighten the tourniquet, but still the blood pumps forth; the shoulder is too close to the machinery to obtain a good position.

"What is your name?

"Johnny, Johnny White. Please help me. I hurt so much."

"Johnny, now listen to me. You have lost your arm. It is crushed and hopelessly mangled." Hating myself, I continue, "We have to cut it off."

"No, Doc, don't cut it off! It will be all right! Please don't—"

"Listen, Johnny, listen good. We can't stop the bleeding. You're too far from a hospital or any fast help. You'll die unless we do something quick."

Johnny closes his eyes in meditation. I'm sure he is pondering his new life, life without an arm, life without a steady job, life in which girls think he is a freak.

He drops his head and then slowly looks up at me, fear on his face. "Okay, do it, just do it," he says, tears streaming down his face, down onto the floor, mixing with the blood.

I turn to Steve, the head paramedic, and say, "Get me ten milligrams of morphine, start two more IVs in his legs, and find me a saw." I turn to the workers and say, "Do any of you have fishing gear in your car?" Several give nods, and I send one of them off.

Soon everything has changed from disorganization to organization. We have a plan of action. We all have a purpose. The IVs are started, fluids run wide open, a plant worker brings a workman's saw from the back of his pickup truck, and another brings fishing line and hooks with the barbs cut off. I cover the saw with alcohol and then pour Betadine all over the tiny visible remnant of Johnny's upper arm.

"Okay, what is our pressure?" I ask.

"90 systolic, pulse 150," comes the reply.

"Okay, let's give him ten of Valium and ten of morphine. We have to act quickly."

Johnny fades into unconsciousness. Quickly, as if I were a Confederate surgeon out of chloroform, I slash away at Johnny's flesh, sawing bone, tying off major bleeders with fishing string. Johnny is awake now and screaming; the screams resonate in my head. Bone dust and flecks of blood fly off into the air, mixing with the motes of factory dust. The lamplight shines, multicolored, through these grisly particles. In less than five minutes, Johnny's stump is free and the bleeding is controlled. The ambulance rushes off into the distance, toward Nashville General, the sound of the siren receding. God, I hate myself.

The machine is turned back on, and out the other end pops the mangled extremity. It looks as if it has been through a meat grinder: flesh all in disarray, bones all crushed, tissue all dead. I feel queasy in my stomach, and I want to vomit. God, I hate myself.

The second ambulance needlessly rushes the mangled limb off to the hospital. I call the emergency room to explain to Jim Cleburne why I am running late, and then I stay for a few minutes and help the policemen fill out their reports. Before leaving, I stoop and pick up the John Deere cap, turning it over and over, noticing the rim stained with sweat and blood; and then I drop it, watching it float in slow motion down to the floor, into the pool of blood. God, I hate myself.

Driving toward the hospital, my senses are numb. I feel like a zombie, neither feeling, smelling, hearing, nor seeing. Did I do the right thing? I imagine the youth as a country music guitarist or a NASCAR driver. Now what is he going to do? Will he wake up tomorrow and curse the day that he was born, the day that I was born? Oh, I wish I had the courage to pay him a visit tomorrow, to see how he feels, but I am afraid, deathly afraid. I feel cut off from the world, neither here nor there and with no place to go.

An abandoned Dodge Ram, black in color, sits on the side of the road, the driver nowhere to be seen. God, I hate myself.

***

"Good evening, Dr. Rutherford," Jay, the nurse, greets me. His proud mustache waves in the air; his Italian teeth gleam in the light.

"Good morning to you."

"Doctor, when are you ever going to learn that it is seven o'clock at night—not morning, but night?" he replies, with the same response I have heard dozens of times before.

"It's morning for me, not night, for what fool would be working at night? Where's the coffee?"

"There he is, my precious baby doctor," calls Mrs. Jones, full of cheerfulness. "I'm glad you finally made it. Dr. Cleburne says you had a little excitement on the way to work today. He says you're a real hero."

I change the subject. "Mrs. Jones, what are you doing here tonight?"

"Oh, Doctor, I just couldn't stand the thought of you having to work without me, and besides, I need the money."

"Sure, sure," I reply skeptically. Mrs. Jones is widowed, and her husband left her over a million dollars. "I bet you need the money."

I grab a cup of fresh coffee and greet a weary Jim Cleburne. "Boy, am I glad to see you. All the crazies are out today. The floodgates opened at lunchtime, and it has been a madhouse ever since," he says as his eyes rolls back in his head. "So, Gabe, tell me about the boy you saved. Word has already spread around town."

"Jim, I'll tell you all about it later, but I know you need to get home. So what exciting turnovers do you have?" I say and then look over at the dismal stack of charts of patients waiting to be seen.

"Well, in Room 1 is a little old lady in congestive heart failure. She will need to be admitted when her lab work is back. In Room 2 is a stiff, so you don't need to worry about him. There's a car wreck in Room 5—he is over in X-ray now. He has a nasty cut on his face. You will probably want a plastic surgeon to take care of it. A nosebleed just rolled into Room 8, and back in the observation area, there are four patients whom I know nothing about."

"What about the waiting room?" I say with anxiety in my voice.

"Don't even ask."

"Great, sounds like a Friday night."

"See you in the morning," Jim says, and then the Confederate general limps down the hallway, the echoes of his boots trailing behind.

As I look at the depressing stack of patients to be seen, at the nurses running this way and that in frantic disarray, thinking that it could not get any worse than it is now, the loudspeaker cracks loudly overhead. "Attention, please. Code blue, Room 263. Code blue, Room 263. Code blue, Room 263."

Oh, God, just my luck. "Jay, Ms. Jones, take care of the patients while I'm gone. Order whatever you think is necessary," I say and take off at a brisk walk, joining the electrocardiogram tech rolling her machine to the code.

When I arrive at Room 263, nurses pour out of the overflowing room. The family stands outside the room, along the walls, fear in their faces, tears in their eyes.

As I enter the room, the respiratory technician is bagging the patient, and a nurse flails away, performing chest compressions.

"What happened?" I ask.

"She has been short of breath for about an hour, and then she just stopped breathing. Dr. Smith is on his way."

"Somebody get me her medical records now and hand me a laryngoscope and a size eight tube. Push one amp of epinephrine now."

I intubate the patient in no time and look at the monitor, seeing electrical complexes, but there is no pulse, except with chest compressions.

"What is the patient hospitalized for?" I ask, and then I listen to the lungs, hearing decreased breath sounds on the left.

The nurses all look around at each other, waiting for somebody to reply. Then somebody says, "She has a weird pneumonia. They don't know what it is."

I tap on the left lung with my finger, and an echo resounds.

"Get me an eighteen-gauge angiocath needle and a bottle of Betadine," I say and take the equipment as it is handed to me, splashing Betadine all over the patient's frail chest. Then I insert the needle straight into the chest wall. There is an immediate gush of wind. "Stop chest compressions," I command.

"Doctor, we have a pulse."

"Get me a twenty-eight French chest tube, and call the unit for a bed." The confused patient fights the nurses with her arms.

Soon the chest tube is inserted as the patient's bewildered eyes look around the room, her arms tied to the bed, the tube in her throat blocking her speech.

"Thank you," I call to the room of nurses as I head out the door. I walk up to the family and say, "She had a collapsed lung, what we call a tension pneumothorax, probably secondary to her bad pneumonia. She is stable now, but it will be many hours before she is out of the woods. She is going to the intensive care unit now, and Dr. Smith should be here in a few minutes."

"Thank you, Doctor," the frightened family calls to me as I take off back to the emergency room, back to the morass awaiting me. The door looms in front of me. EMERGENCY ROOM: AUTHORIZED

PERSONNEL ONLY. Oh, if I could just turn in the opposite direction and run off, disappear from this world.

"Dr. Rutherford," Jay begins, "we have a possible heart attack in Room 3 now. He seems to be in severe pain." Jay's old-fashioned curlicue mustache wags with his every word.

I enter the room and see a huge American Indian, about six feet, five inches tall and over three hundred pounds. He reminds me of the mute Indian in *One Flew Over the Cuckoo's Nest*. He clutches his chest with crossed hands, moaning. The fetid smell of alcohol flows from his body; his arms, neck, and legs are crisscrossed with tattoos, scars, and old venous cutdowns.

"Sir, I'm Dr. Rutherford. How long have you been hurting?"

He looks up at me with his drunken face and slurs his words as he speaks, "Doc, I was at a bar in town, drinking, when this pain just came on. It feels just like all my previous attacks. My last heart attack was three months ago, when I was passing through St. Louis. My doctor is Dr. James McKinley in Louisville, Kentucky. Get me some Demerol—I'm really hurting."

Great, a drunken Indian with a heart attack. Just what I need. I am skeptical of his story, but when the nurse hands me the ECG, I see that the patient has Q waves in his anterior leads, but no ST-segment elevations or depressions. At least I know he has had a heart attack in the past. I look at the patient's driver's license and see that he is from Louisville.

"Some Demerol, please," the patient pleads.

"Give him four of IV morphine, and call his doctor in Kentucky," I say to Jay.

"Not morphine. It makes me break out in hives."

"Okay, give him seventy-five of Demerol," I say with mounting frustration.

"Doc, I have a high pain tolerance. Seventy-five will not touch my pain. I need at least 200 milligrams," he says with saliva drooling down the corner of his check.

"I can't start an IV anywhere," Jay responds. "Would you like to try a central line?"

I try to insert a central line for almost thirty minutes, but the patient is scarred from head to toe; even his groin is scarred.

"Give it to me in my butt," says the patient. "That's what they have always done before."

Just when I am about to comply with the patient's request, Rhonda, the nursing assistant, runs into the room and drags me out by my sleeve.

"Dr. Rutherford, there is no Dr. James McKinley in Louisville, Kentucky. So I called up one of the emergency rooms in Louisville and asked if they have heard of this patient. They said they know him well. He had a heart attack two years ago from shooting up cocaine, and ever since, he goes from hospital to hospital, faking heart attacks."

I enter the room and address the patient. "Sir, we will be glad to put you in the hospital, but no Demerol for your chest pain, only Tylenol."

The patient's eyes bug out, and he sits bolt upright in the bed.

"What kind of hospital are you running here?" he yells, "I need Demerol! The pain is too great. I want to speak to the hospital administrator."

"Sorry, but we have talked with people in Louisville, and there is no way we can give you any narcotics."

The patient, realizing the game is up, ceases his chest pain act, rips the monitor pads from his hairy chest, and places his flannel shirt on his massive torso. Before we can stop him, he is gone.

"Tammy," I say to the unit clerk, "call all the hospitals in town and tell them who to look out for."

"Pronto."

Tammy starts going down her list, and I start to try to catch up, the patients now backing up, the frustration mounting.

"Dr. Rutherford," Tammy calls, "guess what? Just as I was talking to the clerk at Baptist, guess who came rolling in?"

"A three-hundred-pound American Indian."

"Correct. You win a prize—a free pass to the emergency room of your choice."

"It's certainly not this one."

I grab another cup of coffee and take a breather, smoking a bummed cigarette. The stress is tearing me apart, being so backed up, not sure what's going on with all my unseen patients. Then I scurry around the rooms, trying to catch up, like a monkey on a greased pole. In Room 12, behind a curtain, a man is on all fours on the bed, screaming. His butt stares me down, and a jacket of X-rays lies beside his clothes.

"What is the problem here, sir?"

"It's my back— I can't bear the pain. I was picking up my suitcase when I felt a pop," he says in an overly dramatic fashion, like a bad actor in a B horror flick. "I've already had three back surgeries, and my pain medicines were stolen from my hotel room. I have a letter from my doctor explaining my situation."

"Where are you from?"

"Washington DC," replies the patient. His bottom still waves; moans fill the air.

Another drug seeker. I take a quick look in the X-ray jacket. He has some old, plain X-rays, an unremarkable myelogram, and a CT scan that reveals degenerative arthritis. Inside the jacket is a letter from a physician stating that the patient is permanently disabled from his back condition. The letter is dated five years ago, and its edges are torn and frayed; the center has a small coffee stain.

"I can give you a prescription for Motrin and Flexeril, but nothing more."

"Flexeril gives me a rash, and my doctor told me I cannot take Motrin, due to my stomach ulcers. How about enough Percocet until I can make it back home? I'm leaving next Saturday."

"Sorry, I can't do that. I don't know who you are, and we see too many people who are addicted to drugs or just trying to get drugs for resale."

"What? Are you accusing me of being a drug addict?" he yells. "I want to talk to your supervisor."

"That would be me," I reply with a smile on my face. "What would you like to talk to me about?"

The patient pulls up his pants, glares at me, and then walks out of the emergency room without signing out, his pain resolved, like Lazarus leaving his tomb.

"Tammy?" I call.

"I know, I know, call the local hospitals."

A migraine awaits me in Room 5. She lies in bed, and a wet washrag covers her face. She has long blonde hair, and her face is pockmarked with old acne scars.

"Is this like your typical migraine?"

"Doctor—" She looks at my nametag. "Dr. Rutherford, this is the worst headache of my life. I can't take it anymore."

"What do the doctors usually do for you?"

"They give me a shot of Demerol and Phenergan and then write me a prescription for a pain medicine."

"Well, if this is the worst headache of your life, we are going to have to do a spinal tap, to make sure this is not meningitis."

She sits upright. "Doctor, it's not really that bad. I have had them this bad before. Just a shot, and I will go home and go to sleep."

"Okay, I will give you a shot of Thorazine, and you will go home and go to sleep—I guarantee that."

"I'm allergic to Thorazine."

"Okay, we will give you a shot of Compazine. That will put you to sleep."

"I'm allergic to Compazine."

"What else are you allergic to?" I ask.

"Codeine, Stadol, Nubain, Darvocet, and Talwin," she replies with a thoughtful look on her face, as if he is trying to remember more names. Then she looks up and says, "Oh, yes, I almost forgot. I'm also allergic to Toradol."

I am tired of fighting this patient. It would be so much easier to give in, to give this patient exactly what she wants.

"Okay, we will give you a Tylox capsule and a shot of Phenergan."

"Tylox doesn't work for me," the patient says and glares at me in anger.

"Okay, we will give you a shot of Phenergan and a Motrin," I reply.

"I'll take the Tylox. Can you write me for some Fiorinal #3?"

"But you told me you were allergic to codeine. Fiorinal #3 has codeine," I say with mounting irritation.

"But I can take it if it is mixed with Fiorinal."

"Sorry, you will have to talk to your regular physician."

"I'll never come back to this hospital again. You sure don't know how to take care of sick patients."

Thank God, I think—one less migraine to deal with. The patient takes her medicine and then glares at me with hatred as she walks out through the doors. A slovenly dressed boyfriend greets her.

"Tammy," I call out.

"I know, I know."

I pack a bleeding nose in Room 10, place a splint on a hairline fracture in Room 5, and suture a laceration in Room 3, and soon my emergency room is starting to clear out.

Just as I sigh in relaxation, Mrs. Jones calls out, "Jake's back."

Oh, no, not Jake! Just when I thought the world was safe again, Nashville's most famous Münchausen syndrome patient, Jake Eldridge, is back. Oh, God, what did I do to deserve this?

I walk into Room 1 and find a disheveled Jake peering at me with two tired eyes. He wears a rancid, bloodstained T-shirt; his skin is pale as a ghost.

"What's wrong this time?"

"My ulcer is bleeding again. I have been vomiting blood all day long."

My temper boils. Mr. Eldridge has a several-year history of sticking blunt objects into his nose and bleeding himself down to shock, swallowing all the blood he can manage. As if to add credence to his story, he vomits a cupful of foul, red blood into his lap. Specks of blood shoot up and spatter my clean scrub shirt.

"I'm going to be honest with you, Mr. Eldridge. I know what you do, and I don't like it one bit. I don't like you one bit. We are going to place an IV in you and give you some blood."

"You don't like me. Well, I'm not going to let a doctor who doesn't like me take care of me. Nurse, nurse, I want another doctor!"

"I'm sorry, but I'm the only doctor on duty. Would you like to sign out against medical advice?"

"I'm not signing anything," he says and then stands on his weak legs and walks out into the waiting room. He will be back in a few minutes.

During Jake's hiatus, I take care of a grease burn in Room 9, drain an abscess in Room 8, and splint an arm fracture in Room 12. On returning, Jake lies in the bed in Room 1 again. A line of IVs pours saline wide open, and two units of blood are hanging. His pulse is slowing, and his face is turning pink.

"When was the last time you were hospitalized?"

"I just got out of Nashville General yesterday."

Great, my luck must be turning. I will transfer him back.

I call Nashville General, and I am transferred to the doctors' station. A resident answers, "Dr. Nate Forrest here."

"Dr. Forrest, this is Dr. Rutherford. I'm hoping you can help me ou—"

"Dr. Rutherford?" he says, incredulous. "Is this Dr. Gabriel Rutherford?"

"Yes," I say rolling my eyes upward, afraid of where this conversation is headed.

"Dr. Rutherford, everybody is talking about how you saved that boy. That is amazing, what you did. You're a real hero. He went straight to surgery, and I hear he is doing well."

"I'm glad to hear that," I say and then change the subject. "I have a problem here, and I hope you can help me out."

"Sure, anything," he says eagerly.

"Well, Jake Eldridge just showed up, and he says he was just released from your hospital yesterday."

"Oh, no! Not Jake."

"Yes, I'm afraid it is Jake. We have already given him two units of blood, and he is stable, but he is going to need to be admitted overnight for more blood, as well as for his millionth psych consult."

"Just think, I wanted to be an engineer," the resident replies with resignation in his voice. "I was accepted into Georgia Tech, Carnegie Mellon, Cal Tech, and MIT, but no … My parents insisted I apply to Vanderbilt and then made me go when I received a full scholarship. Now look at me. Yes, we will take Jake back."

"Thank you, thank you. I owe you one. If there is any way I can return the favor, any dump I can accept, just call me."

"Sure. I hope the rest of your night is peaceful. It sure is a zoo here," replies the resident and then hangs up.

"Me too," I say into the dead receiver.

Soon the ambulance arrives, and Jake is wheeled off, despite his protests, his pleas to stay where he is. Sorry, Jake. I hope I never see you again.

It is now 2:00 AM. I am utterly exhausted, and I pray that nothing more happens tonight; I have had enough. If I could just see Sis now, if only I could hear her voice, then everything would be all right. I imagine her sleeping now, a beautiful smile on her face, her soft brown hair pouring out on her satin pillowcase.

I think back to when I first wanted to be a physician, as a kid, playing with my GI Joes. I used to bandage and splint imaginary wounds. I thought being a doctor would be glorious, saving lives, helping humanity, playing God. But no, it is just one big headache. Where are the rewards? Where is the pleasure?

I smoke another cigarette and think back to medical school, when I decided to become an emergency physician, dreaming of taking care of the masses, taking care of all comers, the poor and the wealthy, taking care of all the helpless people with no place to go. Where is my humanity? Where is my compassion? If only I could reach out and yank it back into my soul, then maybe things would be better.

Sometimes it seems that all my patients are vegetative nursing home patients, drug addicts, derelicts, rapists, and murderers. I save these patients as I save the rest, but sometimes I wish I did not have to. For the vegetative nursing home patients, I feel as if I am sending them back to a life of empty convalescence, a life that places a severe emotional burden on the family and often causes all former love for that relative to pass by the wayside. For the derelicts, who often are in shock from exposure or bleeding or alcohol poisoning or drug overdose, I feel as if I am a sadist for allowing them to return to their squalor, to crawl on the dirty streets and curse the day that they were born, the day that I was born.

I believe quite strongly that there are worse things in life than death, and living on the streets from bottle to bottle, from needle to needle, is one of them. Letting these people die would be easy; it is saving them that is hard. I know it is not my duty to play God, but if God is real, who, I ask, is this god for making these people suffer so much? And as for the rapists and murderers and criminals, I ask, how many innocent victims have been raped, beaten, robbed, or shot by people whose lives I have saved? Is their blood on my hands too? And if God exists, who, I ask, watches over this god?

Oh, Monday, hurry up and arrive. I need the peace and quiet of my houseboat, the pleasure of reading in the autumn breeze, the ecstasy of Sis's naked body against mine.

* * *

Things have slowed now to an intermittent line of mild complaints. At around 5:00 AM, a sad mother brings in her four-year-old daughter with a hurt arm. The mother is attractive, with curly, bleached-blonde hair and deep blue eyes. Her lower lip quivers, and her clothes seem a bit ragged.

"Hi, I'm Dr. Rutherford. And who do we have here?" I say as I stoop down on one knee.

"This is Kelly, and she fell down some steps yesterday afternoon. I think she hurt her arm," the mother says, forcing a smile, and then she looks past my gaze with a faraway expression.

Kelly is dressed in an immaculate yellow dress; her hair is natural blonde and curly like her mom's. She also has her mother's beautiful blue eyes. Kelly whimpers in pain but does not cry, refusing to look at me. Am I so scary?

"Kelly, how old are you?"

Kelly looks toward her mother, as if for approval. Her mother nods her head, and Kelly holds up four fingers with her left hand.

"Kelly, you sure are a pretty girl. I need to see you arm. I'm going to be real careful and try not to hurt you."

Gently, I lift Kelly's right arm. There is an obvious deformity in the mid-shaft: the bone curves off to the right.

Kelly still does not cry, merely whimpers. Why isn't she crying? I examine Kelly's body, noting various bruises of different sizes and shapes. The mother notices my interest.

"Kelly falls a lot," she says, avoiding my eyes.

I look into Kelly's right ear and see an old ruptured eardrum. The anger wells up in me. My hair stands on the nape of my neck. Goose bumps swell up all over my body as my blood surges through my arteries and boils in my head.

I look at the mother and see what looks like the shadowy traces of a contusion on her right cheek, under her makeup.

"Ms. Brown, are you married, or do you and Kelly live alone?"

"No, we live with my boyfriend," she says, her lower lip quivering.

"Ms. Brown, I will be honest with you. I don't think Kelly fell down any stairs. I think somebody did this to her, and I don't think it was you."

Ms. Brown averts her eyes to the ground. Kelly now cries softly, sensing that something is wrong.

"Did your boyfriend do this?"

Ms. Brown does not answer; her eyes remain fixed on the ground. Tears run down her cheeks, distorting her face, like a clown's face, her makeup all in disarray.

"Is he outside waiting for you?"

Ms. Brown nods her head and bursts into tears. Kelly sobs freely with her mother. Her tears mix with her mother's on the floor below.

"After we send Kelly to get X-rays, we will be admitting her to the hospital for a day or two. We will also have to notify the police and the child protection agency."

"No, you can't do that! Please don't. He will kill me," she pleads.

"It's required by law for any suspicion of child abuse."

Ms. Brown nods her head, terror on her face. The sobbing continues.

"We can arrange for you to stay at a women's shelter, if you like."

"No, I couldn't do that. My boyfriend needs me."

Yes, he needs you; he needs somebody to beat up. My anger is rising. I walk out of the room and say to my nurses, "Don't let her leave that room. And call security and have them place a guard in front … and call the police and child protection services." The rage seethes through my porous bones. Why is there so much injustice in the world? God, how can you be so thoughtless? It's just not fair. *Quis custodiet ipsos custodes?*

I step out into the waiting room, and immediately Ms. Brown's boyfriend confronts me. He is dressed in a trucker's hat, faded blue jeans, and a shirt that says "I hate fat women." The fetid smell of beer pours forth with his every word.

"Is Kelly all right?" he asks with a drunken slur. The anger wells up in me like a geyser ready to burst.

"What do you mean, is she all right? I think you are the one who broke her arm, and I'm going to make sure you go to jail for it."

"Doc, are you crazy? Has my girl been telling you some lies?" His drunken breath smothers me; it's worse than the spray of an angry skunk.

"She didn't have to tell me anything. It's obvious," I say, rage surging through my arteries, into my fingertips, into my toes.

He grabs me around my left arm with a viselike grip. His veins pop out on his temples, and his eyes glare with fury.

"Now, listen here, you ain't got no right going around accusing me of things I didn't do. Unless you got some proof, you better shut up or meet me around back," he says, his breath smothering me. His grip tightens around my arm like a python suffocating its prey.

His face is now inches away from my face, spraying his foul breath, choking me. The geyser bursts. My right arm knocks his grip off of my left arm, and I push him back. Then my right fist shoots up straight as an arrow and hits him solidly on the left side of his jaw, right into the source of that foul, alcoholic breath. I hear a crack. The boyfriend falls to the floor, confused, holding his jaw, not daring to get up.

Fortunately a policeman has just arrived.

"Doc, I saw the whole thing. He tried to hit you first. You were merely acting in self-defense. That what's going down in my report."

"Thanks."

"Do you want to file charges for assault?"

"Nope. We better just stick to child abuse."

I kneel by the boyfriend and see that I have broken his jaw. The cop takes him back into the emergency room and places him in a bed. I will heal him like I heal the rest.

Looking down, I notice a strange hand with blood oozing from the first two knuckles in a thin stream. Puzzled, I look over my shoulder to see whose hand it is, but then I realize it must be mine. I suck on the blood, but its taste is bitter.

* * *

Around and around I go. The center cannot hold

* * *

It's not my fault …

Not my fault …

CHAPTER 10

The alarm clock blares in the early morning haze of October. I wrap my pillow over my ears, trying to hide the wail, but I hear Sis's voice cry out.

"Shut that stupid clock off! Don't you know it's vacation?"

Fumbling at the bedside table, I hit button after button in frustration until the sound ceases. We drift off back to sleep ...

The clock wails again.

"Gabe!"

I remember our nine o'clock tee time and drag my weary body out from under the covers. This time I hit the correct button, and the alarm clock shuts off for good.

"Sis, we have a tee time. Remember? I will go see if Mark and Mary are awake."

"Couldn't we have gotten a later tee time? I want to sleep."

"No way, I have my best chance of beating you when you are half asleep."

Sis sits up. "The last time you beat me was when I had the flu ... or was it pneumonia?"

"As I recall, it was a hangover," I reply as I rip the covers off her naked body.

Sis looks up at me deviously and says, "You can have this body right now if we can go back to sleep afterwards."

"I'm immune to bribery," I say, and then I pause, rethinking the proposition. "Maybe tomorrow morning."

"Only if you beat me."

"You are one tough cookie, woman," I say. I throw my soft pillow into her face and jump up before she can retaliate. I slip on my robe and go downstairs to check on Mark and Mary. All four of us have finally managed a vacation together, at Sea Island, Georgia. The house we rented is magnificent. It is two stories high, with a fabulous porch around the perimeter, overlooking the ocean just inches away. A heated swimming pool lies in back. There are four bedrooms in all, but two of them have king-size beds. The upstairs master bedroom has a honeymoon touch: mirrors line the ceilings, and the bathtub is made for two. Scattered all through the house are wet bars, perfect for the vacationing folks.

Knocking on Mark and Mary's door, I realize I hear faint moans coming from within.

"Are you up yet?" I call, "We tee off at 9:00 AM."

"Mark sure is up!" Mary shouts, and then I hear laughter from within.

"Well, make sure he gets down in the next ten minutes," I reply. Laughing, I go into the kitchen to see what masterpiece I can create.

Standing in the kitchen, I decide to make two omelets, a half-omelet for each of us. While sautéing mushrooms, onions, and green peppers, I look out toward the morning sun hanging low over the beach. Seagulls are silhouetted against its glare. Docile palm trees lie on all sides, framing the majestic scene. A gentle wind blows through their stubby leaves. I bow my head and thank the golf gods for this wonderful day.

I have been vacationing at Sea Island for years. It is one of the few places in the South that tries to preserve the old Southern aristocratic atmosphere. Everybody dresses up, the men in tacky madras sport suits and the women in long, flowing eloquent dresses. The vast majority of the hired help are African Americans, and they take delight in playing the subservient role, with the words "yes, sir" and "yes ma'am" being slurred into one word.

When I first started coming down to Sea Island as a kid, I was disgusted by the artificiality of the atmosphere, the degradation of the blacks. I remember once trying to treat an African-American waiter as an equal, calling him "sir," but he became very nervous and suspicious. He felt safe in his chosen role. But then I started to observe the other waiters, seeing how they thought of it as a game, a way to flush out heavy tips from stupid white folks. So now when I come to Sea Island, I play the game, but I never forget it is a game: wearing ugly sports suits and drinking mint juleps, pretending I am a Southern aristocrat. I beat the system by knowing it is a game. However, not all of the blacks are playing the same game. Some take delight in ridiculing white folks, and still others are so lost that they want to be degraded; they want to be slaves. They are lost like Ralph Ellison's *Invisible Man,* with nothing else in the world for them and no place to go.

Just as I'm adding cheddar and Swiss cheese, Mark and Mary enter the room, smiles on their faces.

"Sleep well?" I ask.

"Are you kidding? I married an animal. She wouldn't let me sleep a wink."

"Ha, I bet."

"Mmm, something smells delicious. What is it?" Mary inquires.

"Omelets galore," I say and place a plate in front of Mark and Mary containing the first omelet and a quarter of cantaloupe. "Now, the two of you have to share."

"Oh, it's delicious. I hope we get service like this every morning," Mary says.

"Don't count on it."

Soon Sis joins us, and we all feast on our breakfast, the fresh smell of coffee filling the air.

"So are you also up for golf, or did Mary wear out your legs?" I inquire, putting extra emphasis on the word "up."

"Not in the least."

"Just one more cup of coffee," replies Sis.

"I'm bringing binoculars so I don't get bored following you athletes around," Mary says, a smile on her face.

"Don't forget your sketch pad," Mark says. "I want a drawing of Gabe crawling around in the swamp, looking for his ball."

We all laugh and then load the car. The sun beats down with a steady radiance, and there is not a cloud is in the sky. The golf gods are still smiling.

* * *

Driving up the glorious entrance of the golf course, I am reminded of what the South must have looked in her heyday. The clubhouse sits on the site of the old Sea Island plantation house. The old road leading up to the house is framed by a mile of two-hundred-year-old oak trees: a tunnel of beauty and grandeur. Light reflects, multicolored, through the yellowing leaves. The ruins of old slave quarters and other plantation buildings are scattered about. On the horizon, the ocean looms.

We place our three bags and one cooler on two golf carts. Mary does not play, but she takes delight in racing her cart around, binoculars and sketchbook in hand.

"Okay, Gabe, this was your idea getting up so early, so you tee off first," Sis says.

"No problemo. My great shot will just put all the more pressure on the two of you."

I stand on the first tee, the blue tee, and examine the ground, looking for the most neutral spot I can find. I want neither a perfect teeing area nor a bad teeing area, but something in between. I carefully tee up the ball so that half of the ball is above the clubface, and then I proceed through my ritualistic motions of preparing for a shot. I stand behind the ball and take a couple of practice swings, my eyes intent on my chosen landing zone. I walk around to the side of the ball, sight my target, and address the ball with reverence and respect, visualizing in my mind where I want the ball to go: the flight path, the landing site. I wag my club twice, and then my body becomes still as a mountain cat, intent on its prey. My blood surges through my hands, down the shaft, through the clubface, and into the energetic ball. My respiration is slowed; my blood pressure drops. As if in a trance, my club face moves back in a long arc with a mind of its own. Then there is a swish, and my golf ball sails two hundred and forty yards down the right side of the fairway, with just a bit of draw.

"Great shot, Gabe," Mark says.

"Beautiful," says Sis.

Mary merely applauds, and I dip my hat to all.

The course we are playing today is short on the front nine and long on the back. Almost every hole on the front lies on the marsh, and most every hole on the back flirts with the ocean. Every green is well bunkered; alligators lurk in the shadows. Distance is not a virtue on this front nine, only precision and accuracy. Perseverance is the key to the back side, as the ocean wind plays havoc with each and every shot. On both nines, confidence is an asset, but daring and boldness can be your downfall. It is a perfect microcosm of life. You must try your best on every shot, and if disaster occurs, you must take it as a pitfall in life. You must have confidence in the future, confidence that the future holes will equalize the past disasters. That is the only frame of mind that will allow you to succeed in this game, the only frame of mind that will allow you to enjoy this game called golf.

"Oh, that was a good shot, but I think I will lay up so I can put the pressure on you with the next shot," Mark teases.

"You know, it would be all right if you wish to play from the white tee," I say in seriousness.

"The white tee? That is for sissies … oops, my apologies, Sis. I wasn't referring to you," Mark says and gives Sis a mischievous wink.

"Okay, but I don't want to hear any more excuses for your pitiful drive," I say.

"I don't need any excuses. I'll beat you with my deft Ben Crenshaw play around the greens."

"You know, if you would just learn to swing the club a little faster, you wouldn't be accused of being such a wimp off of the tee."

"It's not my style."

Mark lumbers as slow as a tortoise onto the tee, tees up the ball higher than the height of his clubface, takes one wide-arced, slow motion practice swing, and, without stopping, takes a long, steady swing, seemingly in instant-replay slow motion. With hardly any noise, the ball propels itself two hundred and ten yards, straight down the left side of the fairway, away from the bunker guarding the right side of the green, leaving a perfect approach shot.

Watching Mark is a mystifying experience. From the time he tees up the ball until the ball is rushing down the fairway, it seems as if only one motion has occurred. Though Mark is a short hitter, his accuracy is uncanny. You have to beat him on the greens if you want to win.

"Like Iron Byron," I say.

"Great shot," smiles Sis.

"Good one!" cries Mary.

"Okay, Sis, it's your turn to show up these guys. Are you going to play from the red tee?"

"No Mary, I'm playing from the white. I don't want these guys to have any excuses when I beat them."

Watching Sis's graceful but powerful body on the tee, I think that she, more than anybody I have ever seen, embodies what golf is all about. There is a proper method to play golf, a proper set of ethics and morality and respect. You must become one with your mind, body, and soul; one with your clubs, your ball, and the course. You must regard the course with reverence and awe. It is not to be conquered or defeated, but merely endured. A golf course is like that great white whale in *Moby Dick*. You can either try to conquer it, like Ahab, and become rotten in the soul, or you can revere it, and become pure, like Ishmael.

Sis never addresses the ball twice in the same manner. To her, every shot is different; every shot demands a different physical and spiritual awareness. This time, Sis takes out a twelve-degree driver and tees the ball low. She takes two precise practice swings and then lingers over the ball, her mind, body, and soul one. The tanned muscles on her upper arms flex, and the club drifts back. The club face comes to the top of the arc, pauses for an instant, and then, like a lightning bolt, blasts down, sending the ball high in the air with the birds, two hundred and twenty-five yards down the left side of the fairway, thirty yards past Mark's ball and five yards past my ball.

"Magnificent shot," Mark says.

Mary and I applaud and give catcalls.

"I guess I didn't wake you up early enough," I remark.

"It was that last cup of coffee that did it."

We jump into our carts and race down the empty fairway. At this time of year, on a weekday, the course is almost abandoned. All this beauty is ours alone. Mark and I ride in one cart, and Sis and Mary ride in the other. Mary's cart veers off toward the woods, and I hear Sis give a scream. "Slow down!"

After our second shots, Mark is just off the green and almost knocks his pitch into the hole, giving him an easy par. Sis and I are on the green, putting for a birdie. My putt is pulled left of the target, and Sis rams hers home with all the confidence of a victor.

"Hey, guys, do you think that the two of you can beat Sis as a team?" Mary says with a chuckle. "She is already one up."

"So what do you think, Gabe? Do you think we can take Sis on in a low ball?"

"No, Sis wouldn't go for that. We would beat her for sure."

"I'm not so sure about that.'

The front nine is almost flawless for all three of us. Sis and I are two over par, and Mark is four over par. However, the back side is going to be a different story. The holes are long, and the blast of the ocean wind will place Mark at an extreme disadvantage. Sis's closer tees, coupled with her power, ought to give her a good score.

While we are eating hot dogs at the turn, Mary says, "Did you know that Mark has taken up running?"

"Running?" I say with incredulity.

"Yes, I have taken up running. My goal is to run in one of those one-hundred-mile ultra marathons, just to see if I can do it."

"Are you crazy?"

"I think it's wonderful," says Sis.

Mark just grins and grins. "Sis thinks I'm wonderful, Sis thinks I'm wonderful."

"Okay, okay, I have heard enough. Let's tee it up again."

On the back nine, we are all still playing magnificent golf. Mark has taken several bogies and one double bogey due to the fact that the wind is making the long par four holes play like par fives, but he couldn't be more pleased. Mary exalts in the beauty of the course, interrupting our concentration periodically as she points out birds and flowers and the like, drawings piling up in her notebook one by one.

Striding down the eighteenth fairway, I am on my way to my best round of golf in years. I am three over par, and I am sitting one hundred and ninety yards from the pin on this long par four.

Just one good shot, and I am home free. I pull out a three iron and address the ball, but the wind kicks up. Back to my bag, where I retrieve a five wood. A shadow passes over. I look up and see a beautiful bird circling high overhead. It is white all over, with a furry black crest and a bright orange beak. It makes two slow circles around, pauses for an instant, suspended in the air like a kite, and then flies off over to the left, toward the ocean. Again I address the ball. The wind fades, my muscles tense, and a strange sense of déjà vu creeps into my soul. I forget to take my two wags, and swoosh, a screaming duck hook goes firing off into the woods. I hit my clubface on the ground and chide my stupidity. "Gabriel, how could you have been so dumb? You should have hit your three iron," I mutter to myself in disgust.

"Just relax, Gabe, you have only lost one stroke at the most," Mark encourages me as we ride toward my ball.

I walk into the woods and find my ball in a perfect spot, a perfect lie with an open shot straight toward the green. The only problem is that I am standing right behind the old slave graveyard. What do I do? I ponder, and a beam of light reflecting off the nearby historic plaque momentarily blinds me. Do I try to fade the ball around the graveyard and risk losing another shot, or do I elect to hit over these sacred grounds? As I look around, gazing at the scattered tombstones, a cold shudder runs up my spine. A good shot here, and I can salvage bogey, possibly even make par. I pull out a five iron and elect to hit a low punch hook over the cemetery, through the gap in the trees ahead. After all, as my father used to say, trees are 90 percent air. I address the ball and hit what I imagine to be a perfect shot. As my head is rotating upward, I hear the slap of ball against hard wood. I look up and barely dodge an incoming missile aimed straight at the center of my forehead.

"God damn you!" I shout to the golf gods above, waving my club in the air. "If trees are 90 percent air, why do I seem to hit that 10 percent 90 percent of the time?"

I try to find my elusive ball, but to no avail.

"Hey, Mark, come help me find my ball," I shout.

Mark and I search for another five minutes, with no success. Mark's second shot already sits on the fringe in front of the green, and Sis's ball lies ten feet from the pin. Mary is busy sketching the old slave hospital from the cart.

Just as I am about to drop a ball, Mark shouts, "Found it! You can still reach the green with a low fade."

Taking a deep breath, I try to regain some composure. With a three-iron, I hit a perfect soft, low fade that goes winding around the trees, straight for the green. Holding my breath, I watch it roll onto the putting surface, wind by the flagstick, pause, and then trickle over the green and into the trap behind. My head sinks.

"Oh, Gabe, I thought you had hit a perfect shot," Mark says.

"Me too," I say, still focused on the ground below.

My next shot sails over the green into another bunker. By the time I sink my putt, I have recorded an eight, a quadruple bogey. Mark missed chipping in a birdie by inches, and Sis two-putts for a par.

"Oh, Gabe, that's too bad," Sis says. "You really had a great round going. You still broke eighty."

"Yeah, yeah. I let those old slaves put a hex on me."

"Say what?" asks Mary.

"Oh, there is an old slave cemetery in those woods," replies Sis.

"Cool, I'm walking over."

We all add up our scores. Sis has a seventy-six, I have a seventy-nine, and Mark has an eighty-one. Sis and Mark high-five each other, but I am still lamenting my second shot on the eighteenth hole. If only I could replay that shot; if only life could be so forgiving; if only life could give one a second chance; if only—

My thoughts are broken as Mary runs up to me. "Wow, that graveyard is really neat. I want to make a painting of it sometime," Mary says and holds up a sketch she drew in the intervening minutes.

"And I will place it on my wall with my scorecard, as a reminder of what almost was," I say with a terse laugh, still a little frustrated that I was so close, yet so far.

* * *

That night, we eat dinner at the Cloister. I dress up in a horrid red and gray checkered madras sports coat with gray pants, and Mark wears a navy blue jacket with a pair of bright green pants. The pants are so bright that you almost have to squint to look at them. Sis is in a low-cut, long, flowing, yellow dress with white ruffles, and Mary is all decked out in a long, sleek, sexy, dark blue evening gown.

"May I bring you something from the bar?" a cocktail waitress inquires of us.

"Mint juleps for all," I reply.

"Gabe, you are going to be the death of us," Mary whispers into my ear.

Merlin, our waiter, appears from nowhere and greets us, his shiny white teeth contrasting with his ebony skin. Merlin passes out the menus and says to Mark, "Those sure are some pretty pants you have there, sir."

"They're appalling," I say, "almost as appalling as this suit I'm wearing." I wink at Merlin, having noticed the MIT ring on his right hand.

"Yessir, we's all having a good time. Would you like any appetizers?" Merlin asks, his teeth flashing in the low light of the dining room.

"No, thank you, I think we all know what we want." I point to Mary to go first.

"I'll take the New York strip, medium, with baked potato."

"What kind of dressing would you like, ma'am?"

"House dressing will be fine."

"I'll take the filet mignon, medium rare, with loaded baked potato, and house dressing with the salad," says Sis.

"I want fried shrimp and deviled crab, plus French fries, and honey mustard dressing," Mark says.

"That doesn't sound like the diet of a runner," I say with a sarcastic grin on my face.

"How would you know?" Mary interjects.

Merlin turns to me and says, "And you, sir? What can I get for you?"

"I'll take the lobster, and an order of New England clam chowder. No salad for me. And bring us a bottle of good wine—your choice."

By ordering the lobster, I feel safe. It exaggerates the artificiality of the experience, as it is not something from these waters.

Merlin smiles and nods his head a few times. "I'll have your salads out in just a few minutes," he says and departs as quickly as he came.

"So who is going to pay for the dinner?" I say.

"You are, Gabe, unless somebody wins tonight at bingo," replies Sis.

"That sounds fair to me," Mark says.

"I bet it sounds fair to you. But remember, you make more money than the rest of us combined."

Mark leans back in his seat with an all-knowing smirk on his face.

"There goes that grin again," I say.

All laugh, and then we start talking about our activities for the next two days: walking on the beach, playing golf, sunning on the surf, and eating lots of seafood. It is going to be a nice break from the real world.

Merlin brings out a bottle of wine and shows me the label. It is a Château Lafite Rothschild, way too expensive, but you only live once. I nod my head. Merlin uncorks the bottle and hands me the cork to sniff. Then Merlin pours a little wine in my glass.

"So Merlin," I inquire, "Are you in graduate school now?"

"Yes, sir. I'm working on my PhD in biomechanical engineering at Georgia Tech. My family lives in Brunswick, and when I get some free time, I come home and work here to pick up some extra money. I've been working here since high school, first as a dish washer, then a bus boy, and now a waiter."

I swish the wine around the glass a few times and then place a drop on the end of my lip, a libation to the gods. "Just perfect."

Merlin strides around the table and fills each glass in turn. I've always been amused at the ritual of wine tasting. It seems so absurd. It reminds me of the first time I took Sis to Boston, a time when money was short and passion deep, a time when cheap wine was all we could afford. I wanted to show her the ghosts of my past, all of my favorite haunts. First, we toured Harvard Yard. I took her to the exact spot where I vomited on the steps of Widener Library on my first day of school, coming back from the student cafeteria after breakfast, scared to death that I was not smart enough to compete with the bigwigs from Andover and Exeter. Then I took her by the statue of John Harvard, the "Japanese National Monument," as we used to call it, due to all of the Asian tourists flocking to have their picture taken. Next we walked by Thayer Hall, where I lived my freshman year. After eating Bartley's burgers with Western frappés, I took Sis to the Science Center, which was built to look like a Polaroid camera; and then to eerie, gothic Memorial Hall, where I took most of my final exams. A shudder goes through my spine just thinking about those stressful days in that gigantic, haunted house. Whenever I enter Memorial Hall, I will forever marvel at the ghosts who roam the hallways of this building that was built to honor the eleven hundred Harvard graduates who fought and died for the Union during the Civil War. But what about the sixty-four Harvard graduates who died for the South? Where is the justice? Will the wounds ever heal?

After swallowing my first sip I say, "Sis, do you remember the time we ordered wine at Anthony's Pier 4 in Boston?"

Sis shakes her head, rolls her eyes upward, and says, "Gabe, you ain't got no class."

"Spoken like a true lady," I reply. I turn to Mark and Mary and begin my story. "During the first summer after we met, I took Sis with me on vacation to Boston. I wanted to show her all my favorite college hangouts, share with her my memories, both the good and bad—"

"Yeah," Sis interrupts, "like the spot where you puked on the steps of Widener library on your first day of school."

Ignoring her, I continue. "The first night we were in town, we went to eat seafood at a very expensive restaurant called Anthony's Pier 4. Sis was not yet making the big bucks for the TV station, and all of my money was spent repaying loans. We asked for a wine menu, and we were shocked by the prices. My god, we thought, giggling amongst ourselves while pointing out the absurd prices. Fortunately, they had a four-dollar bottle of Blue Nun at the ripe old price of twenty dollars. When we ordered the Blue Nun, the waiter, who assumed we were a couple of Southern rednecks, took great delight in our choice of wine and mocked us with a condescending air. He first showed me the bottle with the year, and I said, 'Yep, looks like Blue Nun.' Next he uncorked the bottle and gave me the cork to sniff, and I said, 'Yep, smells like Blue Nun.' He then poured a small amount of wine into my glass. I swirled the wine around and then took a sip. Looking at the waiter with approval, I said, 'Yep, tastes like Blue Nun.' After the waiter filled our glasses and left, Sis and I started laughing uncontrollably. I thought the manager was going to ask us to leave."

I raise my glass of Château Lafite Rothschild and say, "And here's a toast to Blue Nun."

Everyone replies, "To Blue Nun."

Soon our food is brought out, and we all eat. Mark's slow, steady eating contrasts with the voraciousness of the rest of us. What a feast.

"Mark, you have to check out Gabe and Sis's room," Mary says. "It looks like a bordello—mirrors on the ceiling, two-person jacuzzi in the bathroom, satin bedspreads."

"Hey, I didn't know you had all that! That's not fair."

"Well, remember, I invited you. But maybe if you are a good boy, Sis and I will trade rooms one night."

"Or women," Mark says.

Everyone laughs but Sis. Smiling, I give Mary a wink, thinking of the prospect.

Soon dinner is all finished, and we find ourselves in a huge ballroom, bingo cards all laid out, waiters running drinks from table to table. The room is packed with people, and cigarette smoke fills the air.

"I haven't played bingo in years," says Mary.

"I've been playing here since I was fifteen, and I never have won, just people around me," I reply.

"Poor baby," Sis says.

The ancient announcer drawls out the numbers one by one, just as he has been doing for forty years.

"A pair of ducks, twenty-two."

"Par for the course, seventy-two."

His obnoxious voice whines on and on, just as it has year after year. Sometimes I wish I could go strangle him.

Right and left of us, shouts of "Bingo!" arise, but not at our table.

Finally it is time for the last game, worth two hundred dollars. All squares must be filled in.

"Would you like me to shake the bin?" the announcer whines.

"Yes, yes," comes the cries of the audience.

"Legs eleven."

"Forty-five."

"Cyclops, one."

Once again, I am having no luck, but looking at Mary, I see she only has one square to go. She sits on the side of her seat in nervous anticipation. Soon our whole table is watching her card.

"Record for the course, sixty-three."

"A pair of nickels, fifty-five."

"Bingo!" Mary yells and jumps up like a little kid. The whole audience moans.

"We have a bingo. Silence while we verify the card."

"Yes, we have a bingo."

Mary rushes back to the table, filled with all the joy and glee of a little kid, clutching two hundred dollars in her hand.

"I guess I owe you for dinner," Mary says to me.

"No, you just take us out to dinner tomorrow."

"Deal."

Soon the tables are cleared out of the way for dancing, and a band strikes up "New York, New York."

"May I have this dance, Scarlett?" I say to Sis and give a bow.

"Why, certainly, Rhett," Sis replies with a gentle curtsy.

The band plays on: "Chattanooga Choo Choo," "The Tennessee Waltz," and many more. The band concludes with "The Bunny Hop," with all four of us jumping around like a bunch of idiots.

"I'm whipped," Mary says. "It's bedtime for me. But first, I think I will take a long jacuzzi."

"And I think I will join you," Sis says.

As we file out of the room in the hustle and bustle of the crowd, a voice shouts, "Mark! Gabriel!"

We turn and see one of our classmates from medical school, a real drip. He is so delighted for us to see him, I can tell.

"Scott, how are you?" I ask.

"So I see you two are finally flirting with the upper class. Don't you like how the niggers down here know their place? Hey, I got a good joke for you. What do you call a nigger with ten million dollars?"

Mark and I look at each other and shrug. The nausea wells in my stomach.

"A nigger. Ha, ha, get it?" Scott answers. "And who are these two beautiful ladies?"

"This is Sis, Gabe's girlfriend, and this is my lovely wife, Mary."

"Very pleased to meet you," Scott says as he takes each hand in turn with a gentle squeeze. He leans close to my ear and whispers, "That is some piece of ass you got there. I'll trade you my Mercedes for a night with her."

I nod my head as if flattered, thoroughly disgusted.

"Be sure to look me up in Atlanta next time you are in town," he says and wanders off to spread his obnoxiousness elsewhere.

"What a disgusting human being," Mary remarks.

"I kind of feel sorry for him—too blind to see what others think of him," Sis says.

"You are just too good, Sis," I say and shrug, trying to put the memory of our meeting out of my mind. I guess Scott can't help it. He was just barely smart enough to plow his way through medical school, but not quite smart enough to see the world as it is. He is just a puppet doomed to play the role his parents taught him.

* * *

We all sleep late the next morning and, after a light breakfast of fruit and cereal, head off toward the end of the island. Walking in the hot sun, we soon find ourselves alone, with not a person in sight. We spread out our belongings on the beach, our personal beach, and the pleasant sound of beer cans popping harmonizes with the wind.

Sis wears a beautiful black one-piece bathing suit that unzips in the front, revealing her cleavage; the peeled back portion of her suit is brilliant yellow. Mary dons a thin, sky-blue bikini that reveals her ivory body in all its sumptuous beauty. Mark and I are content in our gym shorts.

"Mary, you better put some of this number 15 sunscreen on."

"Only if you rub it on my back," she says and grasps her ponytail, exposing her upper back.

I look at Mark, who merely smiles as I rub lotion all over Mary's soft, white skin, imagining myself dipping down into the curves of her body.

Sis eyes me suspiciously.

I spread my beach towel and stretch out on my stomach, facing the ocean. On both sides of us, manmade breakers extend far out into the sea, protecting the beaches from the wash of the ocean waves. The waves sway with a steady beat and create a swooshing sound followed by a strange sucking sound as the water rushes backward, back into the sea. Occasional fish leap out of the water, timed with the crest of the waves. High above, seagulls fly, frolicking this way and that. On the distant horizon, fishing boats idle by.

I place my forehead on the edge of the towel, such that my eyes are just barely above the fibers of the fabric. The sun is filtered in a dizzying array through the threads, revealing the full spectrum of light. Digging in the sand below, I am greeted by a funny scraping sound. A little crab about the size of a giant cockroach runs out. I grasp a nearby twig and amuse myself. The crab grasps the twig and then tries to make its escape. But each time I block its avenue, and the crab tries to run off in the opposite direction. Finally the crab escapes and scurries off, scampering by Mark's sleeping head.

Why did I take such delight in torturing the crab, my zodiac symbol, Cancer the crab? It is a dangerous symbol, a volatile element in the cosmos. It can both destroy and create, but its greatest strength is that of moral and physical regeneration. But why do I talk of this nonsense? The only time in my life that I ever followed my zodiac, read my horoscope, were those times when I felt lonely and depressed, when I wanted to read that I was going to meet somebody mysterious and beautiful, or that my luck would change for the better. The horoscope was never correct, but it always gave me some hope in life when there was no hope.

Mark awakens and rolls over facing me. "Throw me a beer."

"Sure," I say, flinging one over to him in a high arc. Mark reaches up and snatches it deftly from the air.

I look up and see Sis playing in the tide, her ankles immersed in water, the foam spreading around her immobile feet. My eyes follow her graceful arms as she bends from one side to the other, sucking up the noon sun, sucking up the fresh air. Love swells in my breast like the incoming tide. Everything about Sis is beautiful: her body, her mind, and most of all her soul. She is such a giving and caring person. I do not think she has a selfish bone in her body. Oh, how can I be so lucky to have Sis as my woman? How can I be so lucky? The Fates smiled upon me when they brought us together.

"Catch," Mary yells to Sis as a Frisbee screams over my head, just missing me by inches.

"Hey, throw that Frisbee somewhere else!"

I roll over on my back, don my dark sunglasses, and pick up *The World According to Garp* once more. I have been trying for months to finish this book, but it just seems so boring. But everybody raves about how it is such a great a novel. If only I could find some redeeming factor in this book. I force myself through ten more pages, and then I throw down the book in disgust. Maybe it really is a good novel. Maybe I am in just the wrong mood to appreciate it.

Mary and Sis run up to me, smiles on their joyful faces.

"Let's go hunting for seashells," Sis says.

"Not now, I want to rest my eyes for a few minutes."

They run over to Mark, who lets out a grunt and falls back asleep. I close my eyes and feel the tiny prickling of heat on my goose-bumped flesh, the ruffle of the wind through my ears. I hear the roar of the incoming waves and the splash of foam in the air. I taste the salty wind blowing through my lips. Relaxed, I relive a memory of playing on the beach with my two sisters while my father watched from behind. We struggled to build a sandcastle, but with every added heap, the castle kept collapsing. Then my father approached us with a gentle stride and, kneeling on the sand, showed us how it was done.

"First, fill your bucket with sand to the rim, and pack it down real tight. Now, this sand is too dry, so you need to add a little water," he said, and we all walked into the surf, where he dipped the edges of the bucket into the tide briefly. "Look at this beautiful shell." He pointed it out to us in the surf. "It will make a beautiful decoration on the castle. And here is a sand dollar." He handed the seashell to my younger sister and the sand dollar to my older sister. "Be real gentle with that sand dollar—it is fragile."

Returning to the site of our castle, my father handed me the bucket. "Now quickly turn it over and knock on the bottom a few times, and you will have the beginnings of a wonderful castle, full of knights and kings and queens and fairy godmothers …"

* * *

I open my eyes with a smile on my face. I look up and see Sis and Mary building a huge sand sculpture. I walk over and watch the sculpture unfold. Sis and Mary are busy at work. They hardly seem to notice my presence.

Sitting on the beach, I cross my legs and feel the sun beating down on my warm shoulders, the wind wafting through my chaotic hair. Soon it becomes apparent that they are creating a sculpture of a godlike man lying on the beach. Just as I am about to make out the face, wondering whose face it is, a large wave rushes in and dissolves the statue away.

"Oh, hell, Sis, there goes our dream man."

"That was your dream man. Uh! He seemed to be awfully small between his legs."

"We hadn't even begun to work on that part," Sis teases.

Soon, Mark is awake, and all four of us are running and splashing in the surf, a Frisbee flying this way and that.

"How about some skinny-dipping?" Mark says.

"No, thanks," Sis says, "the water is too cold."

"And besides," I say, "we would be arrested. After all, this is Sea Island, the playground of the modern aristocracy."

"Wimps."

I remember the last time I went skinny-dipping. As a matter of fact, it was here at Sea Island. It all started when I was vacationing one summer with my family, after my third year in college. My younger sister and her boyfriend and I went out to the Ramada Inn to hear a band and go dancing. Well, the lead singer kept eyeing me and teasing me, practically blowing me on the spot. During one of the breaks, I forced the courage to approach her. We really hit it off, and late that night we found ourselves splashing around in the barren waves, our lithe, nude bodies glowing in the moonlight as we lowered ourselves onto the naked surf. And then we returned just before sunrise to my room and continued our lovemaking. My mother awoke that morning and found my sister's boyfriend sleeping on the couch and figured out what was going on.

"Does John Gabriel have a girl in there?" my furious mother asked.

My sister's boyfriend did not respond.

"Well, I'm going to kick them both out!"

And then my sister, hearing the commotion, came to my rescue, grabbing my mother by the arms, pleading, "Mom, don't go in there! Gabe will never forgive you." And my mother did not enter, and not until later that day did I learn, from my sister, of the events that had transpired that morning. My mother was so shocked that her son had finally grown up that she spent the rest of the vacation saying things such as, "You really ruined my vacation," and "How could you be so thoughtless?" I have to admit, though, it was pretty stupid of me.

Mark drains another beer and approaches me with a serious look on his face. *Oh God*, I think. He's had too much beer. Mark sits down next to me and grasps a handful of sand, letting it sift through his fingers like the sand in an hourglass.

"Do you know how many millions of years it takes for nature to make sand?"

"No."

"And just think, this beach is only a few hundred years old." Mark pauses and then he continues, "If it wasn't for these manmade breakers, this beach and island would be gone in another one hundred years."

"True."

Mark grows even more serious and puts his hand on my shoulder, his face just inches away from mine, his eyes peering into my very soul.

"So Gabe, how are you and Sis getting along?"

"Just fine."

"You know, Mary thinks the world of you."

"I think the world of Mary also."

"Have you talked about marriage yet?"

"With Mary?"

"No, silly, I'm being serious."

"Some."

"You know, life is short, and if I were you, I would think about getting married."

Mark pats me on the shoulder and strolls back to the cooler. *Saved by a beer*, I think.

We continue for the rest of the afternoon frolicking in the waves, imbibing beer, and sleeping in the sun until it is time to return to our house.

* * *

That night, while devouring fried shrimp and deviled crab at the Crab Trap, Mary is driving me crazy with her cock teasing. This is just not the Mary I know. She raises each raw oyster to her mouth, smiles at me, tongues the edge in a seductive manner, and then slurps it down, all in one motion.

Mark leans over and whispers in my ear, "How about a little mate swapping tonight? Mary said she would really enjoy it. Do you think Sis would go for it?"

"I hope so," I respond with eagerness.

"What are you boys whispering over?" Sis inquires.

"Men talk," I reply.

* * *

Soon we all find ourselves in our rented pool, splashing around, our limbs all entwined. Pegasus and Andromeda loom high overhead. We drink up, and soon we are giddy with pleasure.

"If I had my telescope," I say, pointing up to the sky, "I would show you the Andromeda Galaxy. It's so beautiful."

"I want to make a painting of you gazing through Sis's antique telescope sometime ... if that is all right with you?" Mary says.

"Only if it is abstract. I always wanted to be in a Picasso."

"Sure."

Mark swims over to Mary and whispers to her softly. Then they both are grinning.

"What are you two whispering about?" Sis asks.

Mark smiles and then jumps up high in the air, shouting, "It's skinny-dipping time!" He disappears under the surface, and then his bathing suit flies out of the water onto the concrete deck.

My bathing suit and Mary's soon follow.

"Okay, Sis, it's your turn."

"We could all get into real trouble here," Sis says, her voice quavering.

"Let's hope so," I reply.

Soon we are all naked. I approach Sis with gentle breaststrokes and then entwine my arms around her.

"Mark would really like to make love to you, if it is all right with you."

Sis has a very peculiar look on her face. I cannot tell if it is one of delight or horror.

"And you make love to Mary?"

"Of course. It would be fun. We're all friends."

"Gabe, is this what you really want?"

"Yes, one night of pure, unadulterated pleasure."

"Okay," Sis responds in a neutral voice.

I join Mary in the middle of the pool, and soon Mark joins Sis.

"Do you think Sis minds?" Mary inquires.

"No. I think she is just a little nervous and embarrassed, though. Why don't we go upstairs? I think Sis will feel more comfortable in our absence."

Soon Mary and I are lying in bed, mirrors all around, taking delight in our newly discovered bodies, sucking and kneading each other's sweet flesh.

"Oh, Mary, you feel so warm inside."

"Yes, yes, yes … Gabe, give it to me. Give it to me good."

Mary then pushes me off her and rolls over onto her knees and elbows, her divine ass reflecting off the ceiling. She looks over her shoulder at me with a sly grin.

"Mary, I had no idea you were such an animal."

"There are lots of things you don't know about me."

Finding some lubricant, I obey my sweet desires.

* * *

I roll over to Sis and take her in my arms. "Thank you, Sis. I love you so much." Sis lies as still as an iceberg, and then she rolls over away from me, cutting me off. *Sis, why do you have to be so old-fashioned?* I think to myself as I drift off into a peaceful sleep, reliving the pleasures of Mary's smooth body, the tightness of her ass.

CHAPTER 11

Cyndi Lauper's "Girls Just Want to Have Fun" blares on the radio, the wind rushes through the car like a hurricane, the earth and trees fly by like a runaway train. Everywhere is beauty, and the only signs of civilization are rows and rows of quaint, air-conditioned Fords and Chryslers and Pontiacs, all scurrying down the highway like ants returning to their nest.

"Wow, what a vacation!"

Sis does not look over but continues concentrating on driving my car down the winding highway. Intent on the task at hand, she seems oblivious to her surroundings. The muscles of her jaws are taut; a furrow creases her forehead.

"Didn't you have a great time?"

"Part of the time." she answers in a noncommittal voice.

"Didn't you have fun with Mark? I didn't mind."

"No, I didn't have fun! Did you have fun with Mary?"

"Yes, I did. And I don't feel guilty over it. It was just pure pleasure. It was a nice diversion."

"A diversion? Is that all it was? Is that all I am, a diversion?"

"Sis, lighten up. You're the one I'm in love with."

"Then how could you want to sleep with another woman?"

"Sis, it was just sex, nothing more. If you would just learn to relax, maybe you could enjoy such diversions. Don't you find Mark handsome?"

"Handsome? He's gorgeous, but I'm not in love with him."

"Love? What does love have to do with it?"

"Everything!"

"Sis, just lighten up. There is a place for love, and there is a place for sex, and there is a place for just pure fun."

"Gabriel, you don't know what you are talking about. Something happened to me when I was a little girl, something at camp, something I have never told anybody before." Sis pauses, as if she is going to continue, but there is only silence.

"I'm listening."

"Never mind. You wouldn't understand."

Again Sis and I are wrapped in a dead silence. The whole idea about worrying about life seems unimportant now. I have discovered the meaning of life, and it is pleasure. There are no more mysteries to uncover, no more riddles to solve. I can settle down and marry Sis and live out a peaceful life in a two-story suburban house. I can buy a pack of barking hounds, have screaming children, and join a nice country club. I can travel to mammoth malls and buy sparkling suits and leather shoes with my Visa and MasterCard. I can sit back in my comfortable reclining chair and read my newspaper and watch my children grow up. Everything is now so simple.

"Do you feel threatened?"

"Of course I feel threatened!"

"Sis, you are the one I love. You are the one with whom I want to spend the rest of my life, and you are the one whom I wish to be the mother of my children. Let's get married now. We can skip having a formal wedding and just go straight to a judge."

"How can you talk about marriage at a time like this?"

Again we are enshrouded by silence, and I relive the wonderful vacation in my mind, the golfing and swimming and my newfound sexual awareness. Thinking of these wonderful thoughts, I slide down in my seat and prop my knees on the dashboard. The blast of wind through my open window wreaks havoc on my blond hair. Seeing a small piece of bird dung on the window in front, I stare at it blankly, projecting its image on the horizon beyond. Moving my head just a fraction this way and that way, I can bounce the image over the distant highway, over towering trees, over two-story farmhouses, and even over heaven-bound mountains. Just what is the nature of perception, anyway? In this case, I can take a simple piece of bird dung and magnify its significance so that it is greater than the tallest mountain on the horizon. Nothing can impede the motion, and all of it occurs just by moving my head a fraction of an inch, just by staring blankly out onto the horizon. Could this not be some sort of clue? In this case, it is obvious that the significance of the far objects, mountains, outweigh the significance of the near object, bird dung. Is this not a clue to the meaning of events in my life? Could it not also be true that events in my life on which I have placed so much significance are merely pieces of bird dung on the cosmic windshield of the universe?

Seeing some cows grazing in a nearby field, I let my mind wander back to the childhood games we would play on long trips. Without even realizing it, I start counting cows: one, two, three … eighty-seven, eighty-eight … whoops, there is a cemetery; I must bury all my cows and start over. One, two … four hundred and thirty-six … only sixty-four cows to go … damn, another cemetery. My wandering mind starts playing the roadside alphabet game: A, B, C … O, P … now, where is a Q? We need to pass a Quaker Oats truck, or something similar—

"Do you remember our trip to Lake Lanier State Park, when we rented the cabin?" Sis asks, interrupting my concentration.

"Do I remember? Of course I remember. That is one of the most beautiful memories of my life."

"Remember how we declared our love for each other and exchanged pinky rings?"

"Yes, we exchanged vows by candlelight. I still have the white candles in a memory box. And then we made beautiful love, no inhibitions."

"Gabriel, to me that candlelit ceremony was like getting married. I thought you were mine for life, and I thought you felt the same about me."

"Sis, I still am yours for life," I declare and take Sis's smooth hand in my hand, but her hand is cold and limp.

Again the silence creeps into the car, like a wildcat stalking its prey. A Quaker State Oil sign sits up ahead. Q … R, S, T, U … V … W, X … Y … now, where can I find a Z? My eyes close in fatigue, and my hand drifts out the window, as if with a mind of its own. The blast of the wind drives it hard into the door awakening me from my slumbers. *Zone*—Z, I win, as pain seers through my throbbing extremity. Ignoring the pain, I start varying the angle at which my palm cuts through the oncoming wind. Like an airplane rudder, I find I can make my arm travel up and down, flying through the breeze, flying through the oncoming hurricane. Up and down my hand goes, under the fine control of my intent muscles. I smile to myself at my discovery, at all my discoveries. The skin prickles on the nape of my neck. Goose bumps form all over my legs. I can smell all the various odors in the air: the fresh aroma of pine needles, the pungent smell of fresh burning hickory smoke, the not-too-unpleasant fragrance of diesel fuel. I hear a hundred different whistling tones as the vortex of air rushes over the car, through the front windows, and out the back.

The sun reflects in dizzying proportions off a thousand different surfaces of our car and the surrounding cars. Suddenly the car slows down.

"What are you stopping for? Is something wrong?"

"I just want to help this family. Their car has broken down."

"But we have to be back in Nashville by six."

"Don't worry, we'll still get back in time."

We pull in behind a brown Chevy station wagon. It reminds me of the "Gabemobile" that I had in high school. The father stands by the side of the road, beseeching oncoming cars, and his face lights up with a smile when he sees us. The mother and her three daughters wander at the side of the oil-stained road, along a cross section of cut-out rock.

Approaching the father, a cheerful man wearing dark pants and a white shirt, Sis says, "It looks like you need a hand."

"Thanks so much for stopping. My name is Peter, Peter Manuel, and I have a flat tire, but I can't find a jack. I've looked everywhere."

Peter is a giant of a man with the body of a grizzly bear, well over six feet tall with dark Mediterranean skin. His hands are powerful and look as if they could crush granite with a mere grasp. In contrast to his body, his face is that of an innocent boy; it has a look of gentleness and sweetness.

"No problem. My name is Sis, and this is Gabriel."

We all shake hands, and I retrieve the jack from the trunk of my car. Peter and I are soon busy replacing the punctured tire. I look over at the three children playing along the rock sediment; all three are wearing Walt Disney shirts. Sis is busy pointing out the various layers in the sedimentary rock, helping them find fossils. The cheerful mother stands by, occasionally looking over our way, seeing how our task is proceeding. The mother is tall, with long, tan, sleek, muscular legs. Her blonde hair whips in disarray at the blast of the cars rushing by.

"Coming back from Florida?" I ask, handing the wrench to Peter.

"Yes, we just spent three wonderful days in Disney World. The kids just loved it. Have you ever been?"

"No, I haven't. I guess one of these days, when I have children."

"Better not wait too long," Peter says and then points over at his children. "They're beautiful and sweet, but I'll rue the day when they are teenagers. I still can't believe I have three daughters. The oldest is Julia. She likes to have tea parties with her cats and says she is going to be a Pokemon master when she grows up, but I suspect she will join the Peace Corps. Elizabeth, the middle one, thinks she is a fire-breathing cat and says she is going to be the dictator of the world someday, but I think she will be a veterinarian. The youngest, Catherine, is only four years old but acts like she is twenty-four. She wants to be a unicorn and climb rainbows, but I picture her as an actress."

The flattened tire comes off easily, and we continue to chat while I put the nuts in place and Peter does the tightening. The fresh smell of new rubber saturates my nostrils.

"So what kind of work are you in?" Peter inquires.

"I'm an emergency physician." I pause and think of the accomplishments of Sis. "My girlfriend, Sis, is a news anchorwoman in Nashville. You may have seen her on TV."

"Yes, as a matter of fact, I think I have seen her on TV—a commercial for one of the charity organizations."

"Yes, that's probably her. She's been doing ads for the March of Dimes for the past few years." I ask him, "So what about you?"

"I am an insurance salesman." The wrench slips and almost hits me in the face, but I dodge it just in time.

Laughing, I say, "I think I may need some life-insurance now."

"I got lots to sell."

"So what about your wife?"

"She's a tennis pro at a private club in Knoxville. Her passion is teaching young kids how to play."

Soon the spare tire is in place, and the joyous kids run up to the station wagon, shouting in glee. Sis follows with a handful of discarded Coke and beer cans. The mother looks one last time at the cut-out sediment and then follows behind.

"Marilyn, you sure have some beautiful children," Sis says.

"Why, thank you. And thank you for teaching my children about geology and evolution. They seem to resist all my attempts at playing teacher, so it's nice to see them pay attention to someone else for a change."

We all turn our attention to the children.

"Look at this fossil of a dinosaur Miss Sis helped me find," the youngest, Catherine says, a beautiful brown-haired, green-eyed angel, as she holds up the imprint of a tiny lizard.

"Catherine, Miss Sis happens to be a big TV star," Peter says.

Catherine's eyes go wide with wonder. "Really? You are a TV star?"

"I am a TV news anchorwoman. That's a little different from being a TV star."

"Well, I hope I grow up just like you," Catherine replies and runs off toward the car, grasping her fossil in her hands.

"And what did you find, Elizabeth?" Peter asks.

"A fern," she says, her brown eyes and brown hair gleaming in the sun, holding the imprint of the fossil with two gentle hands.

The father turns to the oldest, a girl who looks like Shirley Temple, only a half-foot taller. "And Julia, what did you find?"

"It is a secret," she says demurely as she palms a stone in her hungry hand. "It's going to be my good luck charm."

As she turns, I can barely make out the rich purple reflection of quartz gleaming in the air.

"Sis, thank you again. My children had such fun," Marilyn says.

"I had fun. Your children are so wonderful."

Peter turns to Sis and me. "Here, take one my business cards. If you are ever in any car trouble in Knoxville, or if you ever want a ticket to a Tennessee football game, just call this number. Marilyn and I sure do appreciate your help. Thanks so much."

After saying one last good-bye, we are on our way again, rushing headlong down the seemingly immaculate interstate.

"Now, don't you feel good about helping that family?"

"I feel okay. Somebody else would have stopped, though."

"Gabriel, where's your humanity?"

Where's my humanity? The words echo through my head. I remember my first humanitarian stage of life, my first religious stage. I was a kid of twelve. I read a book called *The Late, Great Planet Earth* and became convinced that the end of the world was near. My mind was still in that concrete stage when I thought that everything in print must be true. I prayed nightly to Jesus to save my polluted soul. I gave up looking at naked girls in *Playboy* and *Penthouse* magazines, and I started to think about all the good things I could do to help save the world. This stage lasted for a few months, and then I started wondering about the fallacy of basing one's religion on the belief that God was going to destroy this evil planet. Is religion not something that is supposed to make you feel good about life? Is not religion supposed to be based on loving and helping your fellow man?

I then started to look around at the most devoted Christians. Oh, they were all so righteous, and they were so quick to condemn others who did not maintain the same standards of morality. Hypocrisy seemed to pile upon hypocrisy, and then one day came the straw that broke the camel's back. I was in the community drugstore that day, when I saw a very pregnant young girl shopping for what appeared to be supplies for her soon-to-be-born child: diapers, bottles, formula, and such. An elderly lady approached her and started scolding her for her sins.

"Miss," the old lady began, "I know all about you, and I don't appreciate a tramp like you polluting the morals of our neighborhood."

The girl looked this way and that, looking for an avenue for escape.

"Remember, God knows what you have done, and you will pay for your sins. Both you and your bastard child will fry in hell."

The girl now was sobbing, looking for somebody to come to her rescue, somebody to help her. I was filled with anger, and I wanted to go to her aid, but I was afraid. I realized right then that this Christian morality was a bunch of bullshit. Our world has enough problems already.

So I rejected Christianity, and I rejected morality. Soon I was again breathing heavily over my *Playboy* and *Penthouse* magazines. I formed my own personal religion based on ethics. My religion was devoid of morality, for morality is a form of bigotry based on society's hang-ups. My religion was simple. It consisted of a single code of life: "Be true to yourself, and never, ever do anything to anybody that you wouldn't want done to yourself." If only established religions could be so simple. If only they could forget this nonsense of heaven and hell and leave people to focus on their lives, now, in the present. Then there would not be any of this bogus condemning of souls, this absurd, condescending morality.

* * *

Onward my car rushes, the air now chilly, the sky now gray, past Atlanta, toward Chattanooga. The windows are rolled up. The leaves on the trees are multicolored: some yellow, others red, and a few already brown. Symbols of civilization surround us. A factory squats on a hill to my left, pouring billowing smoke through giant chimneys. A police car sits behind a tree on my right, pointing its radar gun at unsuspecting travelers. Up ahead, an unkempt boy and girl stand on the side of the road holding a sign saying NEW YORK. They both wear blue jeans and old flannel shirts; their disheveled, long hair flaps in the breeze; their nameless faces stare blankly at the vortex of oncoming cars. *What kind of search are they on?* I wonder.

I am reminded of the movie *Easy Rider*, with Peter Fonda in search of the truth. My favorite line in the whole movie is when Peter Fonda and Dennis Hopper are sitting around the campfire, having just failed miserably in their search. Peter says, "We blew it." It is this realization that signifies that he has actually found the truth. He admits to himself that he has made a mistake. Like Jesus, he is now ready to accept responsibility for his fellow man, and as a result, society blows him away at the end, crucifies him on his motorcycle, because civilization is not ready to be saved. It wants to rot and stagnate and spread its foul odor like a plague.

Up ahead I see a sign announcing Kennesaw Mountain.

"Look, Sis, we are near Kennesaw Mountain." There is no response, and I continue, "Here the Yankees tried to repeat Missionary Ridge. But this time they were beaten. General Thomas sent three divisions charging headlong up the wooded slopes, but unlike before, the Confederates were placed just below the crest so that they could see the entire advance. At Missionary Ridge, Bragg foolishly placed his men on the middle of the crest such that they could not see the approaching Yankees until it was too late. Anyway, General Johnston's troops remained calm in their fortifications and picked off the advancing Yankees one by one. In just a few hours, three thousand blue bellies lay on the muddy ground."

"Gabriel, when are you going to live in the present?"

"Sis, why are you trying to pick a fight? I'm sorry I slept with Mary. Why don't we just forget about it?"

"Elephants don't forget," Sis says in a soft whisper, as if speaking to herself.

I again think of Kennesaw Mountain. After the battle, General Howard remarked that it would always be futile to attack a well-entrenched enemy line by direct assault. If only General Hood had learned this lesson, then there never would have been a Franklin the following fall.

"I'm hungry. Let's pull over at the next exit."

"I thought you had to be back at six," Sis says in a mocking tone. I just shake my head in frustration.

Soon the car slows down and veers off at an exit, into the parking lot of a yellow-roofed Stuckey's. As we walk into the restaurant, a table of five frantically waves at us.

"Look, it is the Manuels," Sis's voice booms in my ear, a smile now on her face.

We walk over and greet them. They are all feasting on cheeseburgers.

"Would you please join us?" Marilyn says.

"We would love to," Sis replies as we sit down at the end of the table.

Elizabeth sits by herself at the opposite end of the table, her fossil lying next to her fries. Julia and Catherine sit across from each other. Julia reaches over and steals a French fry from Catherine. Catherine responds by kicking Julia hard in the shin, despite being half her sister's size. Julia reaches over and strikes Catherine on top of her head with the palm of her hand. Catherine lets out a yelp. Marilyn grabs Julia by her arm and says, "Cut that out. Now apologize to Catherine."

"She kicked me first. I'm not going to apologize."

"Okay, you both apologize to each other, or no more vacations!"

"I'm sorry," Catherine says meekly.

"I'm sorry," Julia returns half-heartedly.

Aren't children wonderful? I think, as I am immediately reminded of the fights between my two sisters and me, of the kicking under the table, the hidden pinches, the crying.

"Have you ever been to Six Flags Over Georgia?" I ask Julia.

"Yes, on a church outing, last summer. It was pretty neat, but not as neat as Disneyland."

"I remember going to Six Flags when I was about your age and buying a bullwhip at a souvenir shop. I was rejoicing in walking around, cracking my whip, pretending I was an African explorer. Looking at my younger sister's legs, gleaming in the noon sun, I just could not resist the temptation, and I popped her good, leaving a pink welt on her tender skin."

"What did your parents do to you?"

"My father grabbed my whip, looked me straight in the eyes, and said, 'When we get home, I'm going to do the same thing to you.'"

"And did he whip you when you got home?"

"Yes, as soon as we pulled up in the driveway, we got out of the car, and my father took the whip in his hand, and before I could blink, there was a welt on my leg. But that wasn't the worst part of it. It was the five-hour drive home, looking at my legs, wondering what was going to happen to them—five hours of pure torture and anxiety."

The children all giggle at my story.

"How did you manage to get your children out of school at this time of year?" Sis inquires.

"Between Peter's job and my job, we just can't ever seem to find vacation time together. This was the best we could do. So we pulled our children out of school on Wednesday at noon. The teachers weren't happy, but I don't know what else we could have done."

Soon Sis and I are munching on cheeseburgers. The children are running around the gift shop, grasping everything in sight. I feel sorry for Sis for not having any brothers or sisters. She missed out on the joys of fighting over the car window seats, fighting over trespassing on your chosen boundaries on the couch, fighting over what TV station you would watch. And in between the fights were those moments of sharing and giving and delighting in your kinship.

"Now, I hope you visit us in Knoxville someday," Marilyn says. "Peter and I and the kids would sure enjoy that."

"And if you ever want a Tennessee football ticket ..." Peter says.

"I'll be sure to give you a call," I respond.

Soon the Manuels pack up in their station wagon and head back toward Knoxville. Sis and I continue eating.

"Sis, don't you just love being around children?"

Sis is silent.

"When I was little, I was always stirring up trouble between myself and my two sisters. It was always my fault. But then one day, my two sisters started up a rip-roaring, screaming, knockout fight. This time I knew it was not my fault, so I went running back to my parents' room to tell them that I had nothing at all to do with it. As soon as I crossed the threshold, my mother's hand latched onto my arm, and before I could protest, five lashes from a belt descended on my unsuspecting bottom. I screamed and screamed in protest, and finally my pleas were heard. My mother apologized but left me with the remark, 'There probably are hundreds of things you have done in your life that you have gotten away with that deserved punishment. Just think of that spanking as back payment.'"

"Your mother was probably right."

Ignoring her derisive tone, I continue, "Yes, she was right, and I had my share of spankings growing up. I used to love to pretend I was a captured Confederate soldier, like Sam Davis, the Yankees trying to force information out of me. Over and over I would tell myself, don't cry, don't talk, you are stronger than they are, as the belt blows descended on my crimson buttocks."

"My parents didn't believe in spanking." Her attitude irritates me, and I give up trying to communicate. She just does not understand.

* * *

Soon we are back in my weary Mustang, rushing down the road, past the pine trees, past the kudzu, past the broken-down cars, the factories, the dismal billboard signs of civilization. I am now driving, and Sis stares abstractedly out the window. Onward we go in our deathly silence, past Chickamauga, over Missionary Ridge, around Lookout Mountain. Sis looks toward me, her eyes staring at me as if I were a stranger.

"Gabriel, you've changed. What happened to the person I fell in love with?"

"I haven't changed. I'm still the same person. I'm just happy now. You need to get over your hang-ups in life. Then you will see."

Again silence looms in the car like a thick fog of despair. The smell of a dead skunk filters through the cracks in the windows.

* * *

That night, I roll over to Sis and take her in my arms.

"Sis, you are the only women I love."

"I find that hard to believe," she says and rolls away from me, facing the wall. I place my arm around her, but her body is as limp as a Raggedy Ann doll.

"Sis, it's true. How can I prove it to you?"

"You can't, Gabriel. You changed so much. I used to think it was just a phase you were going through. But now I see it has become a deeper part of you. It has become your philosophy. I used to think you were the smartest person on this planet, the wisest, the most humanitarian, the most caring ... the person with whom I wanted to spend the rest of my life. But now all I see is somebody who only cares about himself."

"But Sis, I haven't changed. It's still me on the inside."

"But what about what's on the outside?" she says, and the silence again descends on us like a thick winter snowstorm.

* * *

I have not changed …

Not changed …

CHAPTER 12

As I stand high on Sis's balcony in the frigid November wind, my ears burn with pain. I stare out over the city stretching before me, feeling like Sisyphus on top of his mountain. Sis is my stone, and her apartment is my mountain. I accept Sis as she is, but why can she not accept me as I am?

Looking down, the height has a dizzying effect on me. I am afraid. Far below, people scurry like automatons this way and that way, with seemingly little purpose or direction. The cold morning sun reflects off hundreds of metallic projections in whirling proportions. The air is filled with the incessant drone of engine roars and automobile horns.

Thinking about my day ahead, I feel as if I have already lived this day a million times over. I know exactly what is going to happen. I will buy a morning newspaper at the corner bookshop and go into the cafe next door. I will order coffee, munch on a Danish, and start reading over the previous day's events—the murders, the political scandals, the conflicts in the Mideast, the new building projects in the city's slums—the list goes on forever.

Again I look down below. The abyss yawns at my feet. Ennui has grasped me with her evil talons and refuses to let go. I remember in medical school when I was in search of a specialty. Emergency medicine seemed just perfect. I could work my ass off a few days a week, treating the most complex and bizarre cases ever, and then spend the rest of my time living the glamorous life of a playboy.

But now I just feel like a shadow of a person fixing people up and sending them back out into this Sisyphean world. And the patients never stop coming—the sore throats, the sprained ankles, the knifings, the heart attacks. They all look the same to me, the same monotonous faces, and they all seek the same from me: for me to make their dreary world better. But it is so senseless. I'm no God. I cannot do these people any good. Just leave me alone. Just let me be me. I'm the only person that counts. I'm the only person that matters.

The depression settles on my shoulders in a thin cloud, like the radioactive fallout that fell on Hiroshima. I feel the malady creep all over my body. It begins in my extremities with a numbing feeling starting in my distant toes and spreads to my fingers. Next the fog settles in my muscles, and my legs start to go weak. Then all auditory input begins to diminish, becoming a dull ringing. My throat becomes parched, and my head pounds as if my cerebral spinal fluid is running out onto the floor. I feel as if I have a hangover and the flu at the same time.

I stagger inside, without enough energy remaining to close the door, and I fall face first on the spongy, carpeted floor. I am completely paralyzed, catatonic, immobile. Voices from my past taunt me …

"… Help me, help me! The pain is so great …"

"… Why am I not screaming …"

"… Why are you always such a cynic, Gabriel? Try letting go. Stop fighting the world so hard. It's not as bad as you think …"

"… You sure have changed from medical school …"

"… Don't you have a force in your life that pushes you, that beckons you, that makes you create something out of nothingness …"

"… But Gabe, don't you think there is more to life than pleasure …"

"… Doc, are you crazy? Has my girl been telling you some lies …"

"… What happened to the person I fell in love with …"

"… But what about what's on the outside …"

Images of faces from my past beckon me, torment me, and torture me, images of nameless faces on the streets, images of starving children in Africa. Just leave me alone; just leave me alone. I just want to be left alone. Then, just as suddenly as it came, the fog begins to lift. I pull myself up, and I see a strange man standing across from me. He has blond hair parted on the right and deep green eyes that penetrate like arrows into my soul. A faint scar is on his left cheek, grinning at me. Who is this person? Why is he here? But then I realized it is me, merely reversed, staring back at me from my mirror. I look down at my hands—yes, my hands—carefully noting the calluses and scars and lifelines. Looking at the clock, I see that only one hour has passed—only one hour, but it seemed like an eternity. I shut the cold door and drag myself into the shower, where the warmth of the water awakens my senses, refreshes me.

* * *

On the street down below, I see all the nameless faces; the warm, enclosed cars; all the clutter of civilization that looked like tiny toys from above. Looking straight up, I can just make out the edge of Sis's balcony, so tiny, so far. I feel like danger is everywhere, lurking around every corner. I must proceed with caution. I feel like a wise man walking along the edge of the Grand Canyon. A wise man protects himself by imagining all the many ways disaster may befall him. A rock may slip from beneath his foot; a gust of wind may throw him off balance; a bird may suddenly fly out from a nearby crag. This wise man protects himself by considering all of these possibilities. He walks slowly and with balance. He calms his nerves so as not to react too suddenly to any unexpected changes. And in this manner, he safely reaches the end of the canyon.

Now, a foolish man perceives none of these dangers. He walks forth boldly with his head held high and a sneer on his lips. He ignores all of the warnings and challenges the Fates to wrestle with him. And chances are that this man will also safely reach the end of the canyon. But in his false pride, he has neglected the forces of the world around him. He has lost sight of his utter insignificance in comparison to the universe. He has forgotten how to experience life, and he has forgotten how to learn.

I now see the world in its entire foolish splendor. Everybody and everything is out to get me, but I am prepared. A bus careens around the corner, but I jump out of the way. A nameless stranger bumps into my shoulder, but I am too quick for him. A dog jumps out from around the corner, but I dodge it as I would dodge a rattlesnake in the woods. There is the cafe ahead; just one foot in front of the other. Remember, a quarter for the newspaper.

There, now. See? It's easy. Just pull on the door really hard and sit in that empty booth in the corner.

"Are you ready to order, sir?" a beautiful waitress says with a smile. She is not more than nineteen years old.

"A cup of espresso and an apple Danish," I say and concentrate hard in order to form my lips in a thin smile.

"I will have your order in just a few minutes," she says and departs, her smile still burning into my cheeks.

I glance down at the newspaper in front of me. A pitiful five-year-old Lebanese girl sits on top of some burned-out ruins in Beirut, like Job on his ash heap. Both of her arms are in bloody bandages. The rage wells up inside of me, like a volcano ready to burst.

I scratch the table in front of me, but I leave no mark on the hard Formica top. I pinch my arm, and a tiny drop of blood appears. Tasting it, I find that it is bitter, salty. Looking out the tinted window, I see countless blank faces go streaming by. I can see them, but they cannot see me. I am invisible. I am the invisible man.

The cheery waitress brings my food, and I gulp it down. I throw the newspaper aside. I must see Sis. I must see Sis. Something is up; I can just feel it.

* * *

As I hurry out of the cafe, a horn honks, and a blue Plymouth Barracuda goes racing by, just barely missing me, the shadow of a driver just barely visible behind the dark window. The face somehow looks familiar. I jump into my Mustang and go rushing headlong down the freeway, my eyes scanning back and forth, aware of all obstacles in my course.

Entering the tall building of Sis's network, I dash to the elevator, just barely catching the doors before they close. The ride seems interminable. The walls press in on me, and the pressure forming in my ears is unbearable, but up we go.

The doors open, and the spacious room eases the tension that was growing in me. Sis's secretary greets me.

"May I help you, sir?"

"Yes, I would like to speak to Elizabeth Morgan. Tell her it is Gabriel."

"Just one moment, sir." She buzzes the office. "You may go in now, sir."

When I enter the confines of her office, Sis greets me with a cold hug, her arms noncommittal. "What brings you here?"

"We need to talk about us, now."

"Can't this wait till later?"

"No, it can't. You have been treating me so coldly for the last two months, ever since we went to Sea Island, and I just cannot take it anymore. I need you to accept me as me—otherwise there is no future for us. You just don't seem to understand the purpose of life."

"Okay, Gabriel, but remember, you started it. We are going nowhere. You can be you, as far as I'm concerned, but I want no part of it."

"What are you saying?"

"I want you to move out of my apartment. I was going to wait until after winter, but since you want to force the issue, I want you to move out now."

"But my houseboat is too cold," I protest, realizing this conversation is not going where I hoped it would.

"You can stay in a hotel room until you find a place to live." Sis looks at me like I am a total stranger. Then a look of sadness takes over her face, and she continues, "We both need to be apart from each other for a while, to find out what we really want out of life."

"Sis, is this really about you not wanting to have children?"

Sis looks hurt, pauses for a moment, and then declares bitterly, "Gabriel, I do want to have children, but just not with you."

I'm stunned. My heart bleeds like it has been pierced by a thousand arrows. Nothing so cruel has ever been directed toward me. I don't know what to say. Finally I look up, tears welling up in my eyes. "Okay, Sis, I will move out. We are just too different. You will never learn to sit back and enjoy life. It just would never work, the way things are now. Maybe in time, you will see."

* * *

"Ellen? Ellen Moore?" I say into the telephone receiver.

"Yes?" the voice returns, puzzled.

"It's Gabriel Rutherford."

"Oh, hi, Dr. Rutherford. What is going on?" Her voice cracks with nervousness. I'm sure she thinks I'm calling about hospital business.

"I wanted to see if you could go out for dinner tonight. Sis and I broke up."

"You broke up? Poor baby. Yes, I would love to go out for dinner."

"I'll pick you up at about six. Where do you live?"

"Apartment A-11, 6319 Charlotte Avenue."

"I'll see you at six."

"Great. And Dr. Rutherford—oops, I mean Gabriel. Don't worry, I'll take care of you. And if you need a place to say, feel free to stay at my place for as long as you wish."

"No, I can't do that. I need my own space, but thanks for the offer."

"Okay, but remember, you can stay here whenever you want. I'm just a phone call away."

"Thanks," I say and place the cumbersome phone back on the receiver."

* * *

Blazing down the interstate in the dreary November mist, I find myself looking at a pleasant two-story condominium that overlooks the nearby Hillsboro Pike. It sits high up on a hill. The Nashville skyline is in the distance, and I can just barely make out the letter C through the barren trees.

"It is only ninety thousand dollars, nothing down. We provide the financing and also pay for the closing costs. It's a steal," the beautiful blonde real estate agent announces with an all-knowing voice, her young, succulent flesh enticing me, inviting me. "Did you know that it is said the Confederates encamped on this very hill, just prior to the Battle of Nashville?" she says as she leans forward, her loose dress revealing her pert nipples on her lovely breasts. Her rich blue eyes make contact with my roving eyes, and a thin, enticing smile forms on her sweet full lips.

"Where do I sign?"

* * *

My defiant Mustang misses the interstate entrance ramp and I find myself traveling onto the old Franklin highway, towards the old battlefields, towards the monuments of a forgotten generation.

First, I arrive at the Carter House, my Mustang having parked under an aging oak. The house still stands majestic as ever, over one hundred and twenty years after the war. It is approximately fifty feet wide in the front, with huge double doors framed by majestic Doric columns.

"We ask for a two-dollar donation to visit the museum and tour the house," a pleasant young girl tells me at the museum entrance. I place five dollars in the basket and then stroll through the museum, staring with fascination at the bullets and shrapnel and muskets and bayonets. I come across a photo taken in 1920 of Company B, First Tennessee, the last remnants of an age gone past; their faces burn into my memory. I feel as if I know all of them, as if they were my brothers.

In a case near the far wall is one of the most unique museum pieces one will ever find, the burial casket of Colonel Shy, who was killed on Shy's Hill at the Battle of Nashville. I will never forget the unusual story associated with this artifact. On Christmas Eve of 1977, police were summoned to investigate a report that a grave had been disturbed. Upon arriving at the scene, the police found a corpse dressed in a "tuxedo" sitting on top of a casket at the bottom of a dug-out grave belonging to Colonel Shy. It was assumed that someone was intent on hiding a recently murdered corpse on top of Colonel Shy's casket and must have been scared off for some reason.

In early January, the *Nashville Banner* reported that the corpse was twenty-six to twenty-nine years old and died from a blow to the head. The chief deputy reported, "It looks like we have a homicide on our hands." It was not until a week later that the Dr. William Bass, a forensic anthropologist at the University of Tennessee, announced that the body was in truth Colonel Shy. The fact that the body was embalmed and buried in an air-tight cast-iron casket resulted in such excellent preservation of the corpse that no one assumed the body could have been that of Colonel Shy, and no one initially looked in Colonel Shy's casket to see if it contained his body. Presumably, some misguided thieves thought they would find Colonel Shy buried in a full military uniform with sword and buckles, items that would have sold for thousands and thousands of dollars in the collectors' market. I guess these thieves were dumbfounded when they found him buried in dress clothes sans military accoutrements. As I peer intently, seeing if I can see through the glass viewing plate built into the coffin, a young girl in the museum announces that the tour of the Carter House starts in five minutes.

Strolling out front, I am reminded that the Battle of Franklin took place on this very day in November. The cries of wounded lying on the fields in front are deafening; my body shakes from the roar of cannon fire and musketry; the acrid aroma of gunpowder hangs in the air. Feeling dizzy, I close my eyes momentarily and come back to the present.

"Okay, let's gather around," an elderly lady wearing a Civil War period dress says. There are now about ten of us standing around her matronly figure.

"The Battle of Franklin should never have been fought in this lovely and historical community. The Confederate army should have trapped Union general Scholfield's troops in Springfield, Tennessee, located just south of Franklin. However, the Confederates allowed the Union army to escape unmolested at night. Rumor has it that while the Union troops were marching up the road, right through the Confederate army, General Hood was drunk in his tent and General Cheatham was frolicking with the infamous Mrs. Peters in the Martin Cheairs mansion. Whether these rumors are truth or fiction, no one will ever know."

Our tour guide looks to be seventy to eighty years old. Her face is weatherworn and has finely chiseled wrinkles of wisdom. She takes extreme pride in the history of this town, of this house haunted by ancient ghosts. I see a Daughters of the Confederacy pin on the collar of her dress.

"The Carter House was built in 1830 by Mr. Fountain Branch Carter with the aid of his slaves. The house is distinguished by its simple but eloquent architecture, the stone-capped gables, the hand-poured glass windows, and the Doric columns. Just prior to the Battle of Franklin, Union general Jacob D. Cox commandeered the Carter House to use as his headquarters. The Carter family was forced to spend the battle in the cellar, imagining the fierce fighting by the noise and the bullets and cannonballs piercing their very walls.

"Now come around to the side of the smokehouse and plantation office. You can still see the actual bullet holes from the battle. Some of the fiercest fighting of the war took place right here in the backyard of the Carter House."

Looking up, I am astonished at the number of holes in the walls, the chipped brick, the fragmented wood. It looks like a giant piece of Swiss cheese.

"Where were the main works of the Yankees?" I ask.

She points to the ground in front. "The original line of Union works was two hundred feet in front of us. But the Confederates overran that position, and the Union re-entrenched right where we are standing. A battery was placed just to our right. Are there any more questions? Now follow me."

Walking into the house, I marvel at the height of the ceilings, the spaciousness of the rooms.

"Almost none of the items in the house are from the actual Carter family," says the guide. They were donated by families all over Tennessee and are typical antiques of the Civil War time period."

As we walk upstairs, I cannot but help notice the scattered bullet holes through the house, the isolated cannonball hole upstairs. Just think what this house must have looked like right after the battle, before the family had time to start repairing the damage. We proceed upstairs.

"Now, in this room, we have the ending of the most tragic tale of the battle. On the morning of December first, Fountain Branch Carter and his family emerged from the confines of the cellar. The Union soldiers had departed that night for Nashville. Fountain Carter had a premonition that his son was in trouble, and at that very moment, a weary Confederate soldier brought the sad news that their son Captain Todd Carter was mortally wounded charging on the Union breastworks. The family searched the battlefield to no avail before one of the Southern generals, General Smith, led the Carter family to their son. He lay no more than two hundred yards away. He was gently carried off the battlefield and placed in this very room, where he eventually succumbed to his wounds. He died in the arms of his family."

Our guide quickly brushes a tear aside, and then she leads us back downstairs.

"These windows facing the road are the actual hand-poured windows from the Carter House. The only reason that they survived the battle is that they were parallel to the line of fire. The other windows in the house, and much of the brickwork, have been replaced due to damage sustained in the battle."

The tour guide walks out of the house and back into the front yard, and we follow. Pausing, she gazes all about and then, with sadness in her eyes, says, "General Hood, just prior to the battle, accused his men of cowardice. He said they lacked the bravery to charge an entrenched enemy. The Confederate army lost one third of its army, its best generals and officers. As James McPherson so eloquently wrote in *Battle Cry of Freedom*, 'Having proved even to Hood's satisfaction that they could assault breastworks, the Army of Tennessee had shattered itself beyond the possibility of ever doing so again.'"

She pauses, looks at every one of us with solemn eyes each in turn, piercing our innermost souls, making us feel her pain, and then abruptly she smiles. "That concludes our tour for now. There will be a slide show in the museum in fifteen minutes. If you have any questions, I will try to answer them. Thank you."

"Thank you," we all respond.

I wander over to the side of the smokehouse. I am astounded at the number of bullet holes. How could the fighting have been so fierce? I pick one half of the wall and start counting ... one, two, three ... three-hundred and ninety-five ... I stop counting; there are just too many. My god! What must it have been like to be standing on this very spot, bullets whizzing by, men falling left and right? My god!

Still gaping from wonder, I jump into my Mustang and we travel down the road to Carnton, the plantation home of John McGavock. Carnton looms above the horizon, its eight huge columns standing above all. It is closed to visitors today, but I am not interested in the inside, only the outside.

Parking next to the cemetery, for a moment I stand in awe at all the burial markers of the Confederate dead, almost all of them nameless. After the Battle of Franklin, Carnton was converted into the largest of the area's military hospitals. Three hundred wounded Confederate soldiers were cared for within the house, and hundreds more in lawns surrounding the house. It is said that Carrie McGavock, the mistress of Carnton, was an angel of mercy, tending to soldiers' wounds, her dress soaked in blood, giving them water and food, giving them hope when there was no hope.

In 1866, the year following the war, the wooden grave markers of soldiers killed in the battle of Franklin were either rotting or being used for firewood. So that these brave soldiers would not be forgotten, the McGavocks donated two acres next to their house to be used as a Confederate cemetery. For five dollars per soldier, the bodies from all the scattered graves throughout Franklin were exhumed and reinterred in the McGavock Cemetery, almost fifteen hundred rebel soldiers in all. Carrie took great care to record the names and locations of the 780 soldiers whose identities were known. But as I gaze out over the cemetery, at the hundreds of headstones, I realize that the remaining soldiers may be unknown, but they are not forgotten.

After taking one last glimpse of the cemetery, I proceed across an open field, my feet in the damp soil making squishing sounds. There it is: Carnton and her porch, the most famous porch in existence. On this very porch, the bodies of four Confederate dead soldiers were laid to rest—General Patrick Cleburne, General Otho Strahl, General Hiram Granbury, and General John Adams—all dead, all placed on this very porch. I stoop and touch the wood. I feel its rough texture, the grains, the splinters. I look at the many stains in the wood and wonder if these are the bloodstains of the South's glorious generals.

Onward I drive, past the site of General Schofield's headquarters; past the William Harrison House, where Confederate generals John Kelly and John Carter died; past Saint Paul's Episcopal Church, which was used as a hospital after the battle; and past the huge monument in the central square, dedicated to the fallen Confederate soldiers. All about is history; the past and present are one.

Standing on Winstead Hill, the entire battlefield looms in front of me. I can see General Hood ordering his twenty thousand men to charge the heavy fortifications of the Yankee troops; I can hear the gunfire erupting; I can feel the whizzing of the canisters in the air. Everywhere men are falling, but onward they rush, charge after charge, in five hours of senseless slaughter. And when the smoke cleared, six Confederate generals were dead, eight wounded, and one captured. In addition, over fifty officers were killed, wounded, or captured. Eighteen hundred soldiers were killed, and another forty-five hundred were wounded. It was a devastating blow to the once-great Army of Tennessee. *Dreams die hard*, I think as I trudge back to my awaiting Mustang.

* * *

That night I find my naked self entwined in the bare limbs of Ellen.

"So why did you and Sis break up?"

"She was just too old-fashioned. To her, sex had to always be love, and life always had to have purpose. She just did not see the pure fun of pleasure for the sake of pleasure."

"And Gabriel, what do you want out of life?"

"I want to live life to its fullest, to drink it, to taste it, to experience every pleasure imaginable. I want to be a kid again."

"Do you like to play games?" Ellen says with a sly smirk on her face.

"Yes," I answer, grinning, wondering what she is about to propose.

"I'll be your slave tonight and obey your every command—whatever you wish."

I grab Ellen playfully by her hair and push her head down to the softness above my thighs.

"Don't spill a drop, or you will get the spanking of your life."

"Oh, master, don't spank me! Please don't spank me," Ellen says and then eagerly she engulfs my now-swollen manhood. I lift my hand into the air and land a light, stinging blow. Admiring the glowing imprint of my hand on Ellen's rosy cheeks, I whisper, "Good-bye, Sis. Good-bye, dreary world."

PART THREE

Hope is the thing with feathers
That perches in the soul,
And sings the tune—without the words,
And never stops at all

Emily Dickinson

CHAPTER 13

My gloved hands grasp the taut leather reins as I sit astride my faithful steed, Bellerophon, on the summit of Winstead Hill, dressed in full military uniform. My polished saber gleams in the bright November sun; a dark plume of ostrich feathers on the pinnacle of my hat flutters in the gentle breeze. From my vantage point, the entire Union works encircling Franklin are apparent.

"General Hood," I say, "an attack would be insanity. The Union works are all complete. Cannons flank our right on the hills beyond the Harpeth River. You ask the impossible."

General Hood turns his horse and faces me, his debilitated body strapped to his horse in a grotesque fashion. His right arm hangs uselessly at his side; the clothing dangling from his left stump flaps in the breeze.

"General Rutherford, where is your courage? We shall storm the Yankee lines by brute force and press them against the river, annihilate them."

General Nathan Bedford Forrest, his six-foot, one-inch body sitting proudly on his stallion, shakes his head in disapproval, the finely chiseled features of his face forming a frown. "General Rutherford is right," he begins, his rich gray hair and gray beard symbolizing the wisdom inherent in his military mind. "A frontal assault would be disastrous. But if you let me lead a flanking maneuver on the enemy's right, we can smash through the weak point of their lines, cut off their retreat. We can capture the entire army."

General Hood turns to General Patrick Cleburne and says, "And what do you think, General?"

"It would be suicide. But if we must make a frontal assault, at least wait until our artillery and remaining troops arrive from Springfield," General Cleburne says, knitting his weighty brows as the wind dances lightly through his rich, black hair.

General Hood's face becomes flushed with anger. "Is the entire Army of Tennessee a bunch of cowards? Do I hear treason? Are my generals refusing to obey my commands? We will crush the enemy by an overwhelming onslaught. We shall then move to Nashville and drive the Yankees from Tennessee. And from our new supply base in Nashville, we shall free the entire Ohio Valley."

"But General Hood—" I say, but he cuts me short.

"We shall make the fight," he says and then turns his horse away from us, his hideous body mocking us, as he gallops off to address his aides. General Forrest spurs his horse in a fit of rage and bolts off the hilltop.

General Cleburne and I sit alone, side by side, on top of our beautiful horses, surveying the battlefield before us. The sun rains down with a steady intensity; it is surprisingly hot for a late November day. I am overwhelmed by the futility of our task. General Cleburne, sad and despondent, addresses me.

"Well, Rutherford, if we are to die, let us at least die like men," he says and then spurs his horse, galloping off to his men in the distance.

A sharpshooter lies prone on the ground in front of me, at the top of the crest. His Whitfield rifle resounds with the roar of exploding powder, one shot at a time. In the distance, one can see the Union artillery troops scurry for cover as his bullets rain down methodically.

I dismount and walk up to the soldier.

"Son, may I borrow your scope for a moment?"

"Why, certainly, General. It's going to be a mighty tough fight, isn't it?"

"Yes, son, it sure is," I say as I take the rifle. "May God be with us."

Sighting through the scope, I see three completed lines of Union works sitting astride the Franklin Pike. Cannons flank the Carter cotton gin, and on the peaceful hill beyond the river are two complete Federal batteries. It is suicide, but then again isn't it supposed to be glorious to die for your country? And besides, I am oh so tired of this war.

"Thanks," I say as I hand the scope back to the sharpshooter.

"General, good luck," he replies and then starts shooting his unwavering rifle at the distant Yanks.

As I pull myself astride my trustworthy horse, I become aware of a long line of men standing in front of the chaplain. They are giving him their watches and jewelry and photographs and letters. Some are even having their friends scribble their names on yellow pieces of paper, names to be pinned on their overcoats, names to let the gravediggers know who they are.

"Troops, fall in!" I yell with an earnest fervor. "We shall advance and crush the enemy."

Looking down at my gold pocket watch, I see that it is approaching four in the afternoon. My troops are arrayed in a long battle line, astride and perpendicular to the Franklin Pike. Our band plays "Dixie," and our tattered battle flags wave in the gentle breeze. The sunlight is splintered in a dazzling display, reflecting off the gleaming bayonets, off the worn muskets. It is an awesome sight indeed.

"Dulce et decorum est," I whisper to myself, and then I give the command to advance as I gently spur Bellerophon forward. Our troops march in a steady line, like the steady beat of the incoming tide on the ocean beach. The air is electrified by our intense energy.

As we approach the Federal advance line, my gold compass hangs uselessly from my belt. Suddenly all hell breaks loose: cannonballs explode above the ground, Minié balls whizz by my fearless head, shrapnel flies through the tumultuous air.

"Hold your fire!" I scream. "Now charge!"

Our men let out the high-pitched Confederate battle cry and rush toward the barricades. Smoke fills the air, and the roar of musketry is deafening. Men are falling right and left, and I feel as if I could ride my horse across the field and never touch ground. Suddenly a six-pound cannonball pierces Bellerophon's neck. Blood bursts forth, and my mortal horse falls dead to the ground, nearly trapping me. An aide rides up to my side and dismounts.

"General Rutherford, take my horse." I jump up and fix my bloodstained boots in the stirrups.

The Yankees have now turned and fled from their advance position, toward the main works.

"Men, fix bayonets, and follow the enemy into the main trenches. We must break the enemy at all costs!" I shout into the roar of powder. Advancing into the black clouds of burnt gunpowder, I notice a tattered foot soldier following at my side. His gray wool jacket has no buttons, and his shoes are full of holes. As I peer into the face of the old soldier, I see that it is my father, my father, my father.

"Father, Father!" I call. "What are you doing here?"

"Son, I am here to be at your side. I will always be at your side," he says as onward we charge, step by step, side by side, step by step …

My ears are numb from the roar of gunpowder, and men are falling like leaves in autumn, but forward we rush, toward the Union entrenchments. I look down at my father, rejoicing in our companionship. He turns and looks up at me, smiling, when suddenly blood bursts forth from his forehead like a volcano erupting, forming a third eye in the center of his face. He falls to the ground, motionless.

"Father, Father!" I scream as I jump off my bewildered horse. There is no response. His body lies limp in the dust, the blood spurting forth like a geyser.

"Please, don't die. Please, don't die!" I cry as I try to plug his bleeding head with my finger. But the blood pours forth; his limp body dangles in my arms. He is dead, dead, dead. "Father, Father!" I cry one last time, and then I let out a scream, a scream like mankind has never heard before, a scream of sorrow and sadness, a scream encompassing the sum accumulation of all the miseries in our world. The sun is blanked out, and the roar of cannon fire is silenced, so great is my scream.

I gently lay my father down in the bloodstained dust and address him one last time. "You shall be avenged."

I leap on my horse and raise my gleaming saber high in the air, spurring my horse diagonally across the field, through the rain of bullets and canisters, calling to my men.

"Men, where is your courage? We must not be defeated! We must charge over the bulwarks, into the trenches themselves."

The dead are piling up in the trenches in front of the Yankee works like logs in a lumberyard, and there is hardly enough room for the living. The screams of wounded men fill the air. My troops have panicked. They are starting to fall back. I must set an example. Waving my shimmering saber high in the air, I rush headlong toward the Yankee works, toward the parapet sitting in front of the Carter cotton gin.

"Onward, men, onward! We must be avenged!" I shout as I spur my fearless horse forward, jumping the ditch and onto the very parapet itself.

"Hold your fire! Hold your fire!" I hear a Yankee officer calling to his men. "No one so brave deserves to die."

"Onward, men, onward!" I call to my troops, and then I reach down and grab the Union battle flag. Suddenly, I hear the sickening thud of lead against human flesh and feel a pleasant sensation of warmth over my right breast. Looking down, I see that my gray uniform is becoming red.

"No! No! No!" I scream, struggling, not being able to breathe, suffocating as if I am drowning in a yellow cloud of thick acid. "No! No! No!"

* * *

"Gabriel! Gabriel, wake up! Wake up!" a voice shouts to my unconscious self, shaking my body vigorously. "Wake up."

My eyes pop open, and I gasp for breath, suffocating from the weight on my chest. "I can't breathe. I can't breathe." My lips are numb, and my hands tingle.

"Hush ... hush ... everything is okay. It's only a nightmare," a soothing female voice calls. Her soft flesh cradles my head; her sweet hands gently caress my forehead, wiping the sweat of the past away. "Sis, Sis, Sis," I call out. But it is not Sis ... *Father, Father, you shall be avenged ...*

I relax and fall back into a deep sleep.

CHAPTER 14

I awake to the din of the alarm clock and reach over, striking the noise dead. I roll over and drape my arms around the soft body next to me, Sis, Sis … but the smell is different; the hair is coarse. Opening my eyes, I am brought back to the present.

"Wake up, Ellen. Wake up, you have to be at work in an hour."

Ellen's eyes open and peer up at me with affection and reckless abandon. "I just love waking up next to you. It is so comforting," she says and then gives me a gentle hug, followed by a long sigh.

"No, I think you just like the warmth of my new waterbed and my jacuzzi in the bathroom," I tease, trying to avoid words of love.

"That's not true, Gabriel. It's only you that matters."

I think to myself that she would not feel the same way about me if I were not a doctor, but then again, I guess being a doctor is part of me.

"Do you remember your nightmare last night? It must have been a bad one. I thought you were dying."

A chill runs down my spine as fragments of the dream flood my consciousness. "I vaguely remember parts of the dream. I think I was an officer in the Civil War, at the battle of Franklin. And there was something about my father." I try hard to remember, but the memory fades before I can grasp it from my unconscious self. "You better jump in the tub now, or you will be late to work."

"Not until I make sure you will not forget me," she says as her head disappears under the covers.

* * *

Traveling on the interstate, I marvel at the emptiness of the land around, at the occasional spot of snow dotting the frigid landscape. I am overwhelmed by a sense of loneliness, of despair. Sis, Sis … but you just don't understand me; you never will; we are better off apart. Sis, Sis …

I pull into the marina and park my Mustang by a deserted Dodge Viper. My houseboat rocks gently in the distance as a cool fog hovers just above the surface of the hidden waters. The naked trees on the opposite bank stand in a silent vigil; the morning sun reflects brilliantly off the icy branches. It is as if I am in between heaven and earth but present in neither one. If only I could become part of this world, part of the serenity, part of the peacefulness—then everything would be okay, wouldn't it?

Entering the frigid cabin of my isolated boat, I pull out a space heater and turn it on high. The peaceful glow of the brilliant coils warms my cheeks, thaws my unfeeling hands. I wish God would come down before me and say, "Yes, I created you. There is a purpose. There is meaning to life." Then everything would be so simple. But where is God? Who is God? And what if God is only a figment of earthly imagination? But it is absurd to hope for or believe in God. He does not exist. He has no plan. He is not directing our lives with some divine plan, nor is he keeping a tally sheet of our rights and wrongs. No, there is no God. God is only a character created out of man's inner weakness, out of his inability to accept life as it really exists, out of his wish to believe that something better lies in another life. Just look at all the religions ever created by man; there are hundreds of them; there are thousands of gods. What gives Christians a right to say that their god is the only god? Maybe the only reason that Christianity has such a large following is that it gives a promise of eternal bliss, but to others it also gives a promise of eternal damnation. Is it any wonder that ancient religions that offered no hope of an afterlife died out? Only happy people can love a religion where death signifies a return of your ashes to the soil from which you sprung. But there are so few happy people in this world; we all want something more—eternal bliss—because life on this planet is so not enough. But what if the real world was like the Disney movie *Tron* where everyone knows who is good and who is evil; where everyone has their own personal deity steering them on the right course, giving them meaning and purpose to life. If only …

So where do I go from here? I've disposed of love, I've disposed of God, and all that is left is me and the universe, and I am no more a part of it than before. I feel as if I am an electron circling an atom. I must go from point A to point B but never actually cross the space between the two points. If only atoms could speak.

Standing, I gaze out over the water. The fog has lifted, and the sun shimmers off the water's surface, calling me, beckoning me. Sis, Sis … if only you could let me be me.

I open up a small cabinet and retrieve a shoebox that contains the passionate letters Sis and I wrote when our relationship was just developing, looking for a clue, looking for how something so wonderful could go so wrong. Initially, Sis's letters were very tentative and cautious:

> Dear Gabe,
>
> Since I met you, I've felt warm, open, and honest, and I'm scared. In the past, I've been very successful at avoiding my emotions in order to carry on a normal schedule, but now I'm beginning to feel very vulnerable, and I'm not sure if I am ready to give up my independence. As a result, I am experiencing a lot of pain and, at the same time, a lot of joy. Do you suppose the two go together?
>
> Gabe, you've been a beautiful friend and lover, and perhaps soon we will be able to explore more areas. I know it's selfish of me to want the best of both worlds. I hope you know what I am saying. I know we've joked about respect, but it means more to me than anything in the world, and at times, respect is all we have.
>
> Before I close this letter, I want to tell you that I'm well aware of your feelings, and, if at all possible, I don't want to cause you any pain. I suppose you'll feel pain no matter how it turns out, because we've grown so close these past few weeks. But please remember one thing: you have made me very happy, and I hope that I've returned some of that warmth as well.
>
> I'll be thinking of you.
>
> Sis

From the onset, I was head over heels in love with Sis:

> Dear Sis,
>
> It has been three weeks since our first date, and I'm still daydreaming about you and our wonderful weekend together. I feel so warm and close to you, and

yet we've only known each other for such a short time.
Just think what it will be like when we've known each
other for three months, or even three years.

I talked to my former college roommate last
night and told him I was falling in love with a strange
and mysterious woman from Memphis. We talked some
about the complication in our relationship regarding
your desires to have "the best of both worlds," and it
helped me get a better grasp of the situation. I just want
to tell you again that no matter what you decide, I never
will be angry or bitter towards you. I may be sad, but I
still will have the same feelings towards you, and I still
will have the same respect for you as a person. I think
the potential is there between us for something beautiful
and long lasting, and I guess all I really want from you
is a fair chance at developing that relationship. We've
already developed something very special between the
two of us in a very short time, and the best thing I can
do is give you the time and freedom to choose your
own path, to make your own mistakes, to grow and
learn. You've got a wonderful mind and a lot of
potential, and I wouldn't want anything—not even
myself—to stand in the way of you developing that.

Love,

Gabe

P.S. If you are free on Saturday, let's cozy up in my
houseboat and drink a bottle of German wine while
listening to Elton John.

Over time, Sis started to be more trusting and began to open up more
about her past, but still she was hesitant:

Dear Gabe,

When I was at Sewanee during my third year in
college, my best friends were five girls and two guys,
but Cathy and David were the closest ones to me.
Things went well for us for about seven months, during
which we did everything together, but it was always

"together." However, about two months before the summer, David and I fell in love, and you can guess what happened to our group. Cathy became vicious, and our other "friends" wanted nothing to do with us. As our passion flourished, we felt liberated from our group's watchful eyes. We dared to break away, and our romance lasted for a beautiful summer. We thought we could conquer the world, but we couldn't, and it ended, and I lost David as a friend, and I had already lost my other friends. Since that relationship, I've been hurting and feeling weak and vulnerable. It has taken me the last several years to learn how to stand up for myself. Since meeting you, I feel I am close to finishing the process, and as a result, I've never felt more alive.

Gabe, I do wish to become much closer to you, but I'm still hesitant. I am afraid that I will ruin our friendship or that someone or something will take you away. In time, I hope I can become more trusting, but the only thing I have learned in life so far is that I am the only one on whom I can absolutely depend. I hope you understand what I am saying.

Je t'aime, mon ami,

Sis

While Sis was being hesitant, I continued to surrender myself to my feelings:

Dear Sis,

When I am with you and when I am not with you, I feel so close and full of love, and I never want that feeling to stop. You are the only person I have known with whom I have no second thoughts about getting closer. In the past when I started a relationship, my first impulse when things started getting a little serious was to pull back. But with you, Sis, I have none of these fears, none of these second thoughts. And I know it's because around you, I am allowed to be me, and I hope you learn to feel the same around me.

Sis, I hope we keep getting closer and closer. I already know that you are a beautiful woman capable of love and insight and affection. There are so many things that are a part of me that I want to share fully with you, and there are so many parts of you that I hope you can share with me someday. I know I said some pretty heavy things to you this past week, and I know it may have been a little too early, but I meant everything I said. I just hope our relationship reaches that stage of security where the word "love" is always implied. Well, Sis, now you know how I feel about you. I hope this feeling never goes away.

Love,

Gabe

P.S. I only wrote this letter because I wanted an excuse to tell you how much I love you.

And finally, after a few months, my insecurity started to take control over me, and I was afraid that I was losing Sis:

Dear Sis,

Last night, when I was trying to go to sleep, I just could not get you out of my head. I wanted to call you so badly, but I was afraid you would not answer my call. I wanted to tell you how much I loved you, and I wanted to tell you how I wished we were together that very moment, not sex, but just in each other's arms. But Sis, it has been over a week, and you have not written me or returned my calls. I fear that I have done something wrong when everything seemed to be going right, and I am scared that I have lost you.

I have been thinking about the last night we were together. You were feeling a little ticked off at life. I could tell you wanted to start a fight. I was feeling frustrated at first, and then the fear of losing you started to set in. Somehow that circumstance led to us opening up towards each other more than ever before. I remember both of us crying a little, or maybe it was just me crying, and I remember you telling me some circumstances in your past which I doubt you have ever shared with anyone else. When we made love to each other that night, it was the most beautiful, loving experience of my life, and that was just the beginning. The best is that I was so acutely aware that you told me that you loved me more times in that time period than you have ever told me in all the months before. And you know something? It never once sounded like you were just saying it to say it, and it never once sounded boring to me. I loved hearing you say it every single time. And the best thing of all, Sis, is that I love you with all of my heart.

But Sis, now I do not understand … now I am afraid. Did I do something to scare you off? Have I lost you? Why haven't you called? Please, I need to know where I stand.

Love,

Gabe

P.S. Sis, I know this letter sounds crazy, but I'm tired, as I couldn't sleep any last night, and that has just made my insecure feelings worse. Just please let me see you this weekend, let me hold you, let me love you. And please be honest with me, and if something has come up in your life that will interfere with us, do what you have to do. I'll still love you, and I'll always be waiting for you, if you ever change your mind. Sis, I love you, please love me back.

And then, when I had about given up all hope, having not received a visit, a letter, or a phone call in two weeks, Sis bared her soul to me:

Dear Gabe,

How I wish you were here and that I might find comfort in your arms. I have tried to love you and give myself to you, but I always found myself pulling back. And when I have tried to separate myself from you and maintain my independence, all I can think of is being with you. My heart and soul have been at war, and it has been wearing me out. But now I have surrendered to my feelings, and I feel so very close to you, and I never want that feeling to end.

I am tired of worrying about my fear of losing you, of losing one more person that I love. But now I realize I must surrender to my fears, or the world will pass me by.

Gabe, I am yours now. I think I have always been yours, and I know I always will be yours. I love you with all my heart. And just as I have been fighting for you in my nightmares, I will always fight for you in life. Gabe, you are my heart and soul. I love you more than life itself.

With all my love,

Sis

Placing the letters aside, tears in my eyes, I pour myself a Jack Daniel's on the rocks and put Beethoven's Ninth Symphony on my stereo. My heart is numb, and my mind aches from living. Turning up the volume full blast, I kneel on the floor in front of the speaker and press my ears against the silky wood. The radiance from the heater scorches my cheeks, the whiskey burns through my taste buds, but best of all is the music. The musical chords roll straight into my head, reverberate around, and fly straight out. The vibrations reach the most impenetrable depths of my bones, of my inert soul. My lifeless body oscillates with every vibration; my body becomes one with the music.

* * *

"Christine," I say on the cold phone, "It's Gabriel."

"Hi, Gabriel. What's up?"

"I wanted to see if you could have dinner with me tonight, have a few drinks, have a good time."

"Well, I don't know. I heard about you and Sis breaking up, and I'm not sure how I would feel—"

"Listen, it's over between Sis and me. Sis won't mind. She wanted something different out of life."

"And what do you want out of life?" Christine asks, her voice now becoming interested.

"I want to live life to its fullest, try everything, experience all my wildest fantasies."

"I know you know about me. Does that have anything to do with your call?"

"Partly, but I have always been attracted to your free spirit. And who knows, you probably can talk me into helping out with some of your projects. I think we could make a good team," I say, resorting to bribery.

"Do you mind if I bring along my girlfriend?"

"By all means," I reply, the wondrous possibilities unfolding in my sordid mind.

"Okay, it's a deal. Let's meet at the Quarter Note around eight. I hope you know what you're getting into."

"Don't worry, I'm a big boy."

"See you tonight."

"Bye," I say, and the phone clicks dead.

* * *

"Gabriel, it's great to see you," Christine says and gives me a hug. "I want you to meet Jenny Robbins."

"Hey, Jenny, nice to meet you," I say as I give her hand a gentle squeeze.

We sit down at the restaurant table, me on one side and Christine and Jenny on the other. Jenny is a beautiful half-Asian girl, tall, slim, with perky breasts that protrude through her cashmere sweater. Her dark eyes are inviting, enticing.

"So what kind of work do you do, Jenny?"

"I play violin for the Nashville Symphony ... or at least I try."

"Gabriel, she is absolutely fantastic. You have to hear her play sometime."

"I will. I will, I promise."

The waitress interrupts us, and we all order drinks.

"So what do you girls feel like eating tonight?"

"Mexican," says Jenny. "They have the best enchiladas."

"Sounds great to me. I think I will have a beef enchilada dinner, and I bet both of you will have chicken enchiladas, as there is no such thing as a tofu enchilada … or is there?"

"Right as always, Gabriel, at least about some things," Christine replies teasingly.

"So tell me, Christine, what projects are you working now?" I inquire, noticing that Christine and Jenny are holding hands under the table.

"I'm still working on my free legal clinic. We are open two days a week, and I have convinced three other lawyers to join us. We offer divorce counseling and information on child custody, and we are just starting to branch out into business law—to keep people from being taken advantage of."

"Wow, I'm impressed," I say, noting how Jenny is gazing at Christine with admiration. Christine's long, dishwater blonde hair is braided down her back; her brown eyes beam in the dim light.

"So Gabriel, what kind of a physician are you?" Jenny asks.

"I'm an emergency physician, of sorts."

"Jenny, Gabriel is one of the last cynics. He spends his days and nights helping people, improving our lot in life, and then he pretends he is doing no good. He actually is a diehard idealist who has been running from it as long as I have known him. But deep down, I know that he really cares, that he really wants to help people. If only he would stop running from himself and his responsibilities."

"Wait a second, let's not get too personal," I say with a laugh, wondering if Christine is right. I can remember being an idealist in the past, talking about taking care of the downtrodden and disadvantaged, talking about flying to earthquake-stricken communities, wanting to help out.

"But aren't we here to get personal?" Christine replies with a sly grin on her face.

"Yes, you're right. I surrender. Maybe I am running away from life. Maybe it is because I am just too afraid of life, afraid that the past will come back and be my present."

"I've always wondered about your past," Christine says. "To me, you act like women I have known who have been raped. I like to think that you have been raped, or maybe killed someone. It's the romantic in me, as Captain Renault would say."

"I think I have both killed and been raped. Don't the two go together? So Jenny, what dark secrets do you have in life?"

"God, I have lots of them. My mother was a piano teacher, and my father was an alcoholic. But oh, how he used to love to hear the violin. I tried and tried to play the violin, thinking that if only I could become better, he would stop drinking, but he never did. So being the brilliant person that I am, what did I do but marry a drunk French horn player? But of course I couldn't save him either. Now I'm too afraid of myself to ever have a serious relationship again with a man. I'm afraid that I will keep repeating the same pattern for eternity. There, you have my life story. Isn't it amazing what a little alcohol will make you say?"

Christine gives Jenny a sweet hug and a soft kiss on the cheek. "You know I will always love you."

The waiter arrives, bringing us our food, and we all dig in as if we haven't had a meal in years.

"Can you believe that oil spill off California?" Jenny says, talking between bites. "They say that if the wind doesn't change, the entire coast from Mexico to Canada will be covered. Did you know that one oil tanker carries enough oil to cover one fifth of the Pacific Ocean? God, I just shudder at the thought of all those poor dead animals, the sweet whales and the joyful dolphins, all dead."

"Yes, I've been following it closely in the news," Christine says. "I wish they would make the oil companies take more responsibility."

"It's not the oil companies to blame," I throw in. "It's us greedy Americans who like our fancy cars and our houses at seventy-two degrees in the winter. It's us Americans who love to blame all our woes on others. If we would just be willing to give up a little of our luxurious life, then we wouldn't have to worry about whether enough oil could be ferried across the ocean. Take Freon, for instance. We all know that it is destroying the ozone layer, leading to deadly ultraviolet radiation, but does that stop us from using our spray cans? Or take recycling—we could save millions and millions of forests, we could save countless tons of coal and oil, if we just learned how to recycle our goods. But do we? No. We throw our aluminum cans and glass bottles into the same container as the one that holds the old cat litter and discarded food. We throw our newspapers and plastics into the same container that holds the disposable baby diapers. Do you know how long a disposable baby diaper lasts? Four hundred years. Just think, in four hundred years, the entire surface of the planet will be covered with disposable baby diapers. I'm sure they will keep the planet Earth dry as she weeps tears of sorrow."

"That's the spirit, Gabriel. See, Jenny? I told you that deep down he was a real idealist. Now if only we can get that part of him to surface for good."

"Good luck," I reply, grinning, noticing that Jenny is now eyeing me in a mysterious way.

Soon dinner is all finished, and we sit back and relax, letting the food filter through our systems. Jenny and Christine disappear to the bathroom. It seems like forever before they appear with mischievous grins on their faces.

"So, Gabriel, would you like to come over to my house for a nightcap? Or do you have to get up early tomorrow?" Christine asks.

"Yes to the first question, and no to the second," I reply with growing excitement.

"Great. Then it is settled."

* * *

That night, I find myself entwined in multiple limbs, the musky aroma of sex all around.

"Okay, lover boy, are you up for round two?" Christine says with a devious grin and then she and Jenny push me down onto my back.

* * *

God, Fuck you!

Fuck you!

CHAPTER 15

Once again I find myself walking down that dim hospital corridor. I am all bundled up in winter clothes, and my gloved hands feel nothing. Listless patients pace the hallways; cheerful nurses make their rounds; orderlies buzz back and forth. The air is filled with the mechanical drone of the heating system, occasionally broken by the paging of doctors overhead. But I am unmindful of all of that. I thought I had found the answer to life, and I thought it was sex and pleasure, but it is not enough. I am still filled with a deep, empty feeling welling up in my heart, a sense of longing, a sense of being needed. I wander onward, one foot in front of the other.

I think hard, trying to remember what day it is today, what month and what year. Time has lost all meaning. There is no future; there is no past, only the here and now, which seems to have frozen at one point in space. It is as if I am standing between two mirrors, my reflection continuing back and forth through infinity, but motionless nonetheless.

As I walk through the emergency room's double doors, the gleaming patient bays overpower my senses. I feel like a swimmer who has just dived into a freezing mountain stream. The initial shock creates overwhelming pain and then a numbing sensation, a sensation of emptiness and loneliness. I want to run back through those double doors, back out into the snowy weather, back to the safety of my condominium. The mirrors will not stop reflecting.

Ellen runs up and greets me. "Good morning, Dr. Rutherford. Aren't you bundled up this morning?" she says, giving me a secret wink. But I only nod.

"Good morning," Lynn greets me. "Let's hope the snow keeps all the crazies out today."

"Don't count on it," I reply.

Looking about, I see that Jim Cleburne is nowhere in sight. I open the doors of the doctors' room and find Jim peacefully asleep. I give a short cough and flick on the lights.

Jim jumps up, confused and disoriented, and then he realizes where he is. He rubs his bloodshot eyes and stretches his arms wide from his body. His mouth opens in a loud yawn, and then he smiles.

"So, Jim, how was your night last night?"

"It couldn't have been more perfect. I've been in emergency medicine for twenty years, and I have never seen a night like last night. I saw my last patient at two AM. I hope this snow keeps up."

"Well, they are predicting that the roads will be clear today but will ice up again tonight. I guess that means I'm stuck with all of the patients that should have been yours last night."

"It's the luck of the draw."

"'Tis true, 'tis true," I respond, feeling despondent on thinking of the day ahead.

I strip off my leather gloves, looking at my hands as if they belong to somebody else. As I pull off my overcoat, a shiver runs down my spine, and then I brace myself for the day to come.

"Catch you on the flip-flop," Jim says, and he gathers his belongings and marches down the hallway with his limp, the steady beat of his boots on the tiled floors resounding through the corridors.

I walk back out to the emergency room and pour myself a cup of coffee, thick and black, having been sitting on the warmer all night long.

"Lynn, what day is it?"

"Why, it's Sunday. This is your last workday for the week, your seventh day in a row."

"Sunday. What month is it?"

"Why, it's January, January twenty-first. Would you like the year too?"

"No, I think I know that one," I lie. I don't even know what year it is. I don't even have any idea how old I am. My god, is this a dream?

Lynn notices my confused state and looks puzzled, "Are you all right, Dr. Rutherford?"

"I think it's the flu, but I'll be okay."

I ponder back on the events in my life, back to the times when I fell into despair—despair over lost loved ones, despair over unattainable goals, despair over lost hopes and broken dreams. And each time, the despair lasted for a few days, months, and sometimes years. But with time, the wounds healed. Maybe it is true that time heals all wounds. No, I take that back. Time doesn't heal wounds; it is growing up that heals wounds. That's all it is. But it is so hard to grow up, especially when your childhood was stolen from you, snatched away from beneath your very nose. Growing up entails so much. It requires you to abandon your past; it forces you to face weaknesses in your character and personality. Oh, if I could only grow up. If I could only give up those parts of myself that I so detest.

"Dr. Rutherford, here is your morning paper," the unit clerk, Tammy, says, interrupting my concentration. Looking about, I see that the emergency room is still empty. Oh, may it stay just so.

Going through the morning paper, I look at the date on the top: the day, the month, the year. I recite them over and over again in my mind. Doing a little calculation in my head, I remember that I am thirty-three years old. Just think: thirty-three years. My life is almost half over.

I turn to the comics to discover how my heroes Opus and Bill the Cat are doing. Opus is still having a mega inferiority complex over his nose. This week he has sent away for a body massager, guaranteed to shrink away those unwanted pounds. Bill the Cat is nowhere to be seen. Oh well, another day.

The phone rings, and Ellen answers it. While reading the paper, I listen in on the conversation.

"Emergency Room ... No, our doctor is tied up. This is a nurse speaking ... What makes you think you have Lyme disease? It is middle of winter, ma'am, the ticks are not out yet ... It doesn't matter if you were in the woods, ma'am, the ticks are not out yet ... Ma'am, the symptoms would not show up in a day anyhow ... Ma'am, if you are that concerned, our doctor would be glad to see you today. However, I would suggest you call up your private physician tomorrow ... A spider bite? Now, what makes you think you have a spider bite? Ma'am, if you are that worried, our doctor would be glad to see you ... It would be quite expensive to be seen in the emergency room ... Ma'am, if you are that worried, our doctor would be glad to see you ... Ma'am, I have work to do. I have to go now. Why don't you call your doctor tomorrow?"

Ellen hangs the phone up and looks over to me in dismay, "Boy was she crazy!'

"Ellen, you need to learn to be more decisive. A simple 'Yes, our doctor would be glad to see you, although it would be best if you called your private physician' would do. And then hang the phone up. They will figure things out."

"I know, I know, but I feel so guilty cutting these people off."

"But you have your responsibilities also. Don't forget that."

"I know, I know," Ellen says as she wanders off to her morning duties.

The entrance door swings open, and a tech leads the first patient into the emergency room; the day has begun. It is a black-haired man in a thick parka, approximately my age. He clutches a briefcase with pale hands. The nurses are busy doing drug inventory, so I step up and greet the patient, not waiting for the nurse to triage him.

"Hi there, sir. I'm Dr. Rutherford. Let's step this way, please," I say as I point to a bed in the corner of the observation area. He leads; I follow.

"So what seems to be the problem, sir?"

"I'm sick."

"Okay, let's try to be a little more specific. What kind of symptoms do you have?"

"Well, to be honest with you, I think I have cancer."

"Cancer? Good heavens, what makes you say that?"

"Well, I have had no energy these last two weeks. I can hardly seem to keep my eyes open. And these glands in my neck have been swelling. I had an uncle with lymphoma, and his glands swelled up just like mine."

"Do you have a sore throat?"

"I did several weeks ago, but it seemed to go away on its own."

"Have you ever had mono?"

"No. Isn't that the kissing disease? I do have a new girlfriend, though."

"Okay, let's lie back while I examine you."

The patient lies back, and I go through my routine. In one hundred and twenty seconds, I have scanned over his entire body, prodded around, and looked in various holes.

"Sir, I think you probably have mono. We will do a blood test to make sure. But I would just lie back and relax. I'm positive there is nothing to worry about."

The man seems reassured. I look down at his chart and note that he works for an accounting firm. Probably reads too much. If his social life doesn't work out, he will probably be in a doctor's office next year, screaming chronic mono. Isn't it amazing how physicians keep inventing diseases to explain depression? Let's see, there's chronic mono syndrome, irritable bowel syndrome, and fibromyalgia. Then there is TMJ syndrome and tension headaches … and best of all, that catch-all diagnosis, hypoglycemia. I can't even begin to count the number of neurotic patients with panic attacks and fainting spells or weakness and malaise from depression who were told they have hypoglycemia. And once these people have a diagnosis, you cannot convince them otherwise. It is their excuse for not taking responsibility for themselves. If only physicians would not be so afraid to discuss personal problems with their patients, to take a little social history, to recommend a therapist. It would all be so easy. But why do I harp on these matters? I'm just an ER doc and I don't really care.

A new patient awaits me in Room 4. I grab his chart and wander around aimlessly until I find the room. This time, I note the name: Mr. Green, a fifty-six-year-old white male. The chief complaint is stomach pain.

"Hi, Mr. Green. I'm Dr. Rutherford. So how long have you been having these stomach pains?"

"For about six months. But the pains seem to be getting much worse."

"Have you been taking anything for the pain?"

"Only Alka-Seltzer and aspirin."

"Hmm," I ponder aloud. "What color have your stools been lately?"

"Brown ... no, I take that back. Sometimes they are dark, almost black."

"Well, let's lay on your back and I will examine you." First palpating his abdomen, I find that Mr. Green has some epigastric tenderness—not too great, though, and no masses. After a cursory exam of the rest to his body, I have a nurse collect a stool sample, which tests positive for blood.

"Mr. Green, I think you probably have peptic ulcer disease. We will be checking some blood counts, and then we will call a gastroenterologist. Are there any more problems?" I ask, ignoring the cardinal rule of emergency medicine: Don't ask for any more complaints than those that the patient first states.

Mr. Green starts to speak, and then he grows silent, his face flushing.

"Mr. Green, I get the impression that you want to tell me something else. Don't be embarrassed."

Mr. Green blushes again, and then he speaks, his voice halting and stuttering. "It's my wife. Well, actually it's me. I'm not able to please her sexually. I'm so ashamed, but I just cannot seem to have sex."

"Is it erection problems?"

"Yes."

I do a quick exam of his genitalia and the blood vessels in his legs; the pulses are greatly decreased on the right leg.

"Tell me, Mr. Green, how far can you walk?"

"Walk? I guess about one block, and then I have to stop and rest."

"What makes you stop?" I ask, the skin tingling on the back of my scalp.

"I get a lot of pain and cramping in my right hip."

"Great," I say. A mark of surprise registers on his face. "I think the two problems are related. I think you have some blockage in your arteries, which hopefully can be surgically corrected."

Mr. Green's face relaxes, and I see him give a sigh of relief. I, *Super Doctor*, can treat all ailments, whether it be stomach ulcers or impotence. Just come, all you masses, and let me heal you. Walking back out front, I whisper over and over, "Physician, heal thyself. Physician, heal thyself," but nothing happens. My emptiness sits in the pit of my stomach like trash thrown into an abandoned well.

"Dr. Rutherford, a patient with a cough awaits you in Room 2," Ellen calls.

I grab the chart and see it is a sixty-one-year-old white female. The chief complaint is cough for six months. Great, I'm sure she is a smoker. If she would just stop smoking, then the cough would clear.

"Hi, I'm Dr. Rutherford. What seems to be the problem?"

"I have a cough that I cannot get rid of. I've taken three courses of antibiotics from my doctor, but I'm not getting any better—I'm actually getting worse. He keeps scolding me for not taking my antibiotics, but I swear I have taken every one."

"Do you smoke?"

"I used to, but I quit four months ago, the cough was so bad," she says and then has a paroxysm of coughing spasms. I hand her a basin, and a thick, green chunk of sputum with blood intermixed appears.

"Um ... How many chest X-rays have you had?"

"None."

"None? Just where were you going for treatment?"

"Some foreign doctor downtown. I did not have the money to pay for an expensive doctor, and I did not feel comfortable going to the city hospital. I don't like charity."

She has another coughing spell, with more chunks of sputum mixed with blood.

"Don't worry, we will take care of you. Now sit up, and let me examine you."

I go through my quick routine. I feel a hard lymph node just above the patient's right clavicle. On listening to the posterior right upper chest, I hear dim crackles and diminished breath sounds. "Now say 'eee.'" The sound changes; I hear "aah" through my stethoscope. She has a pneumonia, secondary to an obstructing carcinoma. It is already metastatic. She does not have long to live.

"Ma'am, we are going to run a few tests on you, and then I'm sure we will be admitting you to the hospital."

"But you can't admit me. I can't afford it!"

"Listen, don't worry about the hospital bill. Just pay what you can. The hospital will write off the rest," I say and place my hand gently on her right shoulder. It is now for the first time that I really look at this patient, her pleasant smile on her waxen face, the softness of her hands, the tiny rivulets of tears in the corners of her eyes. I didn't even pay attention to her name, and soon she will be dead. What a world we live in.

* * *

The day is progressing at a steady pace, one patient at a time, nothing immediately life-threatening. I find time to wander around the hospital, time to have more coffee, time to smoke cigarettes with the respiratory therapist. The cigarettes make me feel alive. The dark smoke goes in, burning my throat and searing my lungs, and then on every exhalation, I see my breath in the air.

"Dr. Rutherford, put that cigarette out," Ellen chides me. "Don't you know they cause cancer and lung disease? You should pay attention to your own warning that you routinely place on the discharge instructions—'Stop smoking, or you will die.'"

"Of course you're right, but I seem to require them at this particular time. And besides, I don't smoke those kinds of cigarettes."

"What are you talking about?"

"See, look right here on the label on this pack. It says, 'Smoking by pregnant women may result in fetal injury, premature birth, and low birth weight.' Since I'm not pregnant, these cigarettes can cause me no harm."

"Gabriel, you're impossible," Ellen says and turns her attention to another matter. I fade out, wondering why I smoke. Is it because they induce a slow death? Is it because it is a way to harm myself without actually shooting myself in the head? Or is it just because I'm weak, incapable of the kind of action required? I really don't smoke that much, but every day since Sis and I split up, I have smoked more and more. So far I have managed to keep from smoking when I am not working, but how long can that last?

"Dr. Rutherford," Lynn calls, "there is a patient back in Room 8. He won't tell us his problem, but he seems to be in real pain."

"Sir, I'm Dr. Ru—" I pause, trying to remember my name. My voice slurs momentarily. "Ruth-er ... ford. What is causing you so much pain?"

"Doc, I haven't been able to pee since yesterday."

"Okay, we can take care of that problem. Have you ever had any prostate problems?"

"No, but ..."

"But what, sir?"

"Never mind," he replies with shaky voice and trembling hands.

While doing a rectal exam on this middle-aged gentleman, I find a hard solid object inside his rectum.

"Sir, what is that in your rectum? You need to be honest with me."

"Promise you won't tell my wife. This is so embarrassing. She just wouldn't understand," he says as his face turns red.

"Don't worry, this is only between you and me."

"Well ... I'm so embarrassed ... there is a Coke bottle in there."

"Um, I see," I say with a detached medical mind. "How long has it been there?"

"Two days. I kept thinking it would come out. I've tried Fleet enemas and Dulcolax and milk of magnesia, but nothing seems to work."

"It's the suction created by the vacuum," I say with cool indifference. "I will have you taken care of in no time."

I retrieve my magic bag of tricks, just for emergencies such as this one. I take a battery-operated drill and insert the point through his dilated rectum. I can just barely make out the base of the bottle as I make a tiny little hole. Suddenly there is a whoosh of air, and the bottle leaps forward. Next I grasp the bottle with some talons and easily pull it out. The Coca-Cola insignia shines bright. I wonder if the Coca-Cola Company would like to know of another use for their bottles. Naw, probably not.

"Sir, I want you to go into the bathroom and see if you can urinate. Otherwise we will have to place a catheter in your bladder. Next time be more careful, and please, if you are doing more than Coke bottles, practice safe sex—and for your wife's sake, please go down to the health department and have an AIDS test."

"Yes, I'll do that," he answers with a quavering voice.

Yes, I think to myself, you can treat all comers, but not yourself. Oh, but what happens to me? Next I will be forty, then fifty, then sixty, and eventually I am dead. Back to the ashes from which I came. *Dust to dust, ashes to ashes.* The words resound through my head, echoing from my past, from my distant childhood.

I try to remember all the fun times I had in life, but there is only nothingness. I feel as if I am sitting on the edge of a cliff in pitch-black darkness, only emptiness in the space beyond. I close my eyes in desperation. Then the image of Sis appears before my eyes: her perfect body and her flowing brown hair, her cheerfulness and easy willingness to help all, her glowing smile and radiant brown eyes. Sis, go away. Just look at all the patients I have seen today, and there still are a lot more for me to see. You have no right to be in this world, Sis. Just go away, go away.

I open my eyes, and the image fades. Is God making a mockery of me today? Is my emergency room a microcosm of the world? If it is, then what kind of world exists out there? Here I sit, on a Sunday, pondering the nature of God and existence while in the same breath pulling a Coke bottle out of some poor soul's rectum.

God, I know you're out there. I know you're laughing at me. Just leave me alone. Just leave me alone.

"Dr. Rutherford," Ellen calls, "there's a real winner in Room 7. She's a thirty-five-year-old female with chronic back pain for two years, and she says she just can't take it anymore. Every test has been negative—myelogram, CT, MRI, and the list goes on. She's already been seen at Nashville General three times last week."

I grab the chart with a heart full of dread. Why me, Lord?

"Hi, I'm Doc … I'm your doctor."

She looks at my name tag. I look too. "I'm Dr. Rutherford. What seems to be the problem?"

"It's my back. It won't stop hurting," she says in a disgusting, whiny voice. "I have not been able to work for over a year."

"Well, ma'am, the nurse tells me you have had every test imaginable, and that they are all normal. What do you hope I can do for you? After all, I'm just an emergency physician."

"I want you to make the pain go away."

"I'm sorry, but I cannot do that. Tell me, are you married?"

"No."

"Have you ever been married?"

"No."

"Do you live alone?"

"Yes."

"Do you have any family or friends in Nashville?"

"No. Hey, what does this have to do with my back?"

"Everything. Have you ever thought about seeing a psychiatrist for your back pain?

"What, a psychiatrist? Are you saying I'm crazy? Nurse! Nurse! Get this doctor out of here. He says I'm crazy, that the pain is all in my head!"

"Ma'am, I'm not saying that at all. I know your pain is very real to you, but you look as if you spend all day lying around your house, concentrating on how terrible your pain is. You have made that the focus of your life. If I sat around and thought about how much my feet hurt, I wouldn't be able to function."

"Nurse! Nurse! Get this doctor out of here. He says my pain is not real! He says I'm crazy! I want to speak to the hospital administrator!" she continues as I walk out of the room, leaving the door half open. "Nurse! Nurse! Call me a lawyer." Maybe she will calm down in a few moments.

After I grab a few bites to eat, I again approach her room.

"Get out of here, Doctor! I want another doctor! I want you to keep your hands off of me!"

Leaving the room for the last time, I ask Lynn to be my go-between. She approaches the patient with the cold facts that no other doctor has ever helped her, and that maybe a psychiatrist could teach her how to live with her pain. Soon the patient is agreeable, although she still looks at me with hatred and animosity. I phone the on-call psychiatrist and soon transfer her upstairs to the psych unit for an evaluation. I feel drained, exhausted. Here I try to do a little good, and all I get are screams and shouts of animosity and hatred. Oh, isn't medicine rewarding? I wish these people would just leave me alone. Just leave me alone ...

* * *

The day drags on. The patients keep filtering through my rooms in a long, steady array. Just as the shift is ending, an ambulance flies into the ambulance bay—a derelict has been hit by a car.

The paramedics rush through the double doors with the figure of an unshaven, smelly, haggard man. He is pouring forth blood from multiple cuts. He's obviously broken both his legs and arms. The smell of alcohol is unbearable.

"Let's move him into Room 1. Start one more line of normal saline, wide open, and somebody run and retrieve some red tag blood."

His eyes stare pitifully at the ceiling, and he moans incessantly.

"What happened?" I ask the paramedic.

The ambulance captain nods his head and says, "The driver of the car said this man jumped out in front of him on Broad Street. He thinks he was trying to kill himself."

"He did a pretty good job of it."

I open his shirt and find that his sternum is broken, but he has good breath sounds. A liquor bottle rests in his coat pocket, untouched. Yes, God is laughing at all of us. He kills his own but leaves the bottle behind.

The techs are busy cutting off his clothes, removing his shoes, placing a Foley catheter. His socks are black and as hard as a rock. I grab some scissors and cut along the sides. The left sock comes off easily, revealing a nasty case of athlete's foot. I grasp the hard edges of the sock on his right foot and pull, but nothing happens; the sock is stuck to his foot. Patiently I peel away the sock, pieces of skin shedding away with every tug. I give a quick yank, and the remnants of his sock come off, and I am met with a ghastly sight. "Oh, God," I murmur. Nausea wells up inside of me, and I break out in a fine sweat. Oh, God ... oh, God. The end of his right foot is missing, and thousands and thousands of maggots are where his toes used to be. Oh, God. Oh, God. Oh, God ...

Suddenly a strange sensation comes over me. I feel as if the room is full of fog, with only myself and the patient visible.

My head clicks like a camera.

Click.

I see the image of his face before me, his teeth rotting away, the maggots crawling out of the end of his foot, the thin oozing of blood from a laceration along the curve of his right jaw ... a shudder runs up my spine. His eyes plead with me in desperation, plead with me to let him die.

Click.

Sis and I are running along the shore of Lake Lanier, laughing, rejoicing. We are one.

"Gabe, I will always be yours."

"Sis, I will always be yours," I respond, taking her in my arms, our sweet lips intermingling.

Click.

"Dr. Rutherford, his blood pressure is falling. He's losing consciousness." Noticing his distended neck veins, I intubate him and place bilateral chest tubes.

Click.

"Sis, I'm a pleasure seeker now. Nothing else matters. I'm the only one that matters."

"Gabe, don't you think there is more to life than that?"

Click.

"Dr. Rutherford, his pressure is still falling." His neck veins are still distended. He must have a traumatic pericardial tamponade. I can save him.

Click.

"Gabriel, I know you are an idealist at heart. If you would just stop fighting the world."

Click.

I see a broken-down man wandering the streets, his crippled arms and legs, the snow on the ground, the booze bottle hanging out of his pocket; he is begging for money, begging for death.

Click.

"Dr. Rutherford, he has no blood pressure. Do you want us to start CPR?"

Click.

"No. He's dead." Dead, dead, dead …

I could have saved him if I wanted. But I didn't. I let him die. I killed him. Liquids well up from my stomach. I go outside the room and vomit.

"Dr. Rutherford, are you all right?" Lynn asks.

"It's that virus again."

I let him die. I killed him. I am a murderer.

* * *

Click ...

    Nothing.

Click ...

    Nothing, nothing.

Click ...

    Nothing, nothing, nothing.

Click ...

* * *

I wander aimlessly around the parking lot in the cold early evening air. Where is my car? I can't seem to remember. What date is today? What is my name? All is a fog. It must be a nightmare. *Wake up, wake up, wake up,* I call to myself, in vain.

I start putting my key into car door after car door, but none of them open. Finally the bewildered door of a red Mustang opens. I sit in the car and start the ignition; the motor roars. Touching the steering wheel, my confused hands feel the sting of cold plastic. My warm breath fills the air with thick smoke with every exhalation.

I pull out on the Nashville roads, and my Mustang leads the way. I follow. Along winding streets we go, through the light snowfall, by stranded motorists, onward we go.

The car parks, and I get out. It is dark, and I can see nothing. Retrieving a flashlight from the glove compartment, I step out into the cold wintry air. Light snowfall cakes my hair. Dark trees loom all around, silent sentries to these hushed grounds.

Flipping on the light, I shine the beam on the objects around: the icy trees, the isolated bench, the gray tombstones in the distance … tombstones? I walk onward, through row after row of forgotten tombstones. Suddenly I come to a stop. My beam shines onto a black stone; the name Gabriel Rutherford III is inscribed upon it. Suddenly my memory comes back: the gunshot in the library, Sis's beautiful body, the dead wino in the emergency department.

I am filled with rage and anger.

"Just who the hell do you think you are?"

There is no response.

"You are the most pitiful excuse for a human being that I have ever seen."

Again there is no response.

"I wish you were never born. I wish I was never born." I am now enraged, and I do not wait for a response from the black tombstone. "What right did you have to rob me of my childhood? What right did you have to make me grow up before I was ready? I hate you."

I kick his grave.

"I hate you."

I spit on his grave.

"I hate you, I hate you, I hate you," I say, falling down by his tombstone, sobbing. "Father, Father … why did you leave me?"

CHAPTER 16

My anesthetized hands clutch the steering wheel with grim determination, driving through the Stygian darkness, through the oncoming vortex of falling snow. Along the dimly lit streets lie rows and rows of bleak houses in which people actually live. But I feel nothing. My soul is completely empty, a giant void like the primordial soup that existed prior to the beginning of time. My warm breath pervades the frigid car with every exhalation.

Why did I let that man die? He wanted to die, and so I let him. Now he doesn't have to go back to his meaningless existence. He can rest in peace. He can avoid his troubles and the troubles of the world. A great sickness wells up in my stomach, and I pull over to the side of the road. A bridge lies just ahead. Panting, I run to the bridge's edge and heave and heave, but nothing comes out. There is nothing inside of me.

Gazing down at the intersection below, I become aware of the possibility that I could end it all here. I could splatter myself before the rush of oncoming cars. Yes, and if a truck should run over me, it would spread my fetid guts all over the South: little red stains from Nashville to New Orleans.

I leap back into my car and, in a stupefied state of mind, drive down the highway, back to the safe confines of my condominium.

* * *

Pouring a strong drink, I place Wagner's "Ride of the Valkyries" on the stereo. I sit back in an alcoholic slumber and let the rush of the music overwhelm me. I see before me the helicopters from *Apocalypse Now* descending upon the isolated Vietnamese village. The missiles and tracer bullets fall like hail in an autumn rainstorm. Destruction is everywhere, death is everywhere, and then the napalm falls …

Suddenly, I find myself spinning and spinning, falling through a whirlpool of blackness. A strange force grips me, and I am paralyzed, immobile. I desperately try to break free, but the force binds me too greatly. I am being suffocated by the squeezing of the air around me. Then the asphyxiating cloud departs. I can breathe now.

I find myself standing on the desolate roof of my home, adjusting my dim telescope sight on Sirius. Oh, no, it's happening all over again. Wake up, wake up …. I gaze out over the still river beyond, the icy haze lingering on the water's surface, the shouts of men and clanging of barges echoing in the distance. Wake up. Oh, please wake up. Oh, please …

I concentrate really hard, calming myself, focusing my energy; the dark, cold sky disappears and is replaced by a beautiful summer night, with green leaves and the fresh aroma of life all around. Cygnus looms high overhead, but the image fades … it is winter again. I am back alone on the roof. My telescope looms in front of me like a statuette to an unknown god. The eerie trees have lost their leaves. My moist breath pervades the air with every exhalation.

I hold my freezing hand before me in the night air, turning it over, back and forth, examining my pale, waxy skin. Am I just a nightmare? Is my whole life just one long bad dream?

As I look up into the night sky, there is beautiful Orion. And along a straight line descending from the belt, there is Sirius, the faithful star of mighty Orion. The light of Sirius penetrates the darkest depths of my hollow soul. The extreme gravity of the invisible companion tugs on every molecule in my inert body.

Patiently I bring the brilliant star into my field of view. There is Sirius, but I unable to see the dwarf star that lies next to it. Oh, Sis, you are as beautiful as Sirius. But if you are Sirius, am I the dim, heavy dwarf star?

Suddenly a shot rings out. Stay calm, Gabriel, it's only a dream. It will pass. My legs give out and I drag my body to the edge of the roof with bloody hands. But where is the ladder? There is supposed to be a ladder. Slipping on the icy roof, I find myself hanging from the jagged gutter by my right hand. My grip loosens, and I fall, downward and downward, around and around, into the dark abyss below. I land on my feet; the loud crack of bone splintering in the cold night air rings out. The pain shoots up my right leg, searing like molten lead into my cold flesh. Looking down, I see a chunk of pearly white bone protruding through the fabric of my worn jeans.

Opening the sliding glass door, I stumble into the dead house. The dull creaks and groans of wood settling in cold air whisper to me, beckon me. Everything is dark; everything is a blur.

As I enter the study, again my weight falls on my broken leg. The pain shoots up into my weighty soul, and I am hurled downward. My right cheek glances against the edge of the desk and I land in a warm puddle of wetness.

I scream …

… but I don't awaken. Oh, God, help me. Help me. Let me wake up … please …

Pulling myself upward onto the aged desk, I flip on a lamp. I am bleeding from the cut on the line of my right jaw. The blood tastes bitter. There before me, a figure lies sprawled out on the floor, blood oozing forth, forming a thick puddle; his back is toward me.

Oh, Father, why did you leave me? I start to weep, and I kneel down next to his prostrate figure. It's been so long since I have seen your face, oh, so long. Just one more time, let me look upon your face. I reach over and grab him by the shoulders, rolling him over onto his back, gazing downward, gazing into his open face, the aquiline nose, the scar on the right side of his face … Oh, my God. Oh, my God, it's … it's … I scream. It's … I scream.

* * *

I wake up with a scream.

I shiver like a leaf.

* * *

Oh, God, Somebody help me …

Help me …

Somebody …

Oh, God …

CHAPTER 17

The warm air of the heater overhead blows on my numb fingers. The noon sun beams down on my squinting eyes. The shouts of children in the lawn below filter through my sensitive ears. My head pounds from too much alcohol; my stomach screams for water. I feel like death embodied. Images of the previous day filter through my mind like rushing water through the sieve of a storm drain. Everything seems so confused. Images of patients, images of a derelict dying haunt me. Then I remember the dream.

Dragging myself out of the vortex of my bed, I pour myself a huge cup of black coffee. The dream is the clue, but the clue to what?

Picking up my phone, I dial Ken Grand's number in New York. Ken answers on the third ring.

"Hello, this is Ken Grand."

"Ken, it's Gabriel, I want to talk to you."

"Gabriel, it's good to hear from you." His voice grows serious. "I've been worried about you lately. I've heard through the grapevine that you have been having a tough time lately. I'm sorry about you and Sis."

"Never mind about that. Listen, I know this is going to sound weird, but I'm on the verge of some important discovery. It has a direct bearing on my life. Do you mind if I ask you some questions?"

"Gabriel, this is more than weird—"

"Look, Ken, ever since I first met you, I've had this feeling that you know something about this world we live in, that you hold some secret to meaning and existence. Can you tell me your secret to life?"

"Gabriel, are you sure you're all right?"

"Come on, just tell me."

"Wow, that's a tough one. Well, I've spent almost my entire life searching for my identity. First I tried to be everything my parents wanted me to be, but that didn't seem to work. And then I tried to be something that other people wanted me to be, but that didn't work either. Finally, I tried to be who I thought was me, but I wasn't even sure who I was. Then the truth dawned on me. I discovered that I could be free, that I didn't have to be this or that, that I just had to put one foot in front of the other and a path will appear before me."

"And what of your responsibility to your fellow man?"

"Sure, I feel responsible. I don't litter, I recycle my trash, I donate money to the Make-A-Wish Foundation, and I will never do to anyone anything that I would not want done to me. But as for joining organizations and pouring forth my energy to help people in need, I don't believe in that. I feel everybody must ultimately assume responsibility for himself."

"And do you believe in God?" I ask.

"God ... God is the ultimate copout. There is no God. There is only the here and now."

"So does this mean you are an atheist?"

"Well, I have never thought about it like that. I do believe in the collective wisdom of mankind, that this wisdom is the only meaningful driving force in our universe, but I don't believe in God. So I guess I am an atheist. I feel sorry for the people who turn in supplication to this fictional character, that they attribute the good and bad in their life to this all-knowing God. They just need to accept the reality of the world around, accept responsibility for themselves."

After exchanging a few cordial parting words, Ken hangs up. The receiver goes dead.

After I dial the phone for a second time, Christine Sanders answers at her office.

"Hey, this is Christine Sanders."

"Christine, it's Gabriel. How are you doing?"

"Gabriel, it's good to hear from you. Jenny is still talking about our great time together. How about getting together later this week?"

"Maybe," I say disinterestedly. "I'm wondering if you have a few moments to answer a few questions."

"Sure."

"These are kind of heavy questions."

"No problem. Go ahead."

"Okay. What is your secret to life? I've heard you talk before about the guilt you feel for having such an easy life growing up, about how that is a strong motivating factor in your life. What I want to know is—how come you find it so easy to help others?"

"Why? Are you sure you are okay? We can meet for lunch if you wish."

"No, I'm fine. I'm just trying to figure the world out."

"Isn't it a little early in the day to be trying to figure this out?"

"It's never too early," I say.

"Remember, you asked for it. But yes, I feel guilty for growing up in such a pleasant world, when others have not had the same chance, and yes that is probably my motivating factor in life. But I feel that the world should be a giant tag-team effort. We are all here together, and we must all help each other out. Some are born smarter than others, some are born richer than others, and some are born healthier than others. It is the responsibility of these people to give back to the world what they were fortunate enough to receive. Gabriel, if you would just stop fighting your guilt and let go, let it become motivation in your life, than everything will fall in to place."

"I agree with a lot of what you have said, but I will never accept guilt as a motivator. What about God? Where does he fit into your life?"

"God?" Christine exclaims, startled by the question. "I've never seen God, and I have never heard from God. It is not an issue on this planet. And besides, who needs God when there is such beauty in the world around?"

"Are you an atheist?"

"No I'm not an atheist. I just believe that if God exists, he has chosen not to reveal himself."

"Well, Christine, I appreciate you talking with me, I know you need to get back to work. I'll talk to you soon."

Again the phone clicks dead. I dial the phone a third time, and Mark Golding answers.

"Mark, it's Gabe. Can you talk now?"

"Sure, I have a few minutes. I am about to start a needle localization of a breast mass, and I'll have to leave soon. So what's up?"

"This may sound a little strange, but what is your secret to life?"

"Whew, you are crazy. You must not be getting enough sex lately. Well, let's see. I think the secret to life is to experience everything possible. After all, we only have one chance here on this planet."

"And do you feel like you should have to help others?"

"Sure, that's why I'm a doctor. But then again, I don't let it control the rest of my life. I trade off my weekly job of helping people into a sort of selfishness when I'm not at work. Then I don't have to feel guilty about looking out for my own interests."

"And do you believe in God?"

"Sure, I believe in God, but in a different manner than most people. Have you ever studied relativity, quantum physics, cosmology? Are you familiar with the concept of parallel universes?"

"Not really."

"Well, according to relativity and quantum physics, the past, present, and future are all equivalent, all existing at any given point in time, just like a photon is a wave and a particle at the same time. And for photons, it is not until you look for one as a wave or a particle that it assumes a given form. The universe is just the same. This universe we live in is actually a resonating form of multiple parallel universes, and it is not until the observer looks for this universe, the one you are in now, that the universe assumes its shape. God is that part of us that gives this particular universe its given shape, its given self-consistency—oops, I have to go now. How about coming over for dinner with Mary and me on Friday night? Maybe we can have some fun, if you know what I mean."

"Maybe," I respond in a noncommittal voice. Again the phone goes dead.

* * *

I sit at the breakfast table silently, drinking another cup of coffee, breathing in the air around. Again I have that feeling that I am on the verge of an important discovery. Each one of my friends has made some important discovery, but I feel as if they have all come up short. Ken senses the collective wisdom of mankind and the importance of responsibility. Christine sees the beauty around and has learned that we must all work together to make this world a better place. And what has Mark learned? In a sense, Mark has seen the beauty of God, the beauty of the universe, but he has missed the point.

Suddenly, the sun glints off a shiny object in the corner of the room. I turn and see a beam of light reflecting off the face of my gold compass sitting on the counter. I am immediately reminded of the bright star Sirius, the beautiful belt of Orion. And just behind the compass stands a picture of my father and myself, standing in front of an old church, the church of his boyhood. In the portrait, I am a tiny boy, dwarfed by my huge father. My head does not yet reach his waist, and my arms clutch his thigh. Our bodies partially obscure the cross on the door behind us. The previous evening's dream floods into my consciousness. Yes, Father, the world was too much for you. But it doesn't have to be too much for me. And it will not be. I refuse to accept the world as you saw it. I refuse to let myself become like you.

My senses perk up. My ears are filled with the joy of the rustling of wind outdoors, the honking of horns beyond, the barking of dogs. My eyes notice the exquisite beauty of the grain in the table before me, the shimmering of the sunlight through the curtains, the dancing of particles in the air. My hands feel the pounding of blood through my nail beds, the warmth radiating from my chest. The hair on the nape of my neck stands at attention. Goose bumps crop up on my naked flesh. A searing flash of heat descends on my right shoulder like a dove and transfixes my heart. I feel suddenly like Robinson Crusoe finding a footprint in the sand, or like Watson and Crick playing with their DNA molecules when suddenly all the pieces fell into place. The belt of Orion ... Sirius ...

... three stars point to one ...

Ἐν ἀρχῇ ἦν ὁ λόγος, καί ὁ λόγος ἦν πρός τόν Θεόν, καί Θεός ἦν ὁ λόγος ...

In the beginning was Logos and Logos was with God and God was Logos ...

... Logos

God ...

And just as my friends each caught a glimpse of a part of God, so had Heraclitus, Aristotle, the Stoics, and Philo. Logos is God, and God is Logos: Logos, the light that shines bright in the darkness, the light that makes sense out of nonsense, the light that holds chaos at bay. God is here; God is there; God is everywhere. God is the past; God is the present; God is the future. God is a part of each and every one of us, part of every molecule in the universe, part of every bit of empty space. There is no such thing as nothingness.

... God

Logos ...

I think I have always known this secret, but I've been running away from myself for too long. I've been trying to convince myself of something in which I do not believe. I must talk with Sis; I must see her at once. I pick up the phone, dialing the number.

"May I speak to Elizabeth Morgan?" I say to the secretary. "It's Gabriel Rutherford."

"One moment, please."

"Hello," Sis says in her professional voice.

"Sis, Sis!" I exclaim. "It's so good to hear your voice. How are you doing?"

"I'm doing pretty good. And you?" she asks in a reserved tone.

"I'm doing great." Excitement grows in my voice. "I was wondering if we can have dinner this week. I've made some important discoveries. I would like to share them with you."

"Okay," she says suspiciously. "How about Saturday night at eight? We can go to Julian's."

"Great," I say. "I think you will be pleased with me."

"Maybe. But I want you to know I have no intention of ever getting back with you. Too much has happened between us already."

"I'm sorry to hear you say that, but I understand that nowhere is it written that everybody deserves a second chance. But that's okay. I will still enjoy seeing you again."

"Listen, Gabe, I have to run. I will meet you at eight at the restaurant. Can you call for reservations? Bye." The phone clicks dead.

"Good-bye, my friend. See you on Saturday," I say into the empty air and place the delicate phone in its cradle.

* * *

I jump in the shower and let the warm water spray in jets all over my lean body. Tiny rivulets of time run across my forehead, over my shoulders, and down my legs, swirling into the vortex of the drain. Energy spreads through every fiber of my body. I feel as if I am being baptized for the first time, born into a new world, a child of God, a child of Logos. Stepping out, a blast of cool air greets me, lingers over me, refreshing me even more than before.

While dressing, through my bedroom window I see a motorist in the parking lot of a neighboring condo, trying to start his car. I rush outdoors to greet him. A tall man with a red trucker hat sits in his tiny, brown Ford Pinto, vainly trying to start the engine.

"Hi there, sir. I'm Gabe. Can I help you start your car?"

"Boy, can you. My name is Steve," he says, and we shake hands, my strong hand tugging on his firm hand. "Like an idiot, I left the glove compartment open all night long, and now the battery is dead."

"Here, let me pull my car up alongside, and we can jump you off."

Soon our cars are lined up side by side, my Mustang and his lame Pinto, the open hoods gleaming in the sun. Steve opens up his trunk and retrieves a set of jumper cables.

"Hey, what's this?" I say, noticing a metal detector in his trunk.

"That's my metal detector," he replies, his voice taking on a new energy. "I like to collect relics from the Battle of Nashville. They are all spread out in this area—even on this hilltop. I will show you my collection after we get my car started."

Soon Steve's Pinto is neighing in the cool afternoon wind, and he points me toward his condominium. I lead. He follows.

"Martha, this is Gabriel," Steve says to his wife cheerfully. "He helped me start my car."

"Nice to meet you," Martha says as I take her hand with a gentle grip.

"Over here is where I keep my relics," Steve says, pointing me to a shelf in the corner. On the shelves sit case after case of three-ringer Minié balls, canister balls, Union eagle buttons, breastplates, buckles, and all sorts of items I do not recognize.

"Wow, this is amazing. I can't believe you found all of this."

Steve retrieves a bayonet. "I found this Enfield bayonet right in the little patch of grass in front of the condo's swimming pool." Next he points to a CSA belt buckle. "And I found this belt buckle on the hillside in front of the main office."

"Wow."

"And here is my great-great-grandfather's diary," he says, retrieving a dusty and worn leather book. "He survived both the battles of Franklin and of Nashville."

I nod my head again in amazement and take the tattered book delicately in my hands, gently turning the pages, one after another.

"How would you like to go hunting with me sometime? There is an endless array of hills in this area, and two detectors are always better than one."

"That sounds great. I'll buy a detector today. How about Saturday morning?"

"Perfect," he says. "Make sure you get a Silver Saber Plus, just like mine. Oh, I almost forgot—you will need a small digging pick or shovel and some gardening gloves."

I repeat the name of the metal detector in my mind. After exchanging phone numbers, I bid them farewell.

Out in the parking lot, I become aware of a small, blue-eyed girl riding her bike, her long blonde hair flapping in the breeze. Looking at my watch, I see that it is already four o'clock: school is out. The girl tries to make a sharp turn, and she loses her balance. Her bike throws her sideways onto the sidewalk. She starts screaming out of fear and pain.

I go rushing up to her. "Are you all right?" I say, pulling the bike off her legs. There are no obvious deformities. She clutches her right arm in pain. A small abrasion bleeds through the elbow pad of her sweater. "Where do you live?" I ask gently.

She points to an apartment door just across the street.

"Do you think you can walk?"

She nods her head, the sobs easing up, but tiny rivulets of tears continue to drip down the sides of her angelic face.

"My bike, my bike! It was a Christmas present," she weeps.

"Don't worry about your bike, little one. I will carry it for you." I pick up her bike, and we walk gingerly to her door.

After I knock on the door, a much older version of the daughter answers. The daughter lets out a shriek and grabs onto her mother's waist. I gently place the bike just inside the front entry.

"Hi, ma'am. Your daughter had a bike wreck, but I think she will be okay. My name is Gabriel Rutherford. I'm an emergency physician here in town."

"Hi, my name is Carol, and this is Alex. Over in the crib behind is Paul."

I notice a fat, bald kid sitting up in the crib, looking at us as if he knows the secret of life.

"We call him Baby Buddha," Carol says, as if she is reading my thoughts.

"Alex," I say with a gentle voice, "can I look at your arm again? I want to see if it is okay."

Alex meekly lets go of her mother. Examining her arm, I am convinced that it is only a mild scrape.

"She will be okay. I would clean the cut with peroxide and place a bandage. Feel free to call me if you think it's getting infected. I live just across the street," I say and then write my phone number on a scrap of paper.

"I sure thank you for your help. Please feel free to drop by anytime," Carol replies.

"I'll be sure to do that. Hope you feel better soon, Alex. And don't worry about your bike, either. It doesn't have a scratch on it."

Alex has now forgotten her tears. A smile of joy pours forth from her face. "Bye."

"Good-bye," I respond, waving at Alex.

Jumping into my car, I take off toward town, looking for a metal detector, looking for a chance to mingle with the world, looking for life itself. But first I have to say good-bye to a departed friend. I lead; my Mustang obeys.

* * *

"Father, Father," I say, kneeling by the black granite tombstone, "we have to talk. I know you meant well in your life, and I understand that life was too much for you."

I place my hand on top of his grave, grasping a handful of brown grass in my agile fingers. "I realize now that there were many good aspects of your being. I also realize that there is no excuse for you doing what you did, and I will never accept your action. I have a right to feel anger because you abandoned our family, abandoned me."

I reach out and place my right hand on the coarse granite, my fingers tracing the indentations of his name. "But you want to know something? I don't hate you anymore. I understand that people cannot always help their actions. I know you were sick."

Gentle tears are now forming in the corners of my eyes, delicately streaming down over the curves of my cheeks, past my chin, dripping on the ground in front of me.

"Father, I love you, and I will always love you. This is good-bye. I won't come back for a long time, maybe not until I have children, when I will have a story of my own to tell. That's right, a story—a story about life, not death, because in a sense, by your death, you have taught me about life, about love and responsibility. You have given me a gift you never thought possible."

I drop the brown grass onto his grave and reach out and touch the marker one last time. "You know, in a few months, all this earth will be covered by green grass. The cycle of life never ends. It always continues. Good-bye, Father," I say. The wind rustles through my hair; a dog barks in the distance; the carefree shouts of kids echo over the hillsides. "Good-bye," I say one last time, and I return to my joyful Mustang.

CHAPTER 18

I feel so alive racing down the freeway. I feel as if I have awakened from a long, deep sleep, like Rip Van Winkle, born anew to a fresh world. My eyes see the sun low on the horizon, the smiling faces in the cars zooming by, the cheerful trees waving in the cool March weather. My ears hear the honking of the horns, the roar of diesel engines. My hands feel the texture of the steering wheel, the vibrations of the pebbles in the road, the pounding of blood.

The world is in slow motion, and I am a part of it. Hi there, smiling faces on the billboard. Here's to you, wise old man rolling down the freeway at fifty miles per hour; may you keep your car until the day you die. Thumbs up to you, cheerful children playing with your hands in the back window; may you inherit the same beautiful world that I have inherited.

Looking up, I see a white pigeon circling high overhead.

"May you always look out for me, O beautiful bird."

To my right, I see a stranded dark-blue Bronco. Two men and a woman wait by their marooned car. I pull back on the reins, and my Mustang trots to the side of the road.

"Hi, my name is Gabriel, Gabriel Rutherford," I say, walking up to them. "Can I be of help?"

"Hey, my name is Reese, and this is my wife, Dianna, and over here is our friend Ross," one man says, his teeth gleaming in the sun. His eyes shine with an all-knowing, sportive glint, and a John Deere hat sits proudly on the top of his blond head. His accent is thickly country, almost artificial sounding.

"So, what's the problem?" I ask.

"Hell, Reese took us out on the freeway without a damn spare tire," Ross says with a funny grin on his face, enjoying Reese's predicament. "Can you believe it? And then to top it off, he runs over the only nail within a hundred miles." Ross wears a cap with a NASCAR logo on the front and a camouflage hunting shirt. His face is cheerful in nature, in contrast to the coarse texture of his skin that reveals the scars of forgotten fights.

"Yeah, Reese, how come you brought us out here without a spare tire?" Dianna chides him playfully, her cultivated Southern accent in distinct contrast to her husband's. She wears a beautiful multicolored wool sweater and has several finely woven, thin gold chains encircling her neck.

"It's not my car. It's your car. How was I to know you didn't have a spare?"

"Excuses, excuses."

"How about we just take the tire off?" I say. "I know of a discount tire store just down the road. It will be a lot cheaper than going to a gas station or having your car towed."

"Sounds like a great idea to me," Reese replies.

Soon Reese, Ross, and I are busy removing the flattened tire. In the front seat, Dianna is engrossed in a book on birdwatching. In the back of the Bronco, I notice a whole arsenal of weaponry through the car window.

"So what are all the guns for?" I ask. "Are you planning on starting a war?"

"Oh, we've been out shooting black powder. These are all replicas of Civil War guns," Reese replies, opening the hatch. "This is a replica of a 1861 Springfield rifle," he says, holding it up before me. I grasp it in my hands, feeling the weight, rejoicing in the smell of gun oil intermingled with the pungent smell of discharged black powder. Next Reese picks up a pistol, its metal black, its cylinder long and intimidating. "This is an 1862 Colt Navy pistol. Feel the weight of this baby. And you would not believe the kick this beauty makes when it is fired."

Reese continues to show me the gun collection, a dazzling array of pistols and rifles. Ross occasionally interjects sarcastic comments. Finally Dianna is distracted from her reading.

"Reese, will you please hurry up and get the car fixed? I have no desire to spend the night out here."

"All right, all right, I'm going. So what do you think of our guns?" Reese inquires.

"They're cool. I would love to learn to shoot one."

"Well, we are going back out on Sunday. Maybe you would like to come along?"

"Would I ever!"

Soon the tire is off and safely tucked into the trunk of my car.

"Ross, you stay here and look after Diana," Reese says. "I wouldn't want her to be kidnap—"

"Look after me?" interrupts Diana. "This must be a joke. Ross is liable to fall asleep in the middle of the road, or get arrested for peeing in public or something."

Soon Reese and I are galloping down the road, intent upon our task. The top is down, and the wind roars all around. In no time at all, we have purchased a new tire and returned to the wounded Bronco.

After the last bolt is tightened, we stand and rejoice in our success. Reese hands me a piece of paper. "Here is my number, Gabriel. Give me a call on Sunday around eleven."

I bid farewell to Reese, Ross, and Dianna, and soon I find myself proceeding along the interstate. Looking in the mirror, I become aware that the large grill of a jacked-up black Dodge Ram is pressed against my rear, obstructing my view. That's okay, impatient one. You will survive.

Just as we approach the narrow bridge ahead, the aggravated Ram veers out of my lane and goes roaring past on the inside shoulder. Gazing to my right, I see an unkempt redneck with a Confederate hat on his scruffy head. He turns toward me and gives me an evil grin. A long scar meanders along the angle of his left jaw, goading me, taunting me. Good-bye, redneck; good-bye, past. Here's to the present.

Up ahead, on the side of the bridge, a small boy of about twelve is playing along the side of the railing, wearing a Braves baseball cap and a Red Sox jersey that says HUNTER on the back. His skin is fair, and his hair, almost white, sticks out from underneath the cap. Just as the dark truck is whizzing by, the driver gives a loud honk. The boy, startled, jumps a bit, and his cap flies up into the breeze. He lunges forward, losing his balance. He teeters momentarily on the edge and then goes tumbling over the railing, into the cold waters below.

Without even having to think, I slam the brakes. My car comes to a screeching halt, followed by a loud *wham* as a surprised Charger slams into my rear. My face is driven hard into my steering wheel, which catches me full in my lips. Blood erupts, but I don't care.

Gabriel, you have to save that boy, I tell myself. Compose yourself; ignore the pain; only the boy matters. I jump out of my Mustang and race to the edge of the bridge. A whole line of irritated cars is backed up behind. Their drivers honk at me and scream at me, but I don't care.

At the bridge's edge, my vigilant eyes scan the water below. Where is he? Where is he? He is too young to die. Fearless, I strip off my shirt and shoes, preparing to jump, when I catch sight of a small figure below, swimming up and grabbing onto a rusty buoy in the cool, murky waters.

"Hold on, son! I will get help!" I shout.

The boy shouts back, but I am unable to make out the words. Sighting a tiny fishing boat near the opposite bank, I shout and scream at the top of my lungs, running and waving my arms. A gray-headed bearded man looks up, sees my agitation, and then sees where my finger is pointing. Immediately the boat is racing to the rescue.

"Son, hold on tight! A boat is on the way!" I shout at the top of my voice, unsure if he can hear me.

Soon the fisherman pulls alongside and drags the boy into the protection of the boat. He places his coat around the frightened boy's frozen arms for warmth.

"He's safe," I whisper. "He's going to be okay," I say a little louder. "He's alive!" I shout to the world. "And I'm alive!" I shriek and throw my shoes and shirt high into the air, up into the gusting wind.

I become aware of the honks and shouts in the distance. Taking a step, my bare foot kicks something on the pavement below. Looking down, I see a knife lodged in a crevice, its blade open. I stoop down and find that it comes loose easily. I grasp it in my palm, roll it around and then close the blade. I straighten up and toss the knife into the river beyond. The faint splash resounds to my attentive ears. A white pigeon alights on the railing in front of me, pauses, looks at me, and takes off, flying once around in a circle above and then into the distant sunset, the contours of its wings silhouetted against the brightness. I take one look at the setting sun, not even having to squint at the bright light, pausing … and then I turn and walk toward my car, my bare feet prancing on the pavement, my bare chest gleaming in the cold air, the sweet taste of blood in my mouth.

* * *

Sirius burns bright in the distance.

The Nashville skyline looms before me on the horizon …

THE PRESENT

Oh, give us pleasure in the flowers to-day;
And give us not to think so far away
As the uncertain harvest; keep us here
All simply in the springing of the year.

Robert Frost

CHAPTER 19

There is only blackness, but as my eyes adjust, I find myself standing in a darkened room. The walls emanate a faint glow and shimmer like the golden wings of a thousand fireflies dancing in a gentle wind. Whitesnake's "Is this Love" plays in the background, filling me with elation for the present and optimism for the future.

On my right, a solitary table stands, an altar to the heavens. On it rest three candles: the center candle unlit, standing tall but alone, surrounded by two small lit candles whose golden flames flicker in the gentle breeze. I realize now that my naked hands are not alone, that they embrace two warm and soft hands. I can feel every curve, every pore, every contour of the delicate fingerprints. Looking up, I gaze into the two most beautiful eyes I have ever beheld, teary eyes, brown eyes … Sis's eyes. Oh, my god … Sis's eyes … Sis … oh, my Sis. Can this be real? Am I dreaming? Am I in heaven? The music plays on …

Sis looks at me, a smile on her face and a tear running down her cheek. Her watery eyes sparkle in the candlelight like diamonds in the setting sun.

"Gabe," she whispers, the tears now streaming down her cheeks like a mountain brook during the spring thaw, "I promise to be open, honest, and faithful to you. When you need strength, I will offer mine. When you need encouragement, I will provide words of encouragement. When you are sad, I will comfort you. I promise to always stand by your side. I will cherish the memories we make together, and I promise I will love you forever. Gabe, will you take this ring as a sign of my love?"

"I will," I reply, and Sis slips the silver ring onto the last finger of my right hand. Sis looks up with a smile and says, "Gabe, may our love and friendship bring us closer every day. May our lives be filled with peace and happiness. May our souls be forever intertwined."

With tears in my eyes, I say, "Sis, you are my best friend, you are my lover, and you are my everlasting companion. From the first time I laid eyes on you, I knew you were the one. When you looked up and smiled at me, my heart stood still, the heavens and earth stood still. My memory of first seeing you is forever burned into my soul. Sis, I will never forget our first kiss, the first time we made love. I will never forget your laughter, your sweet smile, your gentle touch. Sis, you were so beautiful then and are even more beautiful now. Never in my life have I been as happy as I am this very moment. Sis, I promise to love and care for you, through times of joy and times of sorrow. I promise to rejoice when you are happy and to grieve when you are sad. I promise to be open and honest with you. I promise to always be faithful to you and to our love. Sis, will you take this ring as a sign of my everlasting love?"

"I will," Sis responds in a soft whisper muffled by the tears of infinite hope and eternal joy.

I slip a silver ring onto the little finger of her right hand and say, "Sis, you are my life. You are my heart. You are my soul. Whatever road we travel, whatever path our lives take, I will always be at your side. I want you to become part of the story of my life and for me to become part of the story of your life. I want us to be one, forever and forever." I take a delicate, embroidered white handkerchief and dab away the gentle tears on her cheeks; a handkerchief that was given to my grandmother on her wedding day, and then passed to me, so that I might pass it on to the one I love.

We each pick up one of the two lit candles and together light the center candle. A glowing radiance bathes the room as we each blow out the other's candle with an exhalation of warm air from the depths of our souls. Two candles have become one; we have become one.

Taking Sis in my arms, my emerald eyes stare into her brown eyes, a gaze of joyfulness for the present and anticipation for the future. Leaning down, I press my soft lips against Sis's lips, our tongues intermingling; Sis softly bites my tongue. Our noses gently rub as we stare into each other's beaming eyes. Our kiss is such a kiss as the world has never seen before. Our kiss goes on and never seems to end, a timeless kiss, an unselfish kiss, a kiss of enduring love, undying passion, everlasting admiration, eternal friendship … a kiss not of our lips touching, not of our tongues embracing, not of our noses rubbing, but of our souls whispering. Even the gods above look down in jealousy.

The image fades, and I find myself drifting upward like a feather in a gentle breeze, floating neither in earth nor in heaven. Opening my eyes, I am standing on the roof of my childhood home, gazing at the heavens above. Sis is at my side, and we are holding hands. I am not alone; I am no longer a watcher; it is no longer winter. Cygnus the Swan, Cygnus the Northern Cross sparkles off the distant river. There are no gunshots. The warmth of the summer air penetrates every pore of my steadfast body; the light of the stars ignites my soul. The universe is at peace. I am at peace.

I smile …

* * *

Disoriented, unsure of where I am, I sit up and look around, feeling for Sis. As my eyes adjust to the shadowy light, I see my familiar bedroom. It is only a dream. The clock flashes 2:00 AM; the wind rustles through the trees; the moon beams through the slats of the shades, casting a crisscrossed shadow across my bed. Ellen's picture sits on my nightstand, her eyes beaming with love. Getting up, I thank God that the nightmares are gone.

Turning, I stride down the dim hallway to the safe confines of my study. Sitting at my father's desk (the desk of his father's father, and the desk of his father's father's father), I turn on a lamp and move my right hand along the smooth grain of the ancient table. As if with a mind of its own, my left hand reaches up and rubs the scar along my right cheek as my right hand traces the outline of a sharp indentation along the edge of the desktop.

I lean back in my soft chair. The gentle glow of light pervades the darkness. On the left of my desk stand autographed copies of the three greatest Southern novels ever written: William Faulkner's *Absalom, Absalom!*, Robert Penn Warren's *All the King's Men*, and Walker Percy's *The Last Gentleman*. In front of me rests a picture of Ellen, my devoted wife, in her beautiful wedding gown. On the right sits a family picture of Ellen and me with our son Phillip and our daughter Becky. Our children are so small. Phillip clings on my neck, and his sister rests comfortably upon the bosom of her loving mother. *Ellen, the pillar of my soul, the rock of my life,* I reflect while twirling my golden wedding band around my finger with my left thumb. With tears in my eyes, I pick up Ellen's wedding portrait and remember all of the good times we had together. It now has been over a year since she passed away after a long fight with cancer. Since her death, my life has not been the same. I am now alone. My son is a professor of philosophy at Dartmouth and I have no worry about his future. My daughter went to college for two years at Memphis Rhodes prior to marrying a Vanderbilt law student. She now works part time while attending nursing school. She says she wishes to be like her mom. I have no doubt she will succeed in her goal.

I am surrounded by my past: my diplomas, my awards, framed news articles. On the right, sitting down low on my bookshelves, are plaques of gratitude glowing in the faint light: American Heart Association, March of Dimes, American Breast Cancer Foundation .... Looking above, I see photos from around the world, each one a story of the frailty of human existence: New Orleans 2005, Southern India 1993, New York 2001, Thailand 2004, Haiti 2010, Bangladesh 1991, Mexico 2015 .... Human tragedies, not meant to be understood, but a constant reminder of the misfortune that will always remain with us. Above these stretch out pleasant family photos: our trips to Disney World, Paris, London, New York, Boston, San Francisco ... photos of the youth baseball and basketball teams that I coached ... memories of the past ... my past ... my past ...

I have truly been blessed: a beautiful, loving wife; marvelous kids; and a fulfilling career. And yet I feel as if something was always missing; there is a yearning in my soul that I never could explain. Opening the study window, I gaze out at the new moon. The light pierces the branches of a nearby tree and bursts forth into an infinite array of sparkling silver rays. The cool warmth of the March air beckons me; the light of the glowing moon calls to me. I walk out the front door, wrapped in my forest-green cotton robe, and look to the heavens with heaviness in my heart and tears in my eyes.

Falling to my knees, I beseech the sky above. "God, if you are listening, tell me I have been a good person. Tell me I have been a good father, a good husband. God, tell me I have made a difference in this world." But there is no response. "God, please, please, please, tell me I have done more good than bad," I implore once again. But I only hear the whispering of the wind through the nearby trees.

In the eastern sky, I see the beautiful constellation Cygnus, Cygnus the Northern Cross, Cygnus the Swan ... the swan, my swan ... Sis ... the bucktoothed tomboy who turned into a beautiful swan. It has been a long time since I have thought of Sis, felt the pain of lost love. I still remember, as if it were yesterday, when we met at Julian's for dinner shortly after our breakup. I wanted so desperately to win Sis back, to prove to her that I had changed. When I arrived at the restaurant, Sis was already sitting at a table, waiting for me, a pensive look on her face. After a noncommittal hug, Sis sat down and looked at me with questioning eyes. Taking her hand, I began, "Sis, I'm sorry for the things I have done to you, but I ask for your forgiveness. You are my heart, you are my soul, and I cannot bear the thought of life without you."

"Gabe, I'm sorry, but too much has happened, and I must move on."

"Sis, don't give up on me yet. Let's get married. We don't have to have children. Just give me a chance."

"Gabe, I know you always believed that I did not wish to have children, and you were right. But something happened to me, something I never got the chance to tell you. Do you remember the time we made love in your houseboat on the evening of your thirty-third birthday? It was spontaneous, and I had forgotten my diaphragm," Sis said in a soft voice, almost a whisper.

"Yes, Sis, and it was one of the most beautiful moments in my life," I replied with a smile, joyful that Sis still remembered our good times.

Sis nodded her head with her eyes closed, as if she didn't wish to continue. After a short pause, she began with sadness in her voice, "The next month, I was late on my period, and I was terrified that I was pregnant. I was not ready for kids. My career was starting to blossom. What was I going to do? Fearful and frantic, consumed by fright, I took a home pregnancy test, praying to God that I was not pregnant. And while I was waiting for the result, terrified, trembling, a peaceful sensation came over me, and I smiled. I smiled at the thought of motherhood. I imagined being awakened in the darkness of the night by the beautiful cries of a newborn baby. I felt the joy of nursing, the contentment of changing dirty diapers, the bliss of watching my child grow bigger and smarter, day by day. I thought of the happiness of marriage with you at my side. And then I saw the test result. It was negative, and you know, Gabe, it was not relief I felt, but it was disappointment and regret. Yes, I was disappointed that I was not pregnant. My smile turned into tears. I should have told you then how I felt. I wanted to get married. I wanted to have children. Maybe if I had told you, Sea Island never would have happened. But Gabe, you showed your lack of respect for me at Sea Island, and the trust was gone. When I slept with Mark, I was reminded of my dreams of motherhood with you at my side, no one else. When I slept with Mark, I was reminded of an event from my childhood, something I never told you, and something I never will. I was feeling raped by the past, raped by the present, and most of all, raped by you. My love for you was dead, and I do not think I can ever trust you with my heart again."

I took Sis's hands into my hands and looked at her with love and longing and sadness and regret. If only Sis could see into my soul. If only Sis knew how I truly felt, she would give me one more chance.

"Sis, I understand your feelings, and I respect your honesty," I said with all the warmth from the depths of my soul. "I can't help it if the truth sucks, but I still wish to be your friend and, I hope, someday something more."

After that, I told Sis of all my discoveries, the events that had occurred to me in my life since we broke up, my plans for the present, and my hopes for the future. During dinner we relived many of the good times we had experienced in the past, and at dinner's end, Sis wished me the best.

"Gabe, I hope you have a wonderful life. I'm sorry that I cannot be a part of it right now. Too much has happened, and I do not think time can ever erase the pain you caused me."

Over the next month, I wrote frequent letters and made several phone calls, trying to get Sis to give me one more chance, but to no avail. Feeling empty, I went by Sis's place and implored her again to at least be my friend. Then one day a package arrived. In it was the scrapbook she had made several years earlier of our good times together. Also in the box were my grandmother's handkerchief, my collection of Bob Dylan eight-track tapes, a copy of Walker Percy's *Love in the Ruins*, and a few other miscellaneous items. In the box was an accompanying note—harsh, very painful.

Dear Gabe,

Enclosed are our scrapbook, your grandmother's handkerchief, and a few items of yours that you left behind. This is all that remains of our time together.

It is inappropriate for you to ever contact me again. Your presence will cheat me of a future. I won't have that. If you insist on coming by my place— unannounced or otherwise—I will tell you to leave. Our dinner last month at Julian's was an opportunity for closure. That is how it will remain. Enjoy your new girlfriend, your houseboat, and your career. You have been blessed.

Good-bye,

Sis

Though I was glad Sis did not relegate these items to the trash dump, the pain of knowing that Sis was trying to erase me totally from her past was unbearable. My heart was broken; my soul was in tears. But Ellen was there for me, steadfast Ellen, to pick up the pieces.

And one year later, now engaged to Ellen, we had a chance meeting in the Chicago airport, our flights being cancelled due to inclement weather. I was on my way to San Francisco for a medical conference, and Sis was on her way home to Nashville after a business meeting. I looked up, and there was Sis, gazing upward at the monitors listing the flight schedules. I was stunned. And then, as if sensing my gaze, Sis turned and looked at me and gave me that smile, that smile that has always been burned into my soul. And just like old times, we sat in a cafe and talked for hours over coffee, laughing and reminiscing over good times. The past and present were one, and I knew I had made the mistake of my life losing Sis. I knew Sis was my soul mate, and that I wished to spend the rest of my life with her.

After I returned to Nashville, we talked a few times on the phone, had lunch together several times, and even played golf together. I broke off my engagement to Ellen. I thought Sis was having regrets, that she was going to take me back. All the magic in our relationship seemed to be coming together, two becoming one, just like our candles.

Fearful of rejection if I should be the aggressor, I kept hoping and hoping that Sis would come to me and once again pin a "hapless youth" and confess her undying love ... but it never happened. The phone calls stopped; my hopes were fading. I wrote a long letter baring my soul, but I was too afraid to mail it.

Dear Sis,

You once wrote to me when our relationship was first developing, saying, "I am experiencing a lot of pain and, at the same time, a lot of joy. Do you suppose the two go together?" Well, the last few weeks have been some of the best days of my life, and I am still feeling the pain and the joy. To see you again, to talk with you, to laugh with you, to cry with you, to hold you …. Despite the sorrow I feel at having lost you in the past, I am overwhelmed with joy to know you still remember many of the good times we had together. I was sure you had blocked out all the old memories, both the good and the bad. My time with you these last few weeks reminds me of Humphrey Bogart telling Ilsa in *Casablanca*, "We'll always have Paris."

Sis, I will never forget the expression on your face on our first date, when you turned and smiled … talking that night for hours on end over coffee, knowing I had met my best friend … trying to get the nerve to kiss you when you finally took charge … how soft your lips felt on our first kiss … the tingling in my spine when you gently bit my tongue … the passion I felt with our gentle Eskimo kisses … the exhilaration I felt when you placed my hand on your breast … the shock and delight you had on your face when I expectedly showed up the following day with a red rose … the night you pinned my hands above my head and declared your undying love for me … the evening we made our commitment vows and exchanged silver rings.

I will never forget your laughter, the sweet sound of you calling me Gabe … the touch of your hand on my face when you would gently caress me … the glimmering of the moon on your beautiful body when we first made love … how you danced like a reed swaying in the gentle currents of the wind … drinking German wine in the cabin of my boat … the excitement of checking my mailbox each day to see if you wrote me … beating you at golf (or was it the other way around?) … my dismay on opening a set of Christmas luggage with no hidden surprises.

Sis, I will always be a searcher, and I am searching now for the meaning of our "chance" encounter in Chicago. I refuse to believe our meeting was a random coincidence. I have no idea what God has planned for us, but he must have some plan, whether it is in the distant future or in heaven, or just to let us catch a glimmer of his forgiveness and allow us to be best friends once again. I will never give up on my fantasy that someday I might kiss you again. I will never give up on my fantasy that we are destined to become part of the stories of each other's lives. I like to think that I may be blessed to die in the arms of one I truly love.

Sis, I do hope you ponder the purpose of our "chance" encounter and let your heart and soul be the judge of where we go from here, as there is no question in my mind that our lives are forever intertwined. And I was wrong when I said that you haven't changed. You have changed. Though you are as beautiful on the outside as you were when we first met, your inner beauty is far greater than I ever could have imagined.

Always your friend ... and I mean always ...

Love,

Gabe

Was Sis thinking the same? Was Sis waiting for me to be the aggressor, to be the man? If only I knew. Several times I came close to mailing the letter, but I never did. Despondent, I gave up, and once again Ellen was there to pick up the pieces, sweet Ellen, loyal Ellen, my Ellen. But what if I had sent the letter? What if I had told Sis how I felt? Would the present be different?

After my marriage and kids, there were a few times when Sis and I spied each other at a distance: at the post office, at a restaurant, at the mall, me with my beautiful wife and young kids. She was not married, did not have children. I would always smile, but she would look at me and then look away as if she had not noticed me. I could never tell if she was feeling jealousy, pain, regret, longing, anger, or hate. I so wanted to know that Sis did love me at one point in her life, that she did not totally erase me from her memory. All that I knew was that I felt a longing in my soul, a yearning pulling at me, an impulse to grab her, to comfort her, to cherish her, to hold her and never let go.

I have not seen or talked with Sis in years and years. I once ran across an article in the newspaper stating that she had left the news station to become the producer of a company that made documentaries. I also heard from an acquaintance that she was married briefly, but things did not work out. Over the years, I have periodically looked up her name in the phone book, curious where she lived, but she was always unlisted. At times I have thought of calling her at work, to catch up with the happenings of her life—just friends, not lovers. But as always, I was afraid of rejection, afraid of—

The barking of a dog brings me back to the present. The late-night spring air is now damp with a chilly dew. I stand and go inside to the comfort of my home.

* * *

I find myself rummaging through an old storage closet. From the back of it I retrieve a cardboard box, dusty, taped shut. Going back downstairs, I use my loyal Bowie knife, a knife carried by a private killed at Stones River, to cut through the worn tape. Inside are many of the items that Sis sent me in days gone by: the scrapbook, loose photos of us, the love letters I sent her, my grandmother's handkerchief. I open the scrapbook, and on the first page is a picture of us gazing into the camera. In Sis's handwriting are the words, "This is a story about two people who fell in love …" I turn the page, and there is a picture of us gazing into each other's eyes, our soft noses touching, and the words, "… and made their dreams come true." I flip through the pages and revel in the photos of our great times together, our trips to Lake Lanier, to Beaver Creek, to Ponte Vedra, to Whistler, to Boston … the list goes on.

Setting the scrapbook aside, I pick up the bundle of the letters I once wrote to Sis and skim through them, looking for clues of what went wrong.

"… I feel so warm and close to you, and yet we've only known each other for such a short time …"

"… I think the potential is there between us for something beautiful and long-lasting … all I really want from you is a fair chance at developing that relationship …"

"… I just want to tell you again that no matter what you decide, I will never be angry or bitter toward you …"

"… When I am with you, and when I am not with you, I feel so close to you, and I never want that feeling to stop …"

"… I just hope our relationship reaches that stage of security where the word 'love' is always implied …"

"… And of all the memories I have of that weekend, the best is that I was so acutely aware that you told me you loved me more times in that time period than you have ever told me before …"

"… I wished we were together that very moment, not sex, but just in each other's arms …"

At the bottom of the box is a letter I left for Sis on her pillow one evening prior to leaving for work, a letter I wrote the day after our return from our trip to Lake Lanier, a letter that still has the faint smell of the Chaps cologne that I sprayed on it, a letter beside which I placed a red rose.

Dear Sis,

I have never been as happy in my life as I am right now, and I fear I will wake up and find it is only a dream. To wear your ring, to share your dreams, to hold your heart. And to think, this is just the beginning. I know everything in our relationship seems perfect at the present time, but like dreams, life also has nightmares. And despite all the joy we have with each other in the present, I know we are going to have tough times when we cause each other pain and sorrow. I know there will be instances in which we question our commitment toward each other, but as long as we remember our love, the love that we have today, no matter how angry we may get at each other, we will never lose our love, and that is the most marvelous thing in the world about love. If we both want it to be, it's a tie closer than blood. Sis, our tie is closer than blood, and I will never forget it. I am always yours.

Love,

Gabe

The words reverberate through my soul, sadden my heart: *If we both want it to be, it's a tie closer than blood.* How could something so wonderful go so wrong? Setting down the letters, I turn to my desk and retrieve, from the back of the bottom drawer, a small wooden box, a box made by my grandfather and given to me when I was a small child, a box that has not been opened in many years. I open it and find the letters Sis wrote to me, the candles from the time we exchanged commitment vows, my silver ring, and my golden compass. I pick up the compass and flip it over. The words call to me, beseech me ...

Now you can never become lost.
Always yours,
Love, Sis

Picking up the larger candle, I place it before me and light it with a silver-plated lighter that belonged to my grandfather. I drip hot wax on a wooden coaster and press the base of the candle into the sticky center. Some of the wax drips onto my skin and burns like molten lava. The pain feels pure and honest. The candle gives out a bright incandescence. The smoke rises in a thin stream that swirls and dissipates as it wafts up toward the ceiling. Closing my eyes, I relive times gone by. With a mind of its own, my left hand picks up the silver ring and places it on the little finger of my right hand. It fits perfectly after all these years. Opening my eyes, I pick up Sis's letters and pore through them like Sherlock Holmes looking for clues.

"... Since I met you, I've felt warm, open, and honest, and I'm scared ..."

"... I am experiencing a lot of pain and, at the same time, a lot of joy. Do you suppose the two go together?"

"... Gabe, you've been a beautiful friend and lover, and perhaps soon we will be able to explore more areas ..."

"... I know we've joked about respect, but it means more to me than anything in the world, and at times, respect is all we have ..."

"... Gabe, I do wish to become much closer to you, yet I'm still hesitant ..."

"… In time, I hope I can become more trusting, but the only thing I have learned in life so far is that I am the only one on whom I can absolutely depend …"

"… My heart and soul have been at war, and it has been wearing me out …"

"… And just as I have been fighting for you in my nightmares, I will always fight for you in life …"

At the bottom of the stack is a brief note that she wrote on memo paper that she taped to my bathroom mirror, memo paper that an Aunt had given her years before for Christmas, memo paper that misspelled her middle name, Halcyonn, with one N instead of two. To the right of Sis's signature at the bottom of the letter are imprints of her lipstick-coated lips, and I can still smell the faint scent of the Fracas perfume that she sprayed on the paper.

> Gabe,
>
> I can't wait until we leave for Sea Island. I have already packed and will be ready in the morning. I'm working late tonight, so do not wait up for me. I have something very important to tell you, something that I have recently discovered about myself that I hope will make you very happy. I will not tell you tomorrow, but soon, when the time is right. And Gabe, always remember, whatever happens to us in the future, whatever path you choose, I love you. After our first night together, I came home knowing that I had just met my best friend. Time will never erase my love for you.
>
> Sis

The final words *time will never erase my love for you* burn into my soul with fire as intense as a newborn star. These are the last words Sis wrote to me before Sea Island changed everything. I read once that it takes years to build trust and seconds to destroy it. But if only Sis's words were true, if only time had not erased her love for me.

I pick up our old scrapbook once again and return to the opening pages. My fingers trace the beautiful words of Sis, so simple, so passionate. My fingers trace the outline of her face, so gorgeous, so strong, so intelligent, so full of life. Tears form at the corners of my eyes, blurring my vision. The glow of the candle grows brighter with every tear.

I close my eyes and plead, "God, if you are listening to me, please let me be fortunate enough to see Sis before I die. Please, I pray, let me see that smile again, that laugh, that sparkle in her eyes. Please, O God, let me share coffee with her once again and talk for hours, just like we did on our first date. Let me hug her. Let me weep tears of joy. Let me kiss her. Please, please," I implore, the hot tears now streaming down like lava from the eruption of Mount Vesuvius. "Please, oh please, oh please …" My head sinks to my chest, my sobs interrupting the silence of the night.

When the sobs end and the tears dry, I blow out the candle and climb the stairs to the safe confines of my bedroom, scrapbook and compass in hand. I turn out the lights and crawl into bed, falling asleep with the silver ring warming my soul, the scrapbook resting comfortably against the gentle heaving of my chest, the stars peering through my window, a faint smile on my face.

* * *

My compass lies silently on the nightstand.

Its needle points directly away from me …

CHAPTER 20

The morning sunlight awakens me from my peaceful slumber. On opening my eyes, I see the scrapbook lying by my side. The rising sun reflects off my compass with a dizzying array of sparkles; the chirping of birds announces the coming of spring. Compass in hand, I go downstairs back to my study, the scrapbook held tightly against my chest, and sit once again in my familiar chair. The darkness now has receded, and I am surrounded by towering bookcases, by my antique gun and sword collection, by my Civil War relics that I discovered with my trusty metal detectors, all with stories to tell …

… The pendulum Hause sight for a Napoleon cannon that I found in the West Harpeth River, hunting the retreat after the battle of Nashville. I can clearly see the artillery gunner throwing the sight in the river while crossing over the flimsy pontoon bridge, thinking to himself, *What the heck do I need this for when I have no cannon* …

… The Nashville Plow Works cavalry saber that I bought from an old lady in Murfreesboro. She said it belonged to her great-grandfather Captain William Oliver Bennett. Along with the saber, she had a pocketful of CSA buttons that she sold me as well. When I asked her where the buttons came from, she said they were from an old jacket of Captain Bennett's, but that the jacket was not in very good condition, so she cut off the buttons and threw the jacket in the garbage the week before. I almost choked. I can still smell the jacket rotting in the city trash pit …

… The hundred Minié balls I found in the yard of the physician who delivered my son while his wife was on a shopping spree in Atlanta. He told his wife that gophers must have gotten into the yard …

The list goes on. All relics of the distant past, all stories of my past …

Looking outside, the Monday morning sun is hidden by a gray sky. I'm off from work for three days, and today I have a wonderful adventure planned. The mother of one of our new physicians lives on Shy's Hill, just a few hundred yards from the summit where the Confederate cannons stood during the second day of the Battle of

Nashville. He told me that as a kid, he would occasionally find Minié balls while digging in the dirt. To the best of his knowledge, no one has ever hunted in his yard with a metal detector—virgin territory at the site of the last battle of the Army of Tennessee. Having made all my preparations—spare metal detector, extra batteries, pick and shovel, thermos full of hot coffee, snacks, and the like—I jump in my silver Infiniti G and leave Old Hickory Lake in my wake. I rush headlong down Interstate 65, my gleaming golden compass on the dash leading the way. The morning spring air is damp and chilly, so I quickly roll up my window. The white painted stripes on the interstate rush headlong toward me and then separate along each side of my car like shooting stars. I feel like Hans Solo hitting the hyperdrive in the *Millennium Falcon* for the first time.

Driving down the interstate, I turn on the radio to my favorite station. There is a commercial break announcing the new line of Volkswagen electric cars, and then Bob Dylan's "The Times They Are a-Changin'" plays. As the familiar words filter through my head, I am surrounded by Datsuns and Volkswagens and Toyotas and Audis and the like. Where are the Fords, the GMs, and the Chryslers? Look at me: my Ford Mustang is now in the past, and here I am driving a Nissan Infiniti. To my left is the National Cemetery, where the brave Union soldiers of the Civil War and the brave U.S. soldiers from all the subsequent wars rest in their solemn graves.

In the distance, the Nashville skyline appears on the horizon. The sun is still hidden from view. Bob Dylan sings on ....

As I look out toward the skyline, I see my life pass before me. In the center stands the Life and Casualty Tower, built when I was a very small child, the beacon of my youth, the large L&C reminding me that life has its rewards and its misfortunes. It is hard to believe that when this thirty-story building was built, the tallest building in Nashville was twelve stories. And as I grew older, from childhood to grade school to high school, the buildings kept coming: the Parkway Towers, the Andrew Jackson Building, and the Tennessee Tower. And then my father was gone, and a part of me was gone.

After college, medical school, and residency, I returned to a different Nashville skyline: the Regions Center, the Sheraton, the Plaza, and the James Polk Building. And then Sis came into my life, and the buildings kept growing: the "R2D2 building," Fifth Third Center, Renaissance, and City Center. After Sis, Ellen became the inspiration of my life, and every year, as my kids grew older, as my wrinkles grew deeper, and as my gray hairs became more abundant, new buildings appeared, one by one: the Palmer Plaza, The AT&T "Batman" Building, Viridian Tower, and the Pinnacle. And now looming before me, rising into the clouds above, appears the Signature Tower, over twice as high as Nashville's tallest buildings, dwarfing the nearby L&C Tower, dominating the skyline just as the L&C Tower once did. The Signature Tower, its pinnacle shining in white metal and diamond glass, an antenna to God almighty, a reminder that the future is the present and the present is the past.

I take the Main Street exit and cross the Victory Memorial Bridge into the heart of the city. The State Capitol rises to my right. I turn southward and pass the City Cemetery, where one can find the graves of many Confederate dead. I pass Fort Negley, where the opening shots of the Battle of Nashville were fired. When I think of the Battle of Nashville, the only word that comes to my mind is insanity; *insanity, insanity*. After shattering his courageous army against the fortifications at Franklin, Hood marched his demoralized men northward. In Hood's mind, the battle of Franklin was a victory, as the Federal troops had retreated that night to the safe confines of Nashville.

Having attended to the wounded and dead, Hood entrenched his troops south of Nashville, with his line extending five miles in length from Hillsboro Pike to Nolensville Pike. Never mind that the Union army had fifty-five thousand troops concentrated in Nashville; never mind that Nashville at that time was the most heavily fortified city in the entire United States; never mind that General James Wilson's cavalry of twelve thousand men was armed with the seven-shot repeating Spencer rifle, with more firepower than the entire Confederate army. Hood's plan was simple—let the Union army destroy itself in a frontal attack against the Confederate army, and then Hood would follow the fleeing soldiers into the city.

After capturing Nashville, Hood would proceed northward into Kentucky, recruit a new army, and then link up with General Lee in Virginia, thus saving the Confederacy. As a testament to his brilliant military genius, Hood also had the wisdom to send General William Bate with his infantry and General Nathan Bedford Forrest with his cavalry to attack the garrison in Murfreesboro thirty miles away, under the belief that General George Thomas would panic and send a large portion of his Nashville troops to protect Murfreesboro. Never mind that Murfreesboro likewise was well fortified; never mind that

Murfreesboro had three times the number of troops as the attacking Confederates ... insanity.

Going south, I imagine the hasty retreat of the Confederate army after the first day of battle. They were outflanked but not badly beaten. Their spirits were still high, considering the adversity they had faced. I arrive at Battery Lane, pause, and then slowly proceed down the road toward my destination. Along this road the retreating Confederate army formed a two-and-a-half-mile east-west line from Peach Orchard Hill to Shy's Hill.

As I look upward, the sky is full of morning mist; steam rises from my hood. I pass by the stone wall from which General William Loring's troops successfully repelled attack after attack against a never-ending onslaught of Yankee soldiers, and then I start a gradual ascent up Shy's Hill. Arriving at the historical marker, I park my car and proceed on foot to the summit to pay my respects.

* * *

The air is thick and quiet, broken intermittently by the chirps of invisible birds, by the rustle of the wind. Climbing up the hill at a slow walk, I am already out of breath, amazed at the steepness. As I stop to rest, I feel the thundering of the brave Yankee soldiers charging up the opposite slope into the thick rain of hot lead. I look up and see the brave Confederate soldiers valiantly firing their rifles at the wild stampede of troops clad in blue. On the peak of the hill, Colonel Shy stands, waving his sword in encouragement. Just as I resume my ascent, his head explodes with blood and his lifeless body crumples to the ground. The gray soldiers pause, unsure of whether or not to flee. From below, General James Smith encourages the men to stand and fight, but hundreds of Union soldiers immediately overrun the hill. Some Confederates are shot where they stand; others throw down their rifles and flee headlong down the back of the hill; and still others are just too tired and beaten and hold their arms up in surrender.

As I reach the top, my breath running short, two Yankee soldiers hold Colonel Shy's lifeless body against a tree while a third soldier rams a bayonet through his abdomen, pinning his misshapen body in a ghastly stance. They laugh and jeer at their gruesome antics. Nausea wells up in my chest, and I shake my head in disgust. Dead soldiers cover the ground, staining the brown leaves with blood and gore.

As I walk back down the hill, the entire Confederate army flees in panic and almost knocks me to the ground. At the bottom, General Benton Smith tries to rally the troops, but enemy soldiers quickly overrun him, and he holds his arms at his side in surrender. A gruff officer in blue walks up to General Smith, demands his name, and then strikes him three times on his head with his saber. Blood erupts from the gash, mixed with flecks of bone and brain, but General Smith does not die.

Looking below me, rifles and knapsacks and cartridge boxes are strewn everywhere. General Wilson has taken Granny White Pike, so the only avenue for retreat is the Franklin Pike. In the distance, officers are trying to encourage the men to stand and fight, but the mass continues to flee southeast toward Franklin Pike. The once-proud Army of Tennessee is dead. With commanders like Hood, who needs enemies?

Climbing back into my car, the morning fog is starting to dissipate, and the singing of the birds grows louder. Journey's "I'll Be Alright Without You" is playing on the radio. I proceed a short distance and pull into a long driveway framed by trees at the address given to me. No one is home, as his parents are out of town for the week. The music plays on …

I shut off the hushed engine with fervent anticipation of all the relics I am going to find: cannonballs, CSA belt buckles, bayonets, cartridge boxes … My imagination is ripe with all sorts of possibilities. After getting out my metal detector, pick and shovel, I pour myself a hot cup of black coffee and spread my treasure map on the hood of the car. I have taken a modern map of Nashville and marked, with red and blue pens, all of the Confederate and Union battle positions for the two days of the battle. I am standing in the midst of the thickest part of the battle, right in the middle of General William Bates's division.

I pick up my compass to check my bearings. The sun peeks from behind the clouds, revealing a small patch of blue sky. I can feel the engravings of the sweet words of an old friend on my receptive fingertips. As I open my compass, the needle is pointing directly away from me. Just as I look up, a diamond-like flash of light momentarily blinds my vision. Focusing in the distance, I see that the flash of light came from the reflection of a glass door being opened on the house next door. A woman is letting out a repairman. As I gaze at the silhouette of the woman framed in the doorway, my heart stops, and my breath goes silent. Even after all these years, despite the distance that separates the two of us, I know in my heart who it is.

As I walk toward the house, the woman has now descended the steps of the front porch and is thanking the workman. My pace quickens; the pounding in my heart grows stronger; my eyes burn bright. As I near the house, I shout, "Sis! Sis! What are you doing here?"

Sis turns towards me, puzzlement on her face, followed by that smile that I remember so well. "Gabe? Gabe? Is that you? Why, I live here."

As I approach, Sis sees the compass in my hand, and I see a smile of recognition on her face. After I explain the circumstances of my visit, Sis explains to me that she just moved into this house three weeks prior and then exclaims, "It's a small world, isn't it?"

Taking my left hand, Sis says, "Gabe, I'm sorry about your wife. I read about it in the paper and thought of calling you, but I did not wish to cause you any more grief."

"Thank you. It has been tough, but each day I become more and more thankful for having her in my life. I have been blessed," I reply with sadness in my voice.

I gaze into Sis's glowing brown eyes. The sun is now shining bright, and the wind is silent.

"Sis, may I give you a hug?" I ask nervously, afraid of rejection.

"Why, of course, Gabe. It is so good to see you," Sis replies with a dazzling smile.

After a tender hug, we stand apart, facing each other. Sis looks down, and I see her face glow even brighter as she sees the silver ring on my little finger. Her eyes twinkle like a million shooting stars. Sis then takes the compass from my hand, flips it over and reads the loving words. A solitary tear forms in the corner of her right eye as she sighs and once again looks into my eyes.

"Gabe, would you like to come inside for a cup of coffee?" she asks, her eyes shining fervently in the growing light.

"Sis, there is nothing in the world that I would rather do," I say, and I follow her into the warm confines of her home, my silver ring warming my soul, my compass leading the way.

Just as I am about to enter her house, a robin announcing the coming of spring alights on the railing of her porch. It gives a few chirps, looks briefly at me, and then takes to the sky, heading northward. In the distance I can barely make out the letter L through the limbs of the budding trees.

* * *

The gleaming Signature Tower disappears into the clouds above …

The Nashville skyline shines bright.

CPSIA information can be obtained at www.ICGtesting.com
Printed in the USA
239040LV00001B/4/P